I0584098

Sacrifice for Freedom Trilogy | Book One

OF SACRIFICE AND SURRENDER

America's First Abolitionists

Craig Stofko

Black Rose Writing | Texas

©2022 by Craig Stofko

All rights reserved. No part of this book may be reproduced, stored in a retrieval system or transmitted in any form or by any means without the prior written permission of the publishers, except by a reviewer who may quote brief passages in a review to be printed in a newspaper, magazine or journal.

The author grants the final approval for this literary material.

First printing

This is a work of fiction. Names, characters, businesses, places, events, and incidents are either the products of the author's imagination or used in a fictitious manner. Any resemblance to actual persons, living or dead, or actual events is purely coincidental.

ISBN: 978-1-68433-908-2
PUBLISHED BY BLACK ROSE WRITING
www.blackrosewriting.com

Printed in the United States of America
Suggested Retail Price (SRP) $19.95

Of Sacrifice and Surrender is printed in Sabon

*As a planet-friendly publisher, Black Rose Writing does its best to eliminate unnecessary waste to reduce paper usage and energy costs, while never compromising the reading experience. As a result, the final word count vs. page count may not meet common expectations.

For Dawn

OF SACRIFICE AND SURRENDER

America's First Abolitionists

PREFACE....

Ancestorial families of Maryland's County Somerset first stood in defiance of the dark and sinister practice of selling human souls more than 300 years ago. Records authenticating their struggle have been buried by the sands of time. The efforts of these brave abolitionists, hidden as though by design, are shared here as a fictionalized account of the desperate attempt to win freedom for all people. This story is based on real events. Characters and chronology are not meant to resemble actual people or places or to accurately depict historical affairs. Still, the tale should ring true as it visits our country when she was but a child, and to that extent we were all there - if only in spirit.

FOREWORD

Providence shall forever work in her own mysterious and magical ways. As players on this great stage, we can only ask of ourselves, and of those with whom we live, to be willing to respond in a well-prepared manner to our call when it should be heard. There are times, unknown to all, when the world is ripe for change. Planning or predicting our role is a fool's errand. Suffice to say, the days will present themselves to us in an orderly fashion, it is then left to us to embrace the occasion that would change lives.

Many before us have seized their opportunity to push the human condition in the right direction, albeit an inch at a time. As our moment approaches it is enough to know that equality and freedom, and goodness, were borne of men and women who willingly carried torches into the dark corners of our world. Some would make their mark under the brilliant blaze of glory while others accomplished feats so colossal next to the feint flicker of a dying candle. And what of those destined to be forgotten? They met their end without ever knowing they had made a difference. Now at rest, in a peace won and well deserved, they may one day be remembered.

Mine is a tale of ignorant bliss, of names not noted and swallowed by time. The people and places have all but disappeared. The events of those days, now as relevant as an unmarked grave, exist only in history's slumber, hidden and neglected. Long ago, when our country was newly conceived, the days were dire and flush with discontent. Lest the fine people of that bygone era be abandoned in their nameless tombs, a recollection of that day is due. Let the untamed weeds and wild overgrowth of centuries be pushed aside, and strangling vines cut away so that you may know my story. As I remember....

CHAPTER 1
Wicomico

To clear the headwaters of the Manokin I traveled east, and then north to the next river, the Wicomico. In the pockets of my threadbare cotton trousers were six coins and a map folded twice in half. On the reverse side of the brownish parchment were written specific directions explaining how to move across the formidable land and instructions for interacting with the various people I would encounter on my journey.

The Wicomico ferryman's name was Jonah. I was to tell him that I was Steven, nephew to Jedediah Brixton, bid him good health from Uncle Jed and Aunt Mildred, and pay him two shillings for safe passage to the other side of the river. Uncle Jedediah had written it all out, having even inscribed the arithmetic on the paper. He did this out of a tendency toward being thorough rather than thinking I possessed a slow mind. Although anyone reading the information on the back side of the map, with its plural and precise notations, would surely have thought them written to advise either a child or an idiot.

Similar directives were added to advise for the crossing of the more formidable Nanticoke River, and the Choptank, on whose banks was built the settlement of Cambridge. This town was regarded as the last bastion of civilization before entering the vast and untamed wildlands of the Nanticoke. A large wooden sign on the side of the road heading east out of Cambridge read, "*Abandon all Hope ye who Enter this Land of Pirates and Savages.*" I found the message humorous. This land, so desolate by all accounts, is where I had been born and raised.

I set out with an enormous brown stallion we called Thunder and a magnificent black thoroughbred named Blue. The brown horse was packed high with beaver pelts and fox fur that would fetch top dollar in Baltimore. I sat atop Blue with my rifle secured to the side of the horse. My sidearm rested in a holster made of hog hide and was attached to my belt by a piece of ligament fashioned from the stringy tendon of a Red Wolf.

The backwoods that framed the eastern shore of Maryland's coastal marshes and swamps, though beautiful, presented treacherous and deadly terrain. This trip was usually made by my Uncle Jedediah and one or two other men, although never with such a sense of urgency. I had gone on a supply run with Jed once before, but no one had ever made the trip alone. My skills as a woodsman and a hunter bolstered my confidence but could in no way conceal my apprehension completely. Indeed, it would be the pretense of a fool to appear unfazed by the demands of my current assignment.

Some in our town had protested, believing it unreasonable to expect such a young boy to navigate the wild lands of the Nanticoke. But these concerns fell on deaf ears. The Somerton Council concluded I was the only logical choice. There is little doubt that Uncle Jedediah influenced the council members by boasting of my experiences tracking game and harvesting fish and fowl on the lands of the lower peninsula. In a sense, Jedediah was really bragging about how well he had taught me to hunt and to live in the forest. Despite the objections of a few, most in our community did not dispute Jed's claim that I was the best available person to traverse the land north to the Island of Kent and cross the Chesapeake to Baltimore. The issue became mute once the men discussed the importance of choosing someone who had already been infected and recovered from the brutal virus that now ravaged our small, secluded fishing village. Everyone else who had been stricken with the sickness was either dead or could be excluded from consideration because they were either too young, too old, or too weak.

Salt, sugar, and black powder were no longer delivered to the dock at Devil's Island because of the English presence on the bay. These staples, however, were almost inconsequential. The emergency was opium. The townsfolk needed the medicine to endure the violent illness. Those in the throes of the virus screamed in agony while others watched in horror as the misery grew ever closer to them.

Pressing on through the dense thicket and bush, I understood completely that every minute seemed like hours to my sick and dying neighbors. This realization motivated me. Still, I experienced a stifling sense of suffocation by the enormity of the responsibility.

A leather satchel hung loosely over my shoulder and was filled scarcely with some black powder and shot. Otherwise, a deerskin tarp to be used to shelter against inclement weather, a large canteen of clean water, some venison jerky, and an Indian blanket were my only supplies, save my firearms and a few cigars.

The ferry carried me across the Wicomico without incident. Then, adhering to Jedediah's notes, I took my horses back down the river's western banks toward the marshes of the Chesapeake. This made for arduous travel but steered me well clear of surprises. There are places in the wetlands that can swallow men whole were they to take a wrong step. Still, it was a route preferrable to the well-worn roadways on which outlaws preyed regularly. It was with excessive caution that I surveyed the land on which I moved as a fleeting moment of carelessness could doom my horses and myself to the grievous misfortune that had welcomed so many before me. The pace over this land was a slow one, its difficulty being the price paid to avoid unexpected encounters.

The journey was uneventful to the point of being tedious. If not for the incessant attacks of the mosquitoes and biting flies, I might have enjoyed the sublime beauty of my surroundings. The swarming insects were insufferable. Uncle Jed had warned me with regards to these pests.

"For all the buzzing and biting," he had said, "they help keep you alert to any signs of savages or bandits."

I was aware of the many potential dangers and threats to my wellbeing that lurked in the forest through which I now passed. It was my most sincere hope that the lessons and training made available to me during my formative years had prepared me for the mission presently undertaken.

The settlement of Somerton was dependent on the people's contributions to the common good. We were taught at a young age that everyone needed to do their share of work. Though the work was difficult, the more that was asked of any one man or woman, the higher that person's reputation and status was among the families of the town. So it was that I felt honored to be painstakingly maneuvering my horses through the dark forests of the shore, ever vigilant of the Indians or pirates that would hesitate not for an instant to lay claim to my animals and my furs. By keeping off the main road and avoiding the more frequently traversed pathways that cut their way through the difficult landscape I was able to avoid any problems. My course took me three full days of difficult travel to make Cambridge.

The Mid-Shore Ferry, as it was called, carried passengers across the Choptank twice a day. The flat-bottomed barge left the banks of Cambridge at about 10:00 each morning and again at 3:00 in the afternoon. The river was quite near a mile wide at this point and it took the ferry captain and his oarsmen the better part of an hour to cross the spectacular expanse of dark blue water. The lives of people working the river centered around the incoming and outgoing tides. Although, the Choptank was subject to mysteriously unpredictable forces that on occasion would send even the most experienced watermen to shore. It was not uncommon to see the ferry turn around in the middle of the river and make its way back to the dock as swirling currents made pushing the boat across to the other side all but impossible.

"We'll see if she lets us pass a bit later," the ferryman was apt to say. "She's presently a tad too upset."

I arrived in the small waterfront village too late to secure passage across the river. It was likely all for the best as I was exhausted and ravenously hungry. Possessing ample coinage to secure a meal, a room, and stable space for my horses, I undertook these chores all the while paying keen attention to my surroundings. A person would have had to been blind not to notice all the eyes that were directed toward the impressive skins and furs piled high on the back of my giant stallion. It was with great care that every pelt was carried to my room, making sure my sidearm was visible for all to see. Only when my payload was locked securely in my quarters did I make my way down the loosely cobbled road to the tavern.

Contrary to descriptions previously shared with me, the town of Cambridge itself was a sight that would impress no one. The poorly fitted stones in the street that ran for a half mile or so down the side of the river made it difficult for horses or carts to navigate. The wheeled carts and animals tended to frequent the secondary road which ran directly behind and parallel to the main waterfront street. It was a dirt path really, beaten smooth by the feet and hooves of man and animal walking this part of the Choptank for centuries.

"*Her Queens Pub*," read the sign hanging from the rooftop of the dilapidated structure. The name struck me as being inconsistent with a town that harbored few, if any, Loyalists. I entered the establishment having climbed a set of steps built of what looked like planking from a ship sitting atop a crumbling brick foundation. The tavern was a one room building with a dozen or so small wooden tables arranged in no discernable order. On the far side of the room stood a long bar. There were a dozen stools that looked to have been constructed out of barrels lined up alongside the bar. I could not have found an empty seat without squeezing myself in between two people so I instead took a seat at one of the vacant tables. A single candle burned at its center. Next to it, and the only other item on the whitewashed wooden table, was a menu.

Before I had time to even pick up the menu a man dressed in expensive looking clothes walked up to the table. His fashionable attire and pleasant continence served to make me comfortable with being approached by a stranger in unfamiliar surroundings. Similarly, I was not alarmed when a second man, also having the appearance of a gentlemen, walked over, and stood by his side. It was not until the two men, without uttering a word, sat themselves down at the table that I first experienced the sting of anxiety. The weariness that cloaked my mind tempered the degree to which I could get excited. It is probably more accurate to describe my emotion at that moment as one of annoyance at having been disturbed rather than one of fear.

The silk-suited dandies took their seats across the table from me. I was now sitting straight up in my chair, shoulders back, stiff and alert. I stared at the men with a look of dissatisfaction that I tried hard to exaggerate. The calm demeanor of the men was the only thing keeping me from angrily demanding an explanation as to why they were bothering me.

When I detected, out of the corner of my eye, another man approaching the table from my left side my defenses became immediately heightened. When a fourth member of their group assumed his position to the right of me, I readied myself to spring into action. Alas, it was too late. I had barely time to even flinch, making an almost imperceptible move toward my holstered pistol. This last man, an intimidating looking character, looked me directly in the eyes and, with his hand already gripping the weapon protruding from his belt, simply stated, "Don't do that."

The four men all took their seats. They slid the chairs up close to the table giving me a sense of being surrounded. There was a surreal quality to my present circumstances. I was too fatigued to think clearly about why these men had accosted me.

Looking to the man on my right I saw someone who had led a hard and unfortunate life. A deep wound, scarred over many years ago, ran across the entirety of his face. It began just above his left eye and had cut him in a line as straight as a ruler to his mouth on the opposite side of his scowling face. I could not imagine such a mark being produced by anything other than the blade of a sword. He wore another scar on his jawline. I could make not even a guess as to what might have caused this heinous injury. The man's penetrating glare intimidated me most profoundly and I turned away to cast my eyes on the less threatening looking gentlemen seated across the table from me.

"What is it you want?" I asked, the words coming in a more abrasive tone than had been intended.

"My name is Cornelius Armstrong," as he spoke, he stood very slowly.

He extended his hand as a gesture of good will. I reached out and accepted his offer. He had large hands, almost the size of mine. His attempt to impress with a firm handshake was dismissed as I squeezed his hand in mine the way one might crush an orange to force it to surrender its last drop of juice. He let his hand go limp so that I might release it and I obliged.

"Do you mind if we join you?" he asked as he again took his seat.

I was able to muster a weak laugh although it was riddled with fear and insecurity.

"With respect sir," I stated, "it seems as though my opinion in the matter is not to be highly valued."

"I can assure you, ah, I'm sorry," he paused and waited for me to introduce myself.

I made him wait, first looking at the man to Armstrong's left. He wore fine silk clothes and possessed a look of confidence and means. I then surveyed the other two. The man with the scar and the horribly weathered face was no longer looking at me. He had reached down to draw an oyster from his plate and slurped it down. I turned my attention to the fourth man. He was somewhat nondescript. A smallish man with plain features. Clearly not of the same stature of the two gentlemen but far less repulsive than the grotesque deviant that sat on my other side continuing to suck down oysters. This fourth man was clearly a subordinate. I turned my attention back to Armstrong.

"I am Steven Brixton," I declared.

"Ah, an Englishman," Armstrong responded. "I can assure you we mean you no harm."

"I did not say I was English," I protested as if I had been accused of murder.

The southern portion of the peninsula that constituted Maryland's eastern shore was known throughout the rest of the state for remaining loyal to England even after the conclusion of the Revolution. This fact had been considered inconsequential to Marylanders on the western side of the Chesapeake Bay until three years ago when hostilities had erupted between England and America with President Madison's declaration of war in 1812. People living to the south of Cambridge, the halfway point between my hometown of Somerton and the great city of Baltimore, were no longer merely thought to be Loyalists, possessing ignorant and old-fashioned ways of thinking, but enemies of the United States.

"Anyone worth their mother's spit is an Englishman," he said. "You, young man, present as a most impressive individual. I find it impossible to believe that English blood does not course through your veins."

"Forgive my boldness gentlemen," I glanced at the two lesser men with an expression that assured them the term did not apply to them. "But I do not know you. And feel, if I am being honest, that this is a group that may not be worthy of my undaunted trust. No offense is meant, I assure you."

"What might be done to set your mind at ease son of England?" Armstrong inquired.

"This," I said, making a circular motion with my finger and including every man in its circumference, "makes no sense at all."

A slight pause ensued as the two gentlemen briefly exchanged eye contact.

"Agreed," answered Armstrong. "And thank you. I associate with these men," he looked at the men sitting to either side of me, "out of necessity and not by choice I can assure you."

"I will refrain from judging any man's character based on appearance alone," I spoke slowly, making sure to deliver my intended points directly but without insult. "That being the case, I would surely be perceived a fool were I to ignore the blinding discrepancy that exists among this group presently assembled here tonight. It begs the question as to what might bring such a disparate collection of characters together. I will confess to being hard pressed to believe that your business is of an honorable nature."

"Ah!" Armstrong interjected. "Understanding completely your reluctance, allow me to clarify this present situation. And I can assure you as a witness to the glory of God and to the greatness of England that our intentions could not possibly be more honorable."

I waited only briefly for him to state his business. When clarification was not immediately forth-coming I spoke assertively but respectfully.

"I have a long day waiting for me tomorrow," I began. "I am tired and hungry and in need of a good night's sleep. If you have something to say, say it and be on your way."

My abrupt and contentious message drew snickers from the four men.

"Well," Armstrong said, "I'll admit that is a good deal less cordial than I am accustomed."

Armstrong spoke with a pompous arrogance that did not sit well with me. I generally made every effort to afford people an open mind before casting judgement on them, but it was clear to me that I did not care for this man. He possessed an air of superiority that reeked of being unearned and undeserved.

"I travel from Somerton," I spoke respectfully but my patience was now worn as thin as November ice.

"In County Somerset?" Armstrong questioned.

"Yes," I answered. "In Somerset. The people in my village now suffer a savage illness. I am three days into my journey to Baltimore with at least three more yet to travel."

"Somerton," Armstrong interrupted me again. "Not too far from Salisbury?"

"It's in between Princess Anne and Pocomoke," the other dandy offered.

"Southern part of Somerset," Armstrong acknowledged. "Nothing but Quakers and Indians down that way."

"Hidden in the woods back a few miles from Devil's Island," informed the scar faced man sitting next to me.

"The Devil's Island port is a good one," informed the dandy. "We much preferred it to sailing all the way up the Manokin to the Princess Anne docks."

"Nothing worthwhile down that way," Armstrong stated. "Surprised you wasted your time sending tobacco down there."

"Money is money," Armstrong's well-dressed accomplice said with half a laugh. "Besides, with the bay in its present condition, we're not selling to the southern shore. Even the trip from Cambridge to Baltimore is becoming too risky. We lose an entire shipment of tobacco and two or three good men every time a British warship stops us."

"Beg your pardon sirs," I interjected sharply. "I do not understand what is going on here. Please understand it is not my intention to be rude. There are sick people in my hometown. Several have already died. My mission to retrieve medicine is urgent. Every hour wasted puts another life at risk. If I am not well rested come morning my travel will be slowed. It is with respect, and the greatest urgency, that I plead with you to get to your point."

"Ha," Armstrong mocked, "I like this boy. He's got some piss and vinegar pumping through him."

The comment was condescending, and I was now completely confident regarding my initial impression of Cornelius Armstrong. He was a man of flawed character, and I did not like him.

"Very well," he resumed. "We saw you arrive earlier with two magnificent horses. It is our hope you would be willing to sell the animals."

"Absolutely not," I answered matter-of-factly, dismissing the inquiry out of hand, "the horses are not for sale."

"I will pay you twice what they're worth," Armstrong countered.

"They are not mine to sell," I stated firmly.

"Everything has a price," he replied.

"Well," I responded, "I disagree wholeheartedly with that sentiment. But surely in this case you are mistaken."

"How is it," Armstrong mused, "that a commoner from the southern peninsula speaks so well? Why, you might even pass for an educated lad."

"Just lucky I guess." My sarcasm was in response to the irreverent manner with which Armstrong spoke of my home.

Armstrong, who to this point had presented as harmless, even jovial, turned in an instant very somber. There was a sudden seriousness to him that I was not surprised existed, but its rapid onset was unnerving.

"My name, as I have stated, is Cornelius Armstrong. I was an Admiral in the King's Navy during the Revolution. I am now retired." He looked to his left, "This fine gentleman is William Alexander Morris."

My eyes widened, "I've heard of you," I said. The Morris family were wealthy tobacco plantation owners, a family of the first order by every standard. It was the Morris family that had established the trading price of tobacco as the official currency in Colonial Maryland. They were a family of considerable influence.

"You've heard of my grandfather," he said without a hint of emotion. "I've done nothing in this life that anyone would waste time talking about."

"My friend is too modest," Armstrong stated. "He's the richest man in all of Talbot."

Morris seemed indifferent to Armstrong's remark. His stoic glare indicating an awareness that it required neither courage nor bravery to be born into wealth.

"So, you are from the other side of the river?" I inquired.

Armstrong spoke for him, "Alexander has houses up and down the east coast."

I was intrigued by this claim, but my curiosity was no match for my weariness.

"Gentlemen, I will apologize, fatigue has set in and while I will not make it a habit to be impatient with men such as yourselves, I am irritable and fear that further conversation may lead to my offending you in some manner. Accidently, of course, but I am exhausted to the point of dizziness and my thinking is clouded. I really must eat something and get some sleep."

"One hundred dollars," Armstrong said, pulling a packet of notes from the inner lining of his over coat and slamming it onto the table.

"I'll not tell you again," this time there was a noticeable belligerence in my tone, "my horses are not for sale."

"Not for one hundred dollars?" Armstrong seemed incredulous.

"The horses are not mine to sell," I stated with finality.

"And the owner of the animals would not find one hundred dollars a suitable account for his horses?" Morris chimed in.

"I cannot sell what is not mine," I repeated with emphasis.

I was curious what these men wanted with my horses. If they were as rich as they claimed they surely owned many horses. But, knowing that any questions on my part would only prolong the present conversation I refrained from inquiry.

"Are you aware," Armstrong asked, "that the British attacked Washington just a few weeks back?" As my reply was not immediate Armstrong continued. "Burned it to the ground."

It was difficult not to take offense at Armstrong's implied contention that the people of Somerton were so uninformed that an event of such magnitude would elude them. Though news of any kind took its time to reach the lower shore, the information would always ultimately arrive. To suggest that southern Somerset, with its Loyalist population and Tory to a fault, were unaware of the Royal Navy's triumph in Washington was insulting. Nonetheless, I played along as I was certain that Armstrong's version of the siege would provide meaningful insight into the man's true colors.

"The British attacked Washington?" I believed my feigned astonishment convincing. "No, I have not heard this news. Burned it to the ground you say?"

Armstrong's account of the battle was mundane compared to some of the more fanciful tales that had been shared with those in my community. His rendition included details regarding how easily the British had stormed the capital city and how the American resistance commenced a full retreat at the first volley of cannon fire. He mentioned only briefly that England's Royal Marines had set the city ablaze and eliminated completely from his narration the violent storm that, for all practical purposes, ended the British invasion of Washington.

This storm carried with it tornadic winds that threw British infantry and artillery alike into the air as if they were a child's playthings. The torrential rains doused the enflamed city and turned side-streets into quickly moving streams. Reliable sources had described to the people in Somerton how the ferocity, and the timing, of this storm were viewed by the Americans and British alike as the hand of God Himself reaching down and smashing England's advance. It was curious that Armstrong did not consider this an element worthy of inclusion in his story.

"Now, having decimated Washington," Armstrong continued, "British forces are planning to attack Baltimore. We have information," he paused ever so briefly to glare at the hideous man to my right then returned his focus to me, "attacks by land and by sea are imminent. Possibly as soon as tomorrow. Without advance warning the American troops stand no chance of defending the city. If Baltimore falls," he stopped himself in midsentence and then resumed, "Baltimore cannot fall. With victories in Washington and Baltimore the British could well run the table. They would surely move against Philadelphia, and New York, and then Boston. England will have won back America."

I stared at him with a perplexed expression.

"Given more comfortable surroundings I might find it a privilege, even an honor, to sit and discuss these matters with gentlemen such as yourself and Mr. Morris, quite obviously hailing from families of the first order," my speech was deliberate but hurried. "But the current circumstances present such inconsistencies that I cannot help but to feel as though this misaligned group intends to take advantage of me. Whether through wit or force I feel greatly outmatched. My comfort with engaging this conversation in the first place is due to our presence in a public setting. But, frankly, I'm not sure even the presence of witnesses could stop you from obtaining whatever the hell it is you desire of me if you decide to take that course of action."

Armstrong sat back in his seat. He exhaled with a great sigh, his face relaxing almost completely, making him look like a much younger man. Finally, he opened his mouth to speak but waited as if for the proper words to form.

"What is it that we can do," he asked, "to put your mind at ease? We mean you no harm and would see you profit from our interaction. But we find ourselves in dire straits and in need of your assistance, at all costs."

My eyes had not veered from him throughout the course of his dialogue. I now looked to Morris and then to the men sitting on either side of me.

Armstrong read my mind. "Incongruent, to be sure."

I returned to him a look that I hoped conveyed mild amusement. "An explanation perhaps," I requested. "Or, at a minimum, introductions."

Armstrong immediately obliged. He looked at the man sitting to my left.

"Jacob McCabe does some work for us," he paused briefly and scanned the room as if waiting for an acceptable description of the man to pop into his head. "Important work. Difficult work. But, of a covert nature. Not the kind of employment that carries with it a job description. And not the kind of work that is readily discussed in an open forum."

While the introduction piqued my curiosity, it did nothing at all in the way of informing me as to the kind of functions Jacob McCabe performed in the service of Misters Armstrong and Morris.

"Mr. McCabe," I acknowledged him with a nod.

"Ah, please," he said in the thickest and most pronounced Irish accent I had ever heard in my life. "Call me Jake. It'll be my pleasure to make your acquaintance." His heavy accent, despite being somewhat difficult to decipher, carried with it an almost lyrical tone.

"This man," Armstrong nodded in the direction of the scar-faced ruffian. "This man is Coleman Holyday. He works for me presently. Previously he has known many lives but inevitably the man is a privateer. A pirate for hire if you will."

I looked at Coleman Holyday to observe his reaction to the charge. He wore an expression that bordered on condescending, even contempt. His horrific wounds made his face difficult to interpret but he was clearly unimpressed with Armstrong's description. His look was dismissive and implied a lack of respect.

The pirate's pistol wore a gold-plated handle that sparkled in the dim light as it protruded from his thick leather belt. The glimmer caught my eye. On the belt had been burned the words "Holy," and "Day." The two words were separated by a large, polished buckle. I surmised they were not separate words at all but rather the man's name. If my assumption proved accurate Coleman Holyday would be descended from Scots. The Scottish spelled the word "*Holliday*" in such a way, though the pronunciation was the same. This might explain my perception that Holyday and Armstrong did not care for one another. Hostilities between England and Scotland went back millennia.

"You are a young man," Armstrong resumed. "You don't remember. Not long ago this bay was infested with pirates. Hundreds of them fled into the Chesapeake after being chased out of the Caribbean. Common criminals they were, and they had their way with the Chesapeake for decades before the British returned to run them ashore. Those not hanged either scattered to the cities to the west of the bay or disappeared into the wilderness of the eastern shore. Still, a pirate is a pirate on land or sea.

Most of them deserve a walk to the gallows but some of them, well, they are just unfortunate victims of circumstance. Given a second chance, Mr. Holyday made the best of it. And young Brixton I would advise that looks can be deceiving. The pirate seated next to you carries considerable influence in both Baltimore and Philadelphia."

Holyday glared at Armstrong with an expression of disapproval. It was now abundantly clear to me that their existed some animosity between the two men.

"We saw you arrive earlier with two impressive animals and fine furs piled high," Morris interrupted, as if to encourage Armstrong to move in a more direct manner to our business.

The mention of my horses agitated me and as I began to sit up straighter in my chair Armstrong raised his hand in a nonthreatening manner as to calm my anxiety.

"You came in from the south," he nodded as if to insinuate that those facts were a given. "Traveling from somewhere out there," he looked off into the distance. "Raised in the woods and have not weathered your soles on cobbled streets. It says something that a man of your age would make such a journey by his lonesome. There are people out there," again staring off into the distance, "that trust you. That is a high endorsement. Fearless too, to journey through the badlands unaccompanied. I will not pretend to know anything of Somerton. You are moving toward Baltimore where those furs will bring a high price. You travel by the shoreline to avoid marauders. Alone, I suspect a small group of Indians, or a gang of pirates would present for you a formidable issue."

"I've already told you, there is illness in my village," I said. "There are a lot of sick people. Woman and children. And old folks. The whole town is depending on me."

"Nothing on this side of the bay?" questioned Morris. "No medicine in Princess Anne?"

"I have a list of supplies in addition to the medicine," I said. "Our town council works with some folks out of Baltimore. Known them since before the Revolution. Anyway, like you said, with the English patrolling the bay nothing is getting down our way. Princess Anne is fairing no better than Somerton."

"Mr. Brixton, could I interest you in free passage across the bay?" Armstrong was finally starting to get to the point. "You can keep your horses and for your help I will pay you the sum of two hundred dollars."

"You are throwing out numbers that defy credibility," I began. "Assuming for a minute that you possess two hundred dollars with which you are willing to forward in my direction, understanding that my horses cannot be sold, what exactly is it that I could do for you that would merit that kind of prize?"

"We need to get across the bay," Armstrong answered. "If the British take Baltimore," he continued in a tone that was both urgent and distressed, "America itself could well fall back into the hands of King George and we would return to life under British rule."

"And yet but a moment ago you were professing loyalty to England," I questioned. "Sir, your story becomes ever more convoluted each time you open your mouth." He clearly took offense at my contention that he was a liar.

Armstrong now wore a wrinkled brow with eyes so intense I would not have been the least bit surprised had darts begun to fly from them. The relaxed posture he had assumed previously had disappeared and been replaced by a rigidity that implied he might well spring to his feet and fly across the table at the next disagreeable word.

"We are English, descendants of royal blood lines that go back centuries," he spoke slowly and deliberately as if to conceal his growing impatience. He made it clear by moving his eyes back and forth between Morris and myself that he was speaking only of the two gentlemen and not the pirate and the other man. "However, America has made me and Mr. Morris extraordinarily rich men. Wealth that most people could not even imagine. Tens of thousands of acres stand in our names throughout Maryland, Virginia, and New York, boasting dozens of working farms. Houses too numerous to count. Enormous waterfront estates built on the most exquisite lands on the most majestic rivers anywhere in this world. We own hundreds of slaves on the Eastern Shore of Maryland alone." He stopped his frantic bragging and took a deep breath. "If England were to win back America, we stand to lose everything. The King would most surely restructure the land rights as they would be considered the spoils of war."

"Are you not in good standing with Britain?" I asked. "I find it puzzling men such as yourselves are not kept in the good graces of the Crown regardless of whether they considered you Loyalists or Americans."

"Ah, were it so easy to predict the whims of King George," Armstrong answered. "Frankly, and lesser men would hang for voicing the obvious, however, the good king is prone to inconsistent thinking."

"Yes," Morris chuckled. "Inconsistent thinking. The good King it seems has lost a good bit of his mind. Some say he is stark raving mad. Others tend to tone it down a bit. Of questionable mental capacity is a fairly common description of his current state."

"The degree of saneness is inconsequential," Armstrong stated. "We cannot put our fortunes at risk, and so the wellbeing of our families, and those even of future generations not yet born. There is far too much at stake to trust it to the unstable mind that presently sits on the throne."

"If I may sir," I interjected, "how is it that you became aware of this impending attack on Baltimore City?"

Armstrong and Morris shared a knowing glance. It was Morris that finally spoke.

"Our good friend Mr. Holyday here," he said, "is very well informed as to the activities of the military and of the government, be they American or British."

"The story grows greater by the minute," I suggested.

It was this comment that seemed to exhaust Armstrong's tolerance for any further explanation. He swallowed up the remainder of his ale and spoke.

"We need to get to Baltimore to warn the militia. The bay, infested as it is presently with British war ships, makes travel upon its waters most perilous. Moving horses across the bay for sale in Baltimore is a plausible explanation as to why such a journey would be undertaken. We will try, obviously, to avoid detection. However, should the British see us they will surely stop us for inquiry. Your horses provide the perfect cover. We are taking the animals to market in Baltimore. It seems Providence has delivered you to us for this express purpose. And, make no mistake Master Brixton, we are transporting the horses across the bay, and we are leaving post haste. Your cooperation would be greatly appreciated and extravagantly rewarded. However, it is your horses that give us the guise to traverse the bay. They go with or without you."

Hearing such a cold-blooded threat I instinctively reached for my pistol only to feel the barrel of Holyday's firearm pressed firmly into my side.

"Gentlemen," Armstrong announced, "shall we?" The remark could not have been mistaken for a question.

Holyday reached over and pulled my weapon from its holster. Everyone at the table stood and I was escorted from the tavern.

CHAPTER 2
Choptank

Exiting the tavern and stepping out into the street my thoughts ran most forlorn. My present situation was grim indeed. Were there a single soul on the deserted roadway I would have no doubt screamed out in distress. But, seeing no one I remained silent and experienced a sense of helplessness that rendered me distraught beyond compare.

"For God's sake Cole holster your weapon," Armstrong demanded.

I felt great relief upon hearing this and was put even more at ease when, in addition to putting his firearm away, the pirate returned to me my pistol.

At that moment, a carriage of the finest quality pulled up along the side of the road. The driver of the carriage jumped down onto the street and hastily opened the door to the transport. Misters Armstrong and Morris entered first.

The Irishman then directed me to enter by making a sweeping motion with his arm. This nonverbal instruction was accompanied with a bold smile and before I had even time to think it through, I was climbing into the vehicle.

The carriage, led by two unspectacular horses, moved back off the unevenly cobbled riverfront street onto the smoothness of the worn dirt road behind it. With a bellow from the driver the animals instantly had the carriage moving at a very respectable speed. Given my present circumstances I should have been much alarmed. There was a strange awareness of this fact and my calmness puzzled me. I suppose it was the good-natured attitudes possessed by my abductors that permitted me to roll along in silence. Having been taken against my will there would have been every good reason to panic and to fear for my life. Although, my weapon had been returned to me and if these four men did indeed possess evil intentions, they did not convey such plans by their demeanor. There was no conversation as we moved at first away from the river and then back toward its bank. There existed a peculiar calmness among the men. I was aware this could well have been a misinterpretation on my part. Still, I took some comfort in knowing that my captures knew full well that I possessed a pistol the pirate had no doubt inspected and found to be loaded and packed with powder and ball.

We turned onto a well-lit street. The stones under wheel were fitted finely and the horses pulled the carriage along the smooth surface. Looking out the window I saw some fanciful shops and people wandering about talking and laughing. Most peculiar for such a late hour.

"Is this Cambridge?" I asked, finally breaking the silence.

"Yes," replied Armstrong with a chuckle. "In all its glory."

"So, the shanty town?" I inquired.

"You came into town by way of the creek," Morris informed, "tracking close to the bay."

We then veered off the main street and though it was dark I could make out some impressive estates in the distance.

"The shanty town, as you call it," remarked Armstrong, "caters to the watermen and travelers with lesser means. The Nanticoke will occasionally call on some of the shops down there. Indians are not made to feel especially welcome in Cambridge proper."

"I thought the Nanticoke had been driven north," I said with the inflection as to make my statement a question.

"Oh, yes," he replied. "The Nanticoke had several villages along the Choptank not a few miles from here. But they have been run out. Pushed up north over the years. Some Indian families still call the Choptank their home. There is a settlement of them ten miles or so upriver, but they number barely a dozen."

"Harmless, that group" Morris joined in. "But some of them have made off into the forests. Small groups of them. Living off the land as they have for thousands of years, but savages, to be sure. The Nanticoke were the most warlike of all the tribes that used to call this region their home. But they have been driven away, all but a few."

"There are still plenty of Indians down your way, in the County Somerset," Armstrong suggested. "I have heard the tribes of the south, the Accomack and the Pocomoke, they refused to make the move north with the Wicomico and the Nanticoke. Still a lot of natives down your way?"

"I guess," I replied. "There is an Assateague settlement over by the ocean. We have a good relationship with them. I do not know much about the Pocomoke or the Accomack. They live across the border in Virginia. Not a safe place for Marylanders."

"Because of the Indians or the Virginians?" inquired Armstrong.

"Virginians," I answered. "Maryland and Virginia have been at war forever it seems. I do not believe anyone really knows where the border is, but the killing continues. Whether on land or sea, if men see each other anywhere near that imaginary line there will surely be blood spilled."

"I've heard those stories since I was a little boy," Morris offered. "The oyster wars."

"All kinds of different names for it," I answered. "People from Maryland and Virginia don't seem to care for one another. The feud predates memory."

"No problems with the Indians then?" Armstrong inquired. "I mean the Assateague, they are a peaceful people, are they not?"

"Are not all the tribes peaceful until you steal their land?" I laughed as I answered him.

At this point the carriage turned down a long lane. It was dark and I could not see everything in detail but even in the moonless night I could make out the immaculate and impeccable landscaping that lined the path we now travelled. It was at this moment I fully comprehended how utterly surreal was my present predicament. Moments ago, there had been a pistol pressed to my side. Yet here I was with this group of strangers traveling in an extravagant transport the likes of which I had never seen.

We then pulled up to a great mansion. My eyes popped open wide, and a pulse of energy ran through my body as I looked in amazement at the enormity of the building before me. Its size was equaled only by drawings I had seen in books. Even the great Teackle House in Princess Anne, the largest and most grand house in all of Somerset County, paled in comparison to this estate.

We exited the carriage and made our way up the walk of the grand manor. Once inside my amazement became difficult to conceal. I stood in the parlor dumbfounded, my mouth hanging wide open. When I noticed the men staring at me, I became embarrassed.

"I've never seen anything like this," I confessed.

None of the men seemed surprised by my statement.

"Make sure Mr. Brixton here gets a wholesome meal," Armstrong called out to one of his servants.

"Right this way sir," the tall, square-shouldered black man extended his arm and led me down a cavernous hallway to one of the many dining rooms in the enormous residence.

"Bring him to the southside study when he has finished dining. And have the boys prepare the *Pegasus*," Armstrong directed the man.

The four men then stepped in unison toward the southern end of the mansion. The hallway in which they walked was so wide that they moved shoulder to shoulder. Armstrong was out in front by half a step but otherwise the quartet stood four men abreast as they marched down the immense hall. Each of their shoes made a distinctively different sound as they contacted the polished wooden floorboards.

The man who had guided me through the maze of hallways that led to the dining room stood to my right side and behind me by several feet. Though he remained motionless for the duration of my dinner I could sense that he was not watching me but rather observing the four other servants as they catered my meal. These servants, two men and two women, sturdy black specimens with stoic expressions, constantly moved to and from the table. As one plate was removed from the table another was set in its place. My water glass was topped off after each sip I took. The crumbs were even brushed from the table as I ate.

I devoured several biscuits, a serving of chicken and one of fish, along with a bowl of corn and a plate of potatoes. Eating so rapidly on an empty stomach I became full rather quickly. It would have been impossible for me to take another bite. I turned to tell the man behind me that I could eat no more.

"Very well sir," and he raised his arm to halt one of the women as she was entering the room with yet another plate of food.

When I rose from my seat there remained on the table more food than I would normally eat in three days.

"This way please," requested the tall black man. He began walking with a hesitation that suggested I was to follow.

We arrived at the library and my expressionless guide pushed open a massive wooden door. The four men each sat in expensively upholstered leather chairs. The walls were lined with impressive mahogany shelves filled with ancient books. The men rose when I entered the room. The servant closed the immense door behind him upon leaving the study.

"Mr. Brixton," called Armstrong as he motioned for me to join the others as they assumed their positions around an immense drawing table.

Walking over to the table I could see two maps laid out for display. The larger of the two documents was constructed of heavy brownish parchment. Armstrong discarded it by tossing it onto the floor behind him. He then repositioned the remaining map, which was smaller and printed on thinner white paper.

I took my position next to Armstrong. Otherwise, each man stood alone at one side of the rectangular fixture. Armstrong placed his finger on the map. I looked down to observe an intricately detailed drawing of the Chesapeake Bay. Before I was able to ascertain exactly what it was Armstrong was pointing to, I could sense him staring at me. I looked over and met his intense eyes.

"I apologize for the disruption to your travel plans. Surely you had no expectation of being so mightily inconvenienced," Armstrong possessed an overpowering arrogance and it seemed as though it took great effort on his part to speak to me in a polite manner. "I can only promise you that had we another alternative available to us we would have considered acting upon it. Unfortunately, time is of the essence and our mission so extremely critical. Our options have been reduced to what amounts to the impressment of a fine young son of Somerset." The inflection in his voice implored all present to appreciate the irony of the statement.

Whether the present war between England and America was its own entity altogether or merely the logical continuation of the Revolution was by all accounts irrelevant. President Madison had declared war against England in 1812. At issue, he claimed, was the British Navy's impressment of American men. All males of fighting age, a target that was by design subjective and at times essentially all inclusive, were apprehended from ships sailing the waters of the Chesapeake and forced to serve in His Majesty King George's Navy.

Initially this practice was limited to Americans captured at sea. More recently, boys and men were being dragged from their homes and fields to labor on English ships patrolling the bay. President Madison cited these abductions as cause for the two countries to engage in a state of war. However, the men of Somerton spoke of the conflict as another attempt by America to expand its boundaries and wrestle more land from the British. England's current presence on the Chesapeake, if the men of Somerton were to be believed, was due in part to the American invasion of English lands held in Canada.

"I understand," Armstrong continued, "that assisting us in warning Americans of an impending British attack runs contrary to the beliefs held by the people within the region of your homeland. I will not condemn those remaining loyal to our Motherland. English blood will forever pump through the veins of all here, their families, and future generations. But the American dream is legitimate. Freedom is a worthy cause for which to live or die. All men, rich or poor, superior quality and common, deserve the ownership of their souls. You may take solace in knowing that forewarning Baltimore of an impending invasion may mean little in the outcome of this war but, if nothing else, we may be able to save the lives and spare the blood of good men, English and American."

I did not believe that Armstrong entertained the idea that warning the Americans would be inconsequential to the outcome of a British invasion. On some level I appreciated him taking the time to help me rationalize my involvement. On the other hand, the slave owner's assertion that all men deserve the ownership of their souls was evidence his words rang hollow and meaningless.

"Once more, I will remind you that you have no choice in this matter," Armstrong's words came matter-of-factly but carried the weight of a threat. "I do hope you take to heart that I am an honorable man and your reward, should you cooperate without obstruction, will be of an immensely generous nature."

Armstrong returned his eyes to the map and continued speaking.

"You must depart immediately. There is no moon tonight. You will be invisible to any British ships you may encounter unless you run into them broadside. The wind and the tide are precisely in our favor. Once you have Annapolis in sight you are home free. We can only hope there are no ships blocking entrance to the port."

"There will be none," answered Holyday. "The British will have passed that point. They'll be gathering at the mouth of the Patapsco readying to make their run up the river to Fort McHenry."

"If," Armstrong extolled with much emphasis, "you are stopped by the British, you are on your way to Baltimore to sell your horses."

"I have to ask," I interjected, my curiosity finally getting the better of me, "why not just use two of your own horses? Surely you have two you could spare," I added.

"The British," Morris attempted to explain, "are going to be suspicious of anyone moving across the bay on the eve of their attack. If our ruse is to be believable, we need to show them something out of the ordinary. Your horses, young man, are out of the ordinary. If stopped, we stand a much better chance of convincing them there are buyers in Baltimore impatiently awaiting animals such as yours. Ferrying two horses across the Chesapeake under cover of night will have them reluctant to believe anything we say. We need them to look at these animals and think, yes, I can see why a buyer would be willing to pay an extravagant price for horses such as these. The immediacy of the sale is a story I am sure Mister Holyday will be able to concoct. The horses are a distraction. And to answer your question, neither Mister Armstrong nor I possess horses so spectacular in their appearance."

Considering everything that was happening it struck me odd that I should be so aware of the pride I took in the compliment directed at my beloved horses.

"May I proceed?" Armstrong asked, sounding rather annoyed at my interruption. He did not wait for an answer but instead moved his finger up the map, narrating as he traced the intended course. "Keep close to the shoreline. Out, along here, across to Kent Island, up," he drew his finger across the map to Annapolis, "and make your run across the bay."

"Sir," I interrupted, "beg your pardon. Is the destination Annapolis or Baltimore?"

"The British will have the waterways to Baltimore sealed off. Forty or fifty British warships will be preparing to race up the river and bombard the fort and the city. Annapolis is our destination. Mr. McCabe will take care of the rest," Armstrong explained.

My assumption was that McCabe would be making the remainder of the trip to Baltimore on horseback. I understood extraordinarily little about how these men expected to accomplish the task at hand. For the time being I had no choice other than to do what I was told.

"Gentlemen," Morris said, "May you go in God's good graces."

Armstrong reached inside his coat pocket and pulled out a thick packet of American notes. He placed them on the drawing table in front of me.

"Two hundred dollars."

He then handed Holyday an additional packet of bills.

"Two hundred more. Give it to him once you dock in Annapolis. Make sure every precaution is taken to ensure the safety of his horses," Armstrong directed his comment to Holyday specifically.

I started to inquire as to my horses but was decisively cut off.

"A total of five hundred dollars," Armstrong proclaimed. He was including the one hundred he had retrieved from the tavern table and stuffed into my pocket at the onset of my abduction. "And the knowledge that you played a part in saving many lives. On your way," the comment being abrupt and final.

Armstrong turned and walked purposefully out of the room with Morris in pursuit. As I watched the two exit the drawing room my attention was interrupted by Holyday barking a command.

"This way," he gurgled.

I mindlessly followed him along a lengthy hallway that took us down some polished stone steps and passed us through a vestibule out into a courtyard. McCabe had fallen in line behind me and the three of us eventually made our way back to the river. Eight boats bobbed slowly up and down in the outgoing tide, their well tied ropes affording them little leverage against the sturdy wooden docks to which they were secured.

Adjacent to the wharf was a boat house. Behind it, set well back from the bank of the river, were the slave's quarters. They were small and in great need of repair. The dilapidated little rooms stood in stark contrast to the sprawling mansion that towered over the river. It was obvious the slave huts had been purposefully built so they could not be seen from Armstrong's castle. They were buffered by a small hill and a grand strand of oak trees. The oaks were majestic and gave the impression they were as old as the Choptank itself. Their beauty distracted from the rows of weathered wooden shacks that ran back a great distance from the river.

There was also a column of willow trees, more recently planted than the oaks, that provided an obstructed view of the deplorable housing to anyone walking along the river. Even at this late hour, the gates through which the slaves passed squeaked busily. Some of them went toward the great house while others made their way back to their pathetic dwellings.

Buying and selling human beings is repugnant and vile. Its acceptance has bewildered me for as long as I can remember. Surely, there are many besides me that struggle to make sense of how things work in this broken world. But nothing quite defies logic and sensible reasoning more than the enslavement of other people. I suspect there is not a single person alive who does not believe the institution to be repugnant. Yet some allow their greed to overpower their humanity while others, somehow, simply appear to be indifferent. And complicit also are those of us who vehemently abhor the practice but speak out only when in the company of like-minded people, hidden away from the possibility that we might be held responsible. It is a troublesome dilemma and profoundly difficult to comprehend.

We watch England and America lock horns once again. The people of Virginia and Maryland still find reasons to kill one another, and the white man and the Indian are embroiled in a state of constant battle. The carnage, in every case, can be attributed to greed and man's lust for land. Meanwhile, slaveowners and those repulsed by them stand side by side, as if members of the same family. Slaves are stripped of every freedom and forced to the fields but there is no war. The outrage is expressed in condemnation but when it comes to correcting a crime that runs contrary to the very reason America exists in the first place not a sword is raised, or a musket packed, nor a militia assembled.

CHAPTER 3
Chesapeake

The existence of Somerton is easily traced back to the families refusing to adhere to the mandates of either England or America. Somerton people did things their own way. Ever suspicious of outsiders and defiantly resistant to change, our world had been carefully crafted to embrace the beliefs we held dear and to disregard everything else. Buying and selling human beings ran contrary to our principles. We did not engage in it and did not associate with those who were tolerant of the practice.

It was difficult for me to see so many helpless black men and women trapped on this man's estate. I confess to thinking that had I not grown up with a negro man named Theodore, of Somerton, my feelings might be quite a bit less impassioned. Maybe I too would look at these people and, like others, decide they were not really people. But I knew better. I had spoken with Theodore many times and respected him too much to believe that he was less of a man than any person I had ever met. Few people in Somerton, or in the whole of the County Somerset for that matter, were as well read or as well-mannered as Theodore. He had made the trip from England the year before I was born with a contract that was paid off in two years. He arrived with other indentured servants both white and black. Most of them, having worked off the debt of their contracts, had moved north to the Philadelphia area. Theodore was the only member of that group of settlers to have remained in Somerton and he had become a respected member of our community and a trusted friend and neighbor. I considered him an exceptionally good person. He possessed unmatched character and integrity and I cared for him as though he were a member of my family. The thought of Theodore being chained and forced to the fields seemed just as obscene as Uncle Jedediah suffering such a fate.

It was with a heavy heart that I looked away from the countless shacks and directed my attention back to the docks where the expensive and beautifully crafted vessels rocked gently in the water. How painful it must be, I thought, for the slaves to see these ships sitting by the wharf each day. Surely, they must think constantly of boarding them and sailing away. They must look out past the mouth of the Choptank River to the Chesapeake Bay as they toil in the fields and think that out there, just over the horizon, is my freedom.

"I could make Annapolis an hour quicker in this one," Holyday rumbled. He was looking at a single-masted Chesapeake Canoe. "But can't fit two horses on her. Here," he pointed, "this is what we need." He pointed to a vessel with the name *Pegasus* painted broadly across its stern. It was a handsome vessel, richly finished and masterfully carved. She sported two sails that flapped in the light breeze waiting to be hoisted.

Two negro slaves approached us from behind. Each of them was leading one of my horses by loosely held reins. The negros were both tall and slender men but differed greatly in age. They were immensely skilled in the handling of horses. Thunder and Blue were extraordinary horses. Big and strong, they were the smartest animals I had ever seen. Having known each since the day of their birth I had a bond with them that allowed me to communicate certain things with mere expressions. Their eyes conveyed to me a sense of calm. This lack of anxiety on the part of my horses served to comfort me in a strange but important way. Horses, especially these two, possess impeccable judgement of character. It was a good omen that they remained calm in the presence of Holyday and McCabe.

The older black man handed me Thunder's reins and I walked the horse onto the boat as nonchalantly as if we were walking into a stable. The younger negro continued to hold Blue's reins loosely and the horse stepped onto the craft without the slightest coaxing.

Holyday untied the boat and with a strong push from the black men the boat drifted away from the dock and was immediately picked up by the river's current. The outgoing tide grabbed the *Pegasus* and pulled her along so quickly that it seemed we were already under sail.

"My furs?" I asked.

"Admiral Armstrong was hoping the five hundred dollars would be adequate compensation," McCabe answered, his Irish accent terrifically thick and out of place.

"Certainly," I responded, expecting a reply that implied a similar message.

"You got your watch?" Holyday inquired of McCabe.

McCabe did not answer verbally but rather pulled a large silver watch from his pocket. Holding it by the thick metal chain to which it was attached he lifted it above his head so Holyday could see it.

"I've been on the water all my life," I said. "What do you need me to do?"

"Get up front with your animals," Holyday instructed. "Need you to keep them calm. Make sure they stay on separate sides of the boat. The more they move around the slower I am going to have to go. If they behave, I can make old *Pegasus* fly."

"They'll behave," I said. "Not to worry about them. Smartest animals alive."

"When I get this thing going," Holyday continued, "cutting hard, they end up on the same side and we'll end up in the water."

I moved to the front of the boat. Standing clear of the boom, I took Thunder's reins in one hand and Blue's in the other and leaned back against the forward mast.

"Now!" shouted Holyday.

McCabe pulled on one line and Holyday the other and the sail shot skyward like a racoon up a tree. The ship accelerated with such force that both horses took a step backwards.

"Here we go," McCabe announced and loosed a second smaller sail. It unfurled and immediately tightened against the wind. The ship seemed to almost come out of the water as it continued to gain speed.

I was hard pressed to believe we were able to move across the water with such force. We flew by the shanty town which was hardly visible from the middle of the river, being lit up solely by a couple of campfires. Within minutes we were racing along in complete darkness. I began to talk calmly to my horses. It was probably as much to smooth my own nerves as theirs.

I was looking straight ahead. Aside from an occasional whitecap crossing our path we were sailing blind. Both Holyday and McCabe appeared to know what they were doing. The sky was clear on this moonless night and the stars lit up the night. It was one gigantic map for an experienced navigator. However, the appearance of but a few clouds would hide the map and render Christopher Columbus himself completely lost.

Both men had lanterns set next to them on the floor of the boat to keep the glow invisible to any ships that may be lurking on the waters of the bay. Every few minutes they would each bend down and hold their pocket watches up to the light of the lantern. The lanterns would then be held off the starboard side of the *Pegasus*. "Any time now," or, "Peal your eyes," they would call out.

These announcements were always followed immediately by, "There he is," and we would race by a buoy close enough that either man could have reached out and touched it. If the buoy were more than a few feet away from the boat Holyday would correct his course with a slight push of the rudder handle or the pull of a rope. The precision with which these men made their way from one buoy to the next was amazing. Had I not witnessed the miraculous accuracy with which these sailors picked up their next mark in the vast darkness I would not have believed it.

Holyday and McCabe worked the batteau magically. The speed with which this ship flew across the water fascinated me to the extreme. Once out in the open water, engulfed by the vast blackness and smooth seas, the tide seemed to push us rapidly into a forceful wind that the sails inhaled so completely that on one occasion I nearly expected the ship to take flight.

Looking out into the void of a darkness absolute, what little waves there were came at us capped with a pale phosphorescence. The wind blew strong across my face as I held tight to each horses' harness. The animals were both so strong and heavy that my embrace aided my balance much more than it did theirs.

"There he is!" the men cried out simultaneously, having found another buoy.

Armstrong had spoken confidently when, back at his estate, he traced his finger up the map out past the mouth of the river and up toward Kent. He had called out the time as if to give the men targets, although it did not seem they needed them.

"And then," Armstrong had continued across the map, "you hit the tip," his finger pressing firmly into the southern end of Kent Island on the map, pinning it to the table, "and make your run." At this point he drew his finger across the map to the other side of the bay. "The tide should push you right up into Annapolis," he said.

We needed to make the western shore by sunup to avoid becoming too easily seen by the British. There is no place to hide on the flatness of the Chesapeake. Our departure left us barely eight hours of darkness to cover the course. Initially, I had thought this goal monumentally ambitious if not flatly impossible. Now, racing under full sail across seas as flat as glass I had no doubt that we would make the opposite shore well before daybreak.

Being mesmerized by the swiftness with which our ship shot across the bay I gave no additional thought to an issue that weighed heavily on my mind when we first set out. I had worried about remaining on my feet for the duration of the journey. Being responsible to steady my horses as we crashed through the waves for eight hours seemed a task that would exhaust my arms, legs, and back. However, with the seas being so calm, there were no waves of any consequence with which to struggle. I had been convinced that fatigue would overtake me prior to the trip's end but such was not the case. It now appeared that the duration of our mission would be shorter than I had anticipated by a measure of hours. Leaning back against the mast, my feet fit squarely against wooden trim running across the deck, each of my hands were snuggly fastened into a horses' harness. If not so fascinated with our pace and the beauty of the starlit sky, I am sure I could have dozed off, such was my level of comfort. Any anxiety I had with respect to my animals all but vanished. It seemed the pitch black into which we sailed pleased the horses. The warm wind blowing in their faces further relaxed them and but for an occasional whinny I would have thought them asleep.

The lights from the western shore now came into sight and I was overcome with excitement. It was a strange sense of distorted euphoria that pulsed through me as the energy generated by the adventure pushed back against a mind and body depleted by lack of sleep. I reminded myself that, having crossed the bay three days ahead of schedule, time was on my side. I would stable my horses and find a nice room. The thought of a comfortable bed and uninterrupted hours of much needed sleep had a peculiar paradoxical effect. Now completely alert, though aware that I was running on nothing more than adrenaline, my senses were so aroused that sleep would have been all but impossible.

Several torches burned on the docks. Without having made the trip to Annapolis previously, knowing which light to follow would have been anyone's guess. But it was obvious that Holyday and McCabe had frequented this port previously and if they decreased the speed of our vessel as they prepared to dock it was only by an imperceptible degree.

"Hold steady," yelled Holyday.

"Here she comes," shouted back McCabe as he released a rope that flung into the air as the smaller of the two sails fell limp. The boom swung violently across the deck of the ship. Holyday ducked without so much as glancing backward and it flew over his head, clearing him by no more than an inch. The ship suddenly lost all power and, coming to an almost complete stop, bobbed gently in the water two or three times, turned herself around and floated gently up against the wooden pilings.

McCabe passed directly behind me and stepped in perfect unison with Holyday off the ship and onto the dock. Their movements appeared almost choreographed. Through the darkness two men approached the ship with torches in hand. McCabe pushed an enormous wooden plank bridge onto the front of the ship.

"Careful," he said. "The horses will be wobbly."

That was my cue to walk them off the ship.

"Blue first." I called out, walking the horse to the bridge. McCabe met me halfway and escorted the animal onto the dock where he held firmly as the horse got its leg under her. We did the same with Thunder who struggled slightly, swaying on the dock as a drunkard would upon leaving a pub. The giant horse shook its head back and forth a few times to clear his mind and whinnied loudly as if to tell me that all was well.

The darkness had begun to fall away as the *Pegasus* snuggled up to the dock. At the very moment the three of us all stood safely on the western shore of the bay the sun peaked up over the waters of the Chesapeake.

There was a moment on the dock when Holyday, McCabe, and I all looked in concert to the east. The morning sun rising over the Chesapeake is a sight like no other. The enormity of the pristine landscape expanded powerfully as the flaming red star kissed the sea goodbye and began its ascent skyward. Our world stopped. We stood silent, awe-inspired, and humble. All worries and anxiety washed clean from our consciousness by the perfection of the vast and stunning brilliance.

Reality waited only briefly for us to bask in the glory of nature and newness before stealing back our attention. With a stunning suddenness the dock grew busy and deafening. A cart rolled past, its wooden wheels clattering loudly and predictably on the stone-laden street. Voices coming from every direction filled thick the morning air. Holding my horses loosely, I turned away from the majesty of the Chesapeake and there before me stood Annapolis.

I had heard so many stories of this legendary waterfront city that there was a sense of having been here before. The historic landscape stretched out in front of me. Its cobbled streets lined with buildings that climbed their way up and away until they disappeared over the hill on which they had been built. In the distance I could see the State House. It looked exactly like the drawings I had seen in so many books over the years. The magnificent spire reaching toward a sky which brightened by the minute.

"I've no time to lose," I heard McCabe say as he approached. "Some militia will be marching for Baltimore this afternoon. You can fall in with them if you so desire. Otherwise, the road to the city is a good one. You won't have any trouble." He then extended his hand and said, "You seem a fine young fellow. I may see you again one day, until then I hope good fortune finds you. Safe trip and Godspeed back to the Somerset. I must hurry and my departure is immediate. Remain courageous and honest Master Brixton and let God guide you." McCabe shook my hand firmly. Staring directly into my eyes as though he were looking for something he said, "Good." And he was gone. I would never see him again.

I watched as he climbed atop a large and powerfully built white and grey horse. He conversed with two uniformed men briefly from atop his mount. The men looked up at him and nodded in such a way that implied they were being given instructions. McCabe then yanked on the horse's reins and, giving it a swift kick in the rump, began trotting down the street.

"Brixton!" Holyday hollered from the other direction.

I turned and saw him walking toward me. His limp told a story of an injury incurred long ago, never healing sufficiently to negate the permanence that now altered his gait. His hard expression evidenced pain, both physical and emotional, that he had swallowed and accepted in what likely seemed a lifetime ago. The suffering printed across his face as plainly as the headlines of a newspaper was now part of who he was. His wrinkled grimace framed the gnarled disfigurement of his damaged mouth in such a way that looking at him one could not imagine the man having ever possessed a different appearance. The harsh, gravelly afront of his voice was the only sound that could possibly have come from such a face. Holyday was the epitome of a renegade, a man that adhered to an altogether ulterior set of rules. Broken and weary, he embodied the lawless participant, a survivor of misery, tormented, fearsome and intimidating, a pirate.

"McCabe is off to Baltimore," he said. "British ships have been moving up the bay all week." He had obviously pumped the dock hands for information. "Twelve ships passed to the east yesterday alone. They guess there to be almost twenty, even thirty ships up there already. Lucky indeed our paths did not cross in the night. If they are preparing to attack Baltimore there would have been short work made of us. British troops are moving by land as well. On their way up from Washington."

"Appears as though my timing could not have been worse," I responded.

My thoughts ran immensely disorganized. The families back in Somerton surely were counting the minutes until my return. The thought of England sacking Baltimore caused me great confusion and anguish. There was no way for me to determine how this event might delay my trip.

"You might postpone your trip to Baltimore," Holyday offered his recommendation while reaching into his trouser pocket. He pulled out an envelope that looked as old as he. With shifty eyes he glanced discretely in each direction and extended the wrinkled, stained package to me.

I accepted it and instinctively looked to read the lettering printed on it.

"*400 Hogshead Dorchester Tobacco*", printed finely at the top of the envelope had been crossed out with a notation of, "paid in full," written almost indiscernibly directly underneath.

"Put that in your pocket," Holyday whispered with his rough voice. "You don't want people around here knowing you got that kind of money. You can count it later. Two hundred dollars."

Stuffing the money into my pants pocket with the three hundred already in my possession, his comment struck me funny. That I would count a package flush with money, given to me by a pirate on behalf of one of the richest men in Maryland, seemed amusing. What would I say should the payment be light? And to whom would I say it?

I was suddenly keenly aware of the traffic on the street. Another person stepped out from behind one of a hundred different doors every few seconds. The number of people walking up and down and across the street was stupefying. There were now more people scurrying about than would make up the entire population of Somerton.

The loudness of the bustling early morning rush of humanity contrasted the dark quietness of the bay to such a degree that I became overwhelmed. It seemed to me that I could hear every voice, each one louder than the next. They screamed into my ears. The horse's hooves banged on the stone, and wooden wheels of all sizes squeaked and rattled. It was unrelenting. The squealing and screaming never stopped. The Annapolis waterfront at dawn was a continuous roar of sound. It was maddening. My head was spinning.

"I need to get to Baltimore. I have to get the medicine back to Somerton," I blurted out.

The British were preparing to attack the city by land and by sea. Setting out for Baltimore was paramount to suicide. It is possible that the realization that my mission was doomed was more than I could accept. Knowing how many people were counting on me weighed too heavy. The disappointment stung with unacceptable failure. Every negativity flooded my mind in dizzying chaos.

Holyday grabbed the horses from my hands.

"You need to rest," he said, "Come with me. You look like you're about to collapse."

We began walking in the direction of a row of brick buildings that lined the dock as it turned itself around the harbor. I mindlessly followed Holyday, now understanding nothing of my surroundings.

My vision had begun to blur. We walked behind one of the buildings into a large stable. There were many horses under the roof and the interior of the structure provided a slight respite from the deafening noise of the streets. Holyday handed my horses off to a stable boy and walked me through a back door.

"We need a room," I heard him say.

"Certainly, Mr. Holyday," answered the softness of an older woman's voice. She handed him a key and he led me down a hallway to a room on the first floor.

I do not recall anything else of that morning, not even climbing into the small bed in the corner of the dark room. I was asleep before my head hit the pillow and slept as if I were deceased.

CHAPTER 4
The Severn River

I awoke to Holyday pounding on the hotel room door. When I did not answer he opened the hollowly constructed wooden door and entered.

"Are you okay?" he inquired.

It took me a moment to collect myself and he allowed for this. I sat up in the bed, sore and disoriented. Looking around the room did little to assist me in getting my bearings. The room was dark. There was a small window, a few feet in width, that ran along the top of the far wall. It was very narrow, measuring not more than one foot from top to bottom and reminiscent of something you might see in a jailhouse. The opening was much too small for a person to climb through and, as it was positioned at the top of the wall near the ceiling, it allowed the light from outside to illuminate only the upper portion of the room. The remainder of the enclosed space remained almost completely black. Understanding this, Holyday moved the candle he was holding closer to his head. The wretched face peering at me in the flickering darkness through candlelight would have given me a fright had I the energy to summon such emotion. Holyday looked at me and watched as my memory returned and I slowly regained consciousness.

"What time is it?" I questioned.

"Early afternoon," he answered. "Get up. You'll want to see this."

Operating in a haze, I clumsily climbed out of bed and blindly followed him into the hallway. It was a little brighter now but still the place was very dimly lit. The windows running the length of the long corridor were, as they had been in the small room, constructed as thin rectangular openings near the ceiling. There were no candles to increase the visibility. Holyday walked in front of me, his one foot dragging just a little longer than the other across the creaking wooden floor. I could see his bent upper torso quite clearly now, but his lower half remained a shadowy blur. Eventually we arrived at a large wooden door. Holyday pushed it open. The blinding sunlight seared my eyes. I instinctively threw my arms over my face to shield myself from the radiance of the afternoon.

"Christ!" I shuttered.

Holyday snorted as he laughed at my discomfort, making a sound that only a pirate could make.

"Where are we going?" I asked as we turned the corner of the building to see the stables where my horses stood.

As my question had been answered he disregarded it. Stepping up to Thunder and Blue I rubbed my hands down their necks. They appeared well rested, and both possessed a calm demeanor. This assured me they had been well cared for through the night.

"The intelligence was correct," Holyday muttered as he lit a poorly rolled smoke. "British are moving on Baltimore in full force."

Holyday extended his tobacco-filled satchel toward me. I nonverbally declined with a simple back and forth movement of my head.

"Listen," Holyday began, "I got a few reliable folks telling me the British are going to take Baltimore as early as today. They are going to hit them first on land over by North Point and follow up with a naval attack. Going to move their fleet up the Patapsco, blow apart Fort McHenry and bombard the city from the harbor. If we can get over to River Beach, I know people over there. Get a front row seat for the whole affair."

I was somewhat shaken by what I had just heard. The topic of war and a British attack on Baltimore had been thrown around almost casually to this point. For the first time the thought of what was about to happen really sunk in. The words Armstrong had uttered back in Cambridge now echoed in my mind. On the heels of what had just transpired in Washington, a British victory in Baltimore could well mean a victory for England in this second war of independence. I envisioned the inevitable assaults on America's great cities as the English sacked Philadelphia then worked their way north. New York would fall, then Boston.

The thought of England taking back her land from the Americans caused me peculiar and unexpected angst. The people of County Somerset had never fully embraced the American victory. We still referred to the states as colonies and continued to use British currency wherever it was accepted. Having remained loyal to the throne, we would undoubtably be handsomely rewarded. But I knew there was much more in play. Some of the Tory loyalists had reasons to want things to remain as they were. The people in my village of Somerton were of that mindset.

"We can get a boat to take us down the Severn River," Holyday interrupted my thoughts. "Probably not five miles. Will you oblige me the use of one of your horses? We can get ourselves down the Severn over to River Beach in three, maybe four hours. We might get to see the fighting. River Beach is just this side of the Patapsco from North Point. If nothing else, we can find out firsthand what happened."

"Let's go," I said without hesitation.

"Which of your animals may I use?"

"That's Thunder," I said as I climbed atop Blue.

Holyday mounted Thunder with more ease than I would have expected given the horses enormity and Holyday's bum leg. We trotted the horses down to the dock where we loaded them onto a fine-looking schooner and before I knew it, we were sailing down the Severn River due west in the direction of Baltimore.

Once more we found ourselves fortunate regarding the tide. The wind was steady and through the efforts of skilled seamen the schooner moved quickly down the Severn. Having secured the horses, Holyday and I took our places on a comfortable big-pillowed bench. The river fascinated me. It was a beautiful stretch of water embraced by enormous cliffs on either side. To be sure, there was nothing like it on the eastern shore. The cliffs, formed of rock and soil, climbed to heights of almost a hundred feet in some places. The land, covered in dense forest, stretched out to the river before falling off down steep slopes into the pristine blue water. On occasion we would pass a majestic house sitting high on the bluffs. Each residence was distinct in its architecture but all of them were quite stunning.

Holyday offered me another smoke and again I declined. As he lit his and began to puff away, a man approached and asked if we would like anything to eat. Holyday responded hastily in the affirmative. The man began to inform us as to what foods were available, but Holyday abruptly cut him off.

"Just bring us each a plate of food," he said, "we are not of a finicky nature."

Our food arrived promptly, and we wasted no time devouring the delicious crabmeat, smoked fish, and oysters. Sitting to the side of the seafood on each of our plates was a small loaf of bread. We made short work of the feast and when the gentleman returned to collect our plates they had been cleared and wiped clean with the last bite of bread.

"Can I get you sirs anything else?" the man inquired. "Some ale perhaps?"

"Good," Holyday answered immediately. "Ale sounds good. Two ales."

The man returned almost immediately and presented each of us a large tankard.

"How much longer?" Holyday asked as he took his beverage from the man.

Our server looked to the shore to locate a landmark.

"Very good time today sir, we should make Sullivan's Cove in another thirty minutes or so," came his response.

"Very good," Holyday answered and gave the man a dismissive wave.

To this point I had been distracted by the beauty of the river, the quality of the ship, the exquisite lunch, and the rapid pace of the day in general. But now, having time to sit back and relax, I finally took notice of my surroundings. The schooner, magnificent in its construction and impeccably maintained, was staffed with a dozen men. Some worked the sails while others tended to the maintenance of the ship, polishing the handrails, and waxing the wooden floorboards on hands and knees. Another man worked what I assumed was the kitchen and his counterpart served us our plates. There were no other passengers except for my horses. Holyday and I had the ship to ourselves. Suddenly my curiosity got the best of me.

"Mr. Holyday?" I said in such a manner as to imply a question.

"Speak boy," he replied.

"With respect," I began, "how is it that you have such a vessel at your disposal? Such a fine ship. And forgive me sir, but the crew is treating you more like a king than a pirate. And these accommodations are at your beck and call. With but a moment's notice you had us underway. I confess to a sense of bewilderment."

Holyday swallowed down the last of his ale and raised his mug in the direction of our server to request another. He looked at me and I shook my head negatively. I had not finished even half of mine.

"You can take the pirate bit with a grain of salt," he said. "Sometimes stories are whipped up in such haste they resemble nothing of the truth."

His statement left me dumbfounded. Was he not a pirate after all?

"Morris and Armstrong," Holyday continued before I had time to request clarification regarding his comment, "ridiculously wealthy men. Immensely powerful they are, on both sides of the Chesapeake. They own plantations, ships, businesses, and people, both black and white."

"And these men," I looked around the vessel pointing at them not with my fingers but with my eyes, "they treat you with such respect because you run errands for these prominent men? I mean, this crew, they appear to be gentlemen. The fine clothes are hardly befitting a staff of sailors and their speech suggests education. Yet they serve us in such a dignified manner. A pirate and, well look at me," I said, stretching out my arms to display soiled and ragged clothing that might suggest I had just crawled out of a swamp.

The server returned with Holyday's ale.

"Bring him another," he said.

"No, I'm fine," I responded.

"Bring him another," he emphasized, and the server left to retrieve another ale.

Holyday pulled out his satchel and without asking handed me a smoke. He lit mine first, then his. I had taken but one pull from the tobacco before the server was putting another ale in my hand. Holyday sat back, swallowed half his ale in one giant gulp then took a long, hard pull off his smoke. I followed suit, to a slightly lesser degree.

"With respect sir, I'm not trying to address matters you'd prefer not to discuss," I said almost apologetically.

My inquiry into Holyday's access and privilege had been met with only some tobacco and another ale. I took it that my curiosity infringed on subject matter that was off limits to me. I wanted to make sure that he had not taken offense in any way.

"I understand most thoroughly that your affairs do not concern me. But I am inquisitive by nature and admittedly not very well practiced in minding my own business. In Somerton little discretion is required. To the extent that we are essentially one big family, it is nearly impossible to intrude into another's business as most everything is so openly shared. I'll try to do a better job remembering I'm not in Somerton anymore."

"Your curiosity bothers me not in the least," he replied. "It's just that your question has not a good answer. I could explain my access to our current transport a hundred different ways. Some of them would include Armstrong and others would not. My relationship with that man is a complicated one. He is not what he appears, but then again, most people are not. That I helped myself to one of his vessels was just a matter of convenience really. Had this ship not been available I would have used someone else's. I'm not sure I could even answer your question in a way that would make sense to you."

"That's fine," I said. "It's just out of habit that I question things I don't understand. I apologize."

"Don't be apologizing," he responded almost as a reprimand. "If not for questions we'd all be destined to walk the earth as fools."

"I reckon' that's true," I replied.

"You've heard the adage that good things happen to good people?" he asked.

"Of course."

"Well, I can't say that applies here," he said with a chuckle and a snort. "But sometimes things work out for people because they're supposed to. In my case I have done many things I regret, but also some things, or at least one thing, that has garnered me certain privileges. Whether it is deserved or not I cannot say. It causes me great consternation and I generally prefer not to speak of it."

"Again," I said, "I don't mean to pry."

I did not want to appear obnoxious or intrusive. After all, I hardly knew this man but was growing more and more interested in Holyday's story. I could tell by the way that he spoke that he was an educated man. The fact that he went out of his way to conceal this fact just made me more curious.

"I fought as part of Maryland's 1st Regiment at the Battle of Brooklyn," he looked my way to see if I understood the significance of what he had just shared. My comprehension, evidenced by wide eyes and mouth agape, clearly pleased him.

One of the sailors called out, "Ten minutes sir."

"We held the line for General Washington," he resumed. "It was the first real battle of the American Revolution. The first time we would fight the English as Americans. And, as General Washington himself admitted, the war would have ended that very day if not for the 1st Regiment."

"The Maryland Four Hundred?" I responded in awe. "You were there," it was a statement, not a question. "What happened?" I knew the story, having heard it too many times to count. But such events tend to get distorted over time. How much of what I heard had been exaggerated? How much fiction had been rolled into history over the years?

"It was the 27th day of August in the year 1776. It was hot. My God it was hot. The Declaration of Independence had been signed only a month earlier. I was a private serving under the command of Major Mordecai Gist," he paused as if to recall the Major. "We knew they were coming. We were ready for them. Or so we thought," he stopped to pull from his smoke. "But once they attacked, they just kept coming. They were so many. Tens of thousands of British Regulars." The look in his eyes revealed that he was seeing it all again. "Their numbers were so great. No one had ever seen anything like that before. No one could have imagined the British had amassed such a force."

He took a long drink, his eyes looking off into the distance with a haunting intensity. I sat transfixed, eyes wide, sitting straight and motionless.

"The fighting was furious. We went at them with the fury of demons. General Washington knew his men would not shy away from battle," his eyes then closed, as if the images were too painful. "The British were too many. There was nothing that could be done other than to fall back."

He stopped for another sip of ale. His smoke had gone out and he took his time relighting it. He then looked right through me and resumed.

"There was only one course for retreat," he continued. "Washington ordered a counterattack to buy time to evacuate. It was Maryland's 1st Regiment under Captain Sterling and Major Gist that circled around the British and brought up the rear," he said. "When Gist gave the order, we charged the hill."

"The Maryland Four Hundred," I replied.

"Yes," answered Holyday. "The Maryland Four Hundred. We charged the hill. Half our regiment was cut down instantly. We ran into the teeth of 30,000 British Regulars and two cannons they had sitting on top of a hill," his pause was of such a duration that I feared the story was over.

"We fell back and regrouped," he finally resumed. "We could see in the distance the full retreat crossing the river. They were still being torn to pieces. Sterling and Gist again sounded the charge and up the hill we went. We were fewer and fewer with each run but slowly, and with tremendous loss of life, we were inching our way closer to the cannons that were wiping out the retreating American force," Holyday swallowed and clenched his teeth before continuing. "The last time we stopped I did not bother to even load my rifle, only checked my bayonet to make sure it was fastened tight. We were close enough that this would be our last charge. The fighting from this point forward would be hand to hand."

Tears were welling up in Holyday's eyes. I sensed they were not born of sadness but of a fiery anger. That he still carried that rage with him after all these years was incredible. As he continued, his voice grew more subdued. He spoke in a determined, focused cadence.

"Those of us still able to get to our feet made that last charge. We fought our way to the cannons and disabled them," his tormented expression gave way just briefly to a look of satisfaction. "We now numbered but a few dozen. Having taken out the British artillery we heard Mordecai Gist call out for us to, 'Make for the creek! Fall back!' and we turned in unison, maybe fifty of us, and ran for our lives."

He swallowed up the remainder of his ale and set the mug on the table next to him. A tear rolled down his cheek and, meeting one of his many scars, detoured inward toward his mangled mouth.

"They cut most of us down before we made the river," he now spoke less intensely. "I took one in the leg, but it went clean through. We picked ourselves up and limped toward the American line," his tone now almost casual. "I turned to see if we were being pursued and caught a bullet in the side of my face." Stretching out his gruesome cheek by hand, he revealed the teeth on that side of his mouth had been taken out by the ball. He grinned, such that it was, and said, "The way I figure it, had I not turned to look behind me, that ball would have gone clean through the back of my head."

A call came out from the crew that we had made Sullivan's Cove.

"Anyway," he summed up, "when it was over, nine of us made it back alive. Nine out of four hundred. But, by Washington's own admission, were it not for the Maryland Line, he would have lost the whole of the Continental Army that day. So, to answer your question," he declared with a scowl, "I take what I need when I need it because, well, I've paid my dues."

I was numb, having heard the story from an actual participant in one of the most famous battles ever fought. The scars that painted his face no longer appeared to be horrific wounds but rather badges of valor.

"It is said," he continued, "that as General Washington watched the men of Maryland's First Regiment charge the hill, he said..."

"Good God, what brave fellows I must this day lose," I finished the line for him.

Holyday seemed flattered that I could recite the words George Washington used to describe the heroic sacrifice made by the Maryland Four Hundred. We rose together in silence and gathered our horses. Slowly, with very deliberate steps, we made our way off the ship.

We mounted the horses and began moving to the northwest. The mood was solemn as I was still in awe of having heard a firsthand account of the Battle of Brooklyn. Holyday was overcome with emotion having gone back to that bloody day. The story of the Maryland Four Hundred was one that everyone knew. The battle had become mythical. Now I sat astride my beautiful black horse and rode with one of the men who had been firmly etched into the pages of history. I felt honored to be in his presence. This man, so grotesque in appearance and manner alike, was in fact a legend. He was a man possessing bravery and a courage undaunted. I now saw him in such a completely different light that he was almost unrecognizable to me.

CHAPTER 5
Bodkin Creek

The trip from the Severn to the Patapsco crossed mostly wooded countryside but there were periods also where the trees gave way to open fields. When traversing spaces without the cover of forest we asked the horses to pick up their pace. We were aware the British infantry was on the move but had no way of knowing their route.

If a platoon of British regulars were to spot us there was no telling how they would react. It was unlikely we would be given an opportunity to explain to them that I was a Loyalist from Somerset. An attacking force moving toward their target would have their fangs out ready to fight. They would almost certainly assume we were scouts, intent on reporting their position. If that were the case, our first awareness of their presence would be the sound of their rifles firing at us. Although, as the British infantry were renowned marksmen, the shots would never be heard if they found their mark.

We travelled through two small towns on our ride. The townsfolk seemed aware of the possible presence of British soldiers and the towns both looked deserted, the residents locked up securely in their houses. We did allow the horses to slow their pace as we rode through the streets of these towns. In addition to letting the animals catch their breath, two men on horseback racing through these Anne Arundel County neighborhoods would have unduly alarmed the people.

The entire trip from the Sullivan's Cove dock on the Severn River to our destination, a tobacco plantation near where the mouth of Bodkin Creek met the Chesapeake Bay, took little more than three hours. At no time did we have cause to take the horses onto difficult terrain. This made an easy trip for the animals who had much left in them by the time we approached the plantation of Captain Francis Smallwood. Holyday was an acquaintance of the captain and seemed certain we would be welcomed despite arriving unannounced.

"Whoa!" Holyday called out, asking the horses to stop. He sat up in his saddle and wore an expression of grave concern. I turned to follow his line of sight and saw smoke rising in the distance. Holyday pulled a spyglass from his jacket but from our position the source of the smoke was blocked by a long line of thick forest.

"Captain Smallwood's farm?" I asked.

"No," he answered. "The house is over there," he pointed in a direction 90 degrees to the right of the smoke. "There is nothing over there. The forest gives way to the creek. It can't be good," and he pulled his long rifle up from where he had affixed it to Thunder's side just under the saddle. "Be on your guard," Holyday warned, and giving Thunder a strong kick, he began racing toward the farm.

In short order the path on which we traveled widened and gave the appearance of a very well-maintained dirt road. I could see the imprints of wheeled carts that had passed this way recently. Surely, we were presently on the man's property. The sight of a meticulously crafted and sturdily built picket fence confirmed my notion and just as we turned a corner in the lane the farmhouse came into view. It was a small house but impressively built of stone and the grounds maintained with impeccable care. There were several people standing out in front of the house.

Holyday slowed Thunder's gait to a slow trot, and I asked Blue to do the same. We approached the front porch of the old stone house where four men stood looking at us intently. Two of the men were in uniform. One of them, a young red-haired fellow, tall and slender, wore an American Naval officer's uniform. The other uniformed man was much older and was clothed in the outfit of a subordinate naval crewman. The two others were dressed in a more casual manner and wore very handsome and well-tailored trousers and elegantly fitted shirts buttoned all the way up to their necks.

"My God!" One of the men cried out. "Cole Holyday! How the hell are you?" He was genuinely excited and pleased to see Mr. Holyday.

"I am well captain" Holyday answered as he climbed off the gigantic horse.

Holyday and Smallwood embraced as if they were brothers who had not seen each other since birth.

"It is good to see you Cole," exclaimed Smallwood, "Damn, it is so good to see you."

"And you my old friend," Holyday responded.

"Gentlemen, it is my great pleasure to introduce to you the Honorable Coleman Holyday," Smallwood said.

The three men looked puzzled by the formal introduction. Holyday had looked every bit the ruffian when I had first met him. Now with another day's growth on his unshaven face, he could not have looked more like a pirate but for a parrot on his shoulder. Out of respect for Captain Smallwood the men nodded in Holyday's direction.

"A hallowed member of the Maryland Four Hundred," Smallwood advised.

The men's expressions and dispositions were immediately transformed, much as mine had been upon learning that the scraggly man before me was American military royalty. The navy officer and his crewman threw their shoulders back and standing as erect as the mast on a ship, drew stiffened hands to their foreheads and saluted Holyday. He halfheartedly returned the salute, but it was done more as a measure to cease the adulation as much as anything else.

The other man, clearly a civilian, bowed in respect as if he were of Asian descent. Holyday nodded a couple times in his direction to acknowledge the effort. Diverting the unwanted attention from himself he turned and looked at me.

"This is Master Steven Brixton," Holyday stated. "He is a representative from the County of Somerset and has business in Baltimore. He was instrumental in warning us of the Royal Navy's movement up the Chesapeake."

The concocted introduction served to put the Navy men at ease. Hearing the mention of Somerset had made them uncomfortable.

Holyday steered the conversation away from further mention of the Four Hundred which, for some reason yet unknown to me, he had no interest in discussing.

"The smoke?" he inquired.

"Yes," Smallwood replied, "these fine men are of the *Lion of Baltimore*. A British frigate chased them up Bodkin Creek and with no alternative they abandoned the ship."

"We were outnumbered four to one," the officer interjected quickly.

Holyday gave him a look, unintentional to be sure, that reminded the officer that Holyday was painfully familiar with being outnumbered. The officer and his assistant were quite taken with embarrassment, and it was obvious the officer regretted deeply having opened his mouth. It became a somewhat awkward moment as even Smallwood, a seemingly affable and mild-mannered gentleman, suddenly wore a look of disapproval. The explanation did not hold merit. Being outnumbered four to one seemed a poor excuse for abandoning ship while standing in the presence of a man who, when outnumbered fifty to one, chose instead to attack.

"It was the right thing to do," Holyday diffused the awkward moment. "Only a fool gives his life for no reason. Even in New York we attacked only so General Washington's army could live to fight another day. Cannot imagine there would be any great service to the country had you and your men decided to remain on your ship only to be burned alive. No honor in that, only stupidity. You made the right call. I am sure it was a difficult decision, but your leadership saved the lives of your crew. You live to fight another day."

"Thank you, sir," the officer sheepishly but gratefully accepted Holyday's consolation.

"His men are out beyond the tobacco fields burying the sails in the forest," Smallwood stated. "We don't want the British finding anything on my property. Would be difficult to explain given the present circumstances."

During our ride over from the Severn River Holyday had shared with me that Smallwood was currently heading up the Anne Arundel County Militia and that they had once spent time together as part of the 22nd Regiment. He provided no other details regarding the experience but did tell me that Smallwood's plantation was part of the American Signaling Corp used by the military to communicate British maritime movement on the Chesapeake Bay.

"I've heard they have been burning farms and houses up and down the bay," said Holyday, "and quite obviously ships," he added, looking off in the direction of the plume of smoke still rising from the *Lion*.

"Yes, bastards have been ruthless," countered Smallwood. "Showing no mercy, to even civilians. Burning farmhouses, killing livestock, most terrible events. Rape and murder," he paused with a pained expression of anger and sadness. "War," he finally added, "no one knows better than you. Very ugly. Shameful what men will do in a time of war. But these cowards," and the pleasant face I had witnessed only moments ago grew contorted with rage. "These cowards are attacking families and farmers with no way to protect themselves. It is not making sense. Just across the bay they burned homes to the ground. Slaughtered families and slaves. Killed the livestock. It is like nothing I have ever heard of before. Indiscriminate murder. It is not the battlefield for God's sake, it is a man's home and his family. Killing children!"

"They've left you alone?" questioned Holyday.

"So far," answered Smallwood. "Normally I would be with the men up in Baltimore as part of the defense. But things right now are too unpredictable. I needed to keep the militia in place in case they attack us locally. I will die before the British raise their flag on this land. There is no honor in these acts of terror. It is not war. It is evil, I swear to you," he was almost brought to tears.

"So, there is a defense being mounted?" asked Holyday. "In Baltimore, I mean."

"Oh yes," answered Smallwood. "You missed them going at it just across the water," he pointed out towards the Chesapeake. "Seems they got the warning in time to position troops before the British landed. You should have seen them. Not sure who is in charge over there, but it was masterful. They staggered their positions across North Point. They would engage, then fall back. They hit them from one side, fell back and hit them from the other side. It was a sight to see."

"So, we drove them right back into the bay?" questioned Holyday.

"No, we didn't turn them straight away. But our troops fought so well the British advance was delayed by at least half a day. A call has gone out to all militia. And every regiment within a hundred miles is in route to Baltimore to assist in the defense. The additional time could increase our fighting forces by thousands of men. Even if Fort McHenry falls, the British will face a formidable army when they commence to move on land to take the city."

Holyday smiled, more so with his eyes than his crooked mouth and said to me, "It looks as though our Mr. McCabe was successful in his mission."

"If it was your group that gave the warning," Smallwood offered, "you indeed may have given us a fighting chance. The word went out late this morning to send the best men on their fastest horses to retrieve every militia within a three-day ride and rally to Baltimore."

"Well," Holyday added, "knowing McCabe, he has reinforcements in route as we speak."

"Jake McCabe?" Smallwood questioned. He was obviously familiar with the man. "Ah," he laughed, "I guess if anyone could get the job done it would be him."

McCabe was a fascinating character. I did not get to know him as he was clearly a man that spoke only when he had something to say. Although our paths never crossed again, he is a man I will likely never forget. I consider this unfortunate for I am sure that Mr. McCabe, much like Mr. Holyday, possesses a virtuous and courageous nature concealed beneath the cloak of plainness that each wear with such skill.

"Yes," Holyday confirmed. "Jake is a well-connected man. I don't believe there is a person in all of Maryland that is a stranger to Jake McCabe, unless he wants them to be."

"Absolutely true," agreed Smallwood. "It always impressed me how well he was able to associate with the rich and powerful. Given his accent, there would be no way possible to conceal his Irish origin. Still, his reputation proceeds him wherever he goes, and his services always seem to be in demand."

"When a man is renowned for his dependability, Irish or no, he endears himself to people of means," Holyday surmised.

"I have no doubt that if it is Jake McCabe whose charge it is to go for help," said Smallwood, "then help is on the way."

"Surely helps that those boys slowed them down at North Point," Holyday added. "If the British ships are lined up at the mouth of the river, they must be ready to go. Every minute counts at this point."

"To be sure," Smallwood agreed. "Knowing McCabe, he's got the whole damned state on the way," he laughed. "Only Irishman in America that carries that kind of clout. Hell, if General Washington were still alive McCabe would have him on his way as well."

"I wouldn't doubt it," Holyday acknowledged as the two laughed.

"With respect sirs," the Navy officer spoke up, "but this Irishman, how did he come to be so admired? Forgive me for I do not know the fellow but generally an English gentleman would sooner be caught in the company of a negro than that of an Irishman. To hear you speak, a person would be hard pressed to believe you were talking about the Irish."

Holyday and Smallwood were visibly annoyed by the question. But I was pleased to have had it asked as my curiosity had peaked some time ago.

"Not just any Irish," Holyday answered.

"McCabe was charged with burying a chest of silver coins for a plantation owner outside the town of Frederick many years ago," Smallwood was going to oblige the officer which pleased me greatly. "As you are aware it is common practice to be careful with riches. There are yet many thieves running about this land. A smart man never keeps too much of his money in one place. Divide and hide we like to say. Anyway, this man had just won a small fortune on a horse race. Ten thousand dollars in silver. The richest horse race in Maryland history."

"To that point," Holyday corrected him.

"Right," Smallwood acknowledged. "Anyway, McCabe was a trusted hand on this man's farm. So, he was given the task of burying the treasure deep in the woods, which he did. He returned and told the man, a Mister Reed, exactly where it had been hidden. The next day McCabe goes into town for some ale. It seems that one of the gentleman's indentured servants, an Englishman named Winston, had become knowledgeable regarding the fact that McCabe knew where this silver was buried. Winston shared this information with a group of scoundrels up from Virginia. They overpowered McCabe on his way back to Reed's farm and told him that he was going to take them to the treasure or be buried alive. McCabe repeatedly refused even after being beaten most severely. The Virginians threw McCabe into a packing crate and lowered him into the ground. Before they shut the lid on him, one of them asked if he had any last words."

"Ga fook yasef! says McCabe in that thick Irish accent of his," Holyday laughed as he interjected. "So, they shut him in and buried him alive."

"McCabe, lucky bastard that he is," Smallwood again picked up the story, "he'd been followed by a patron at the tavern. Guessing that these thugs were up to no good, this fellow had followed them into the woods. After witnessing the assault, he ran back for help. When they dug McCabe out of the ground, they asked him how it was that he was willing to give his life for another man's treasure. And McCabe says, 'I promised Mr. Reed

I'd not tell anyone where I buried his silver. My word is the only thing I have of any value. The thought of tarnishing my name seemed unbearable. I would be better off dead. At least my honor would remain intact.' So, this story spread like a wildfire."

"So certain people," Holyday would finish the story, "leaders of industry, influential families, and politicians, they began to call on Jake when their business required the utmost discretion. And over the years Jake McCabe has become a very wealthy man selling the only thing he has to offer, his honesty."

CHAPTER 6
The Patapsco

The thunder of cannons rang out in the distance. The startled expressions exchanged among our small group lasted only a second. We knew exactly what we were hearing. The British had begun their attack on Baltimore. History would be forever changed over the course of the next few hours. Whether we would be participants or merely observers had yet to be determined.

Smallwood took off for the nearby woods. He ran much more quickly than I would have expected a man of his age to move. We followed him and within minutes, having traversed a series of well-traveled pathways, we arrived at the water's edge. Smallwood stepped carefully through some bushes that appeared at first glance to be natural growth but upon further inspection had been set in place to conceal a ladder that hugged the trunk of a large oak tree. The ladder had been constructed of identical oak and it blended with its host so precisely that it was virtually invisible. Smallwood began making his way up the tree and as I waited my turn to ascend the ladder, I turned my eyes skyward and for the first time saw the intricate system of lookout stations hiding within the canopy that ran along the coastline of the bay.

It was not until I reached the first platform that the extent of the impressive structures became fully visible. There were dozens of observation towers assembled throughout the top of the tree line. The platforms varied both in size and in height and were camouflaged so skillfully that they were difficult to see by any foot traffic that might pass them on the ground, much less by ships sailing past them out on the waters of the Chesapeake. Some of the decks were small and could accommodate no more than one or two men at a time. Other vantage points were much larger and supported chairs and tables. We moved from one position to another by way of narrow bridge walks and a series of ladders made from wood and rope.

Some of the lookout posts were open air in their construction while others had been enclosed to provide protection against the elements. The presence of cots and blankets were evidence these posts were at times manned throughout the night. Our group eventually settled on a platform approximately twenty feet long and ten feet across. It was perched in the fork of an enormous poplar tree and had been walled off on three sides. The open end faced the bay. Both sides had been fitted with openings that allowed lanterns to signal up and down the bay in either direction. The back wall was fully enclosed and securely fastened to the trunk of the ancient poplar.

Smallwood pressed his spyglass to his right eye and stared off into the distance. The rest of us looked in that direction and could see with unaided eye the sky lighting up with the flare of cannon fire. It was growing darker by the moment which made the mortars and rockets ever more spectacular. Our location, a good sixty feet off the ground, positioned us so that we could see very clearly out to sea, as well as directly up the Patapsco River. The intensity of the bombardment escalated.

"Look down the river," Smallwood advised. Holyday now raised his spyglass. "Off to the right you can see a British ship firing on the fort. McHenry is too far down the river to see but you can tell the fort is returning fire."

Holyday peered through his own instrument only briefly. He looked to the right as Smallwood had suggested and then moved the glass to his left crossing the river with his eyes. His lack of interest in any further observation, I assumed, was borne not only of a limited view of the battle but also by the fact that he knew exactly what was happening just over the horizon. The experiences derived from his military service had endowed him with a keen ear for the sounds of battle.

"How many ships?" Holyday asked.

"Thirty or so would be my guess," Smallwood answered. "We cannot account for any additional numbers that may have passed through the mouth undetected. If they sailed close to the shore just off North Point they could have slipped by unnoticed. More ships could have passed under cover of night. From what we have been able to observe from posts up and down this passage, the British ships number thirty. But I would be surprised if there were not a few more than that. Surely England is going to throw everything they have at Baltimore. If every British ship presently sailing the Chesapeake has not already made their way up the river, they are on their way."

Holyday remained facing the action, but his eyes were not focused on the battle. He seemed to be looking at something directly in front of his face. I surmised he was looking inward, visualizing the battle in his mind, and seeing it not with his eyes but with his ears.

"Only six ships working their cannons so far," Holyday stated. "They're setting distance parameters."

Suddenly the intensity of the bombardment took on a new life.

"Here we go," observed Holyday.

The cadence of the thundering reports grew from an explosion every half minute or so to the continuous roar of attack. Holyday listened intently as if the sound of the artillery could tell him the story about what was happening upriver. The rest of us were left to watch with amazement the flashes of brilliance and the bombs bursting in air. Darkness was coming quickly and with it the spectacle of the British bombardment became more dazzling. Then suddenly, as the roaring of the cannons reached a crescendo, there fell an abrupt silence. Slowly the cannons resumed fire but at a much slower and more calculated pace.

Holyday put the spyglass back to his eye. His aim, however, was not in the direction of Fort McHenry but rather he looked directly across the river.

"The beachhead sticking out into the bay," he addressed Smallwood, "that is where the British came ashore?"

Smallwood, for an instant, looked befuddled.

"Oh, earlier today, yes," he answered, realizing Holyday was asking about the British land invasion at North Point. "The line of trees to the right, back behind the point of the beach, that's where they came ashore."

"How many ships?" inquired Holyday.

"We could see eight," Smallwood answered. "But there may have been more. We cannot see from here what lies around the bend of the land. Based on how they came ashore I feel confident the eight ships within our view constituted their entire landing party."

"They landed at the point to resistance?" Holyday queried.

"They marched around the mound crossing our view directly and then headed straight inland. As they came to that first line of dunes the Americans opened fire. It was magical," Smallwood extolled. "The first line looked to be about a hundred men. They stood and fired in unison and half the British front line went down."

A wry smile crossed Holyday's face. "Supported by a second line then?"

"No," Smallwood laughed. "The Americans took off running in full retreat. It took the British a moment to regroup," Smallwood was amused and excited to tell the tale and spoke in short choppy sentences. "They were caught completely off guard. It was obvious they were unaware of an American presence. Their approach was so casual I must believe that the men had been told the point had been vacated. These men were not expecting to meet the Americans until they were much farther inland. But now they had seen the Americans fall back. They marched over those dunes and a second line of Americans rose from this side, behind that strand of pines. The British were so clueless to their presence that many of them were shot in the back, having marched directly past the men as they lay in the sand. The Americans rose and ran in retreat around the hill to the left. The whole British formation, save those now bleeding out on the ground, turned to fire on the retreating men when a third American platoon sprang from the creek bed and opened fire. Again, we saw dozens of the English go down and again the Americans fell back."

"Sounds like something Major Gist would have done," Holyday offered. "Hit and run, brilliant."

"Yes," Smallwood agreed. "Now the English proceeded much more cautiously. They had already lost close to a hundred men. Eighty-four was our official count but there is no way to be sure we did not miss some. I'm sure we did."

"American losses?" Holyday queried.

"Cole, we did not see a single American go down. They hit so quickly and with such stealth, by the time the British had finished ducking for cover the Americans were racing back away from the beach. So, the Redcoats moved slowly. Inching forward, expecting another line of fire to pop up from behind every bush or out from behind every tree. All the while the British are bringing more men ashore. Sniper fire took a few more as they moved toward the tree line. Their advance was slowed to barely a crawl. It took them two hours to make their way from the beach to the trees."

"Two hours!" Holyday laughed.

"We could see them second guessing themselves from here Cole. It was magnificent!" Smallwood exalted. "By the time they were ready to make their charge into the woods the Americans were heavily reinforced. We could tell by the fire that came from the trees, the Americans were lined up two or three men deep. It was a bloodbath. A glorious slaughter."

"Well," Holyday replied, "It's a safe bet those men fresh off the taste of victory have fallen back to support Fort McHenry. But they're facing a force ten times the size of the one they saw this afternoon."

"Yes," countered Smallwood. "But the time they held the British at bay was critical. And with every minute more men from across the region come storming into Baltimore. I know for certain that when the English send their men into the city, they will face an army twice the size of the one they would have faced earlier today."

"I hope so," Holyday wished.

"I doubt the fort can withstand the fury of thirty British warships, but if McHenry falls the British still have to come ashore," Smallwood continued. "I know one thing for sure. If they want Baltimore, they'll pay for it with their blood. It will not be handed over to them the way they took Washington. North Point gave them a taste of what waits for them in the city."

The British cannons were now pounding the fort methodically. The sky lit up over Baltimore and the water seemed ablaze with smoke and fire as the sound of war blasted our ears and shook the trees in which we were positioned.

We took turns looking through the spyglass but the radiance from the battle looked the same from our distance as it did through the magnification of the glass. None of the ships were visible as those not hidden by the horizon were concealed by darkness. So, we watched and listened to the English take back the land they believed stolen from them some forty years earlier. Blinding flashes of bright white light and deep resonating percussion impaled us with the stark realization that the very existence of America hung in the balance.

The crew from the *Lion of Baltimore* were just now returning from their trek deep into the woods where they buried the sails. Having floundered their way through the thicket, shrouded completely in darkness, they appeared ragged and exhausted. Just the same, they did not flinch when their commanding officer ordered them to make ready to march on Baltimore. Their departure was to be immediate and after the briefest of goodbyes the officer and his mate made the climb off the observation platform and began to descend the series of ladders and platforms. It seemed an arduous task in the blackness of night. They would at times come to a halt waiting for exploding ordinance to illuminate the treacherous next step.

"Our militia will be bringing up the rear early in the morning," Smallwood called after the crew as they commenced their journey out of the woods toward the city. "We'll be coming up behind you. Careful on what you fire at."

"Come with us now then and have no worries," called the officer without slowing his stride.

"We leave at first light," Smallwood answered. "We'll not abandon the county until the new day proves no advances by the British into our towns and neighborhoods. Once confirmed, the Anne Arundel County Militia will find Baltimore. You tell them. Tell them two hundred strong are on the way and ready to fight. You tell them we're coming!"

There was no response from the twenty men of *The Lion of Baltimore*. *They* disappeared into the darkness.

Our attention turned back to the river. The cannons on the warships now unleashed a relentless barrage from the harbor. The fort answered less frequently, but there was still fire being returned. If we knew nothing else, we knew the fort had not yet fallen. On occasion the big guns reported. Red hot flashes that stung the eyes were followed immediately by thunderous punches boasting the power being leveled at Fort McHenry.

The fight raged on throughout the night. At times, the volley of the cannons would diminish to such an extent that we wondered whether McHenry had finally succumbed to the perpetual bombardment. But as that fear became most grave and it appeared all hope was lost, the sound of a single cannon signaled the two sides were yet engaged. We could only imagine the carnage endured by the fort. We had heard thousands of rounds discharged.

The mood among those present, numbering now only four, was grim. Most of the discussion remained between Holyday and Smallwood, although Smallwood's assistant did not hesitate to contribute on the rare occasion when his participation was required. I remained for the most part a silent observer. This I found most agreeable as fatigue again weighed heavy on me. To say I was fascinated by the stories that unfolded as Holyday and Smallwood reminisced would be to understate the issue in the extreme. I came to understand that Captain Smallwood was a war hero in his own right. A veteran of many battles during the Revolution, he once marched his regiment four hundred miles in two weeks to rendezvous with the Continental Army in New York. Listening to Holyday recount the war stories it was clear Smallwood possessed a fearlessness in battle and the kind of courage and calm under fire that made him one of General Washington's most trusted leaders. While he could not lay claim to the immortality bestowed on the men of the Maryland Four Hundred, he did possess that fire, unknown to most, that would have seen him make that charge were he given the opportunity to do so. These men, now bent and broken by time, must truly have been spectacular in their prime.

It is only by listening to men such as these that one can fathom how an impossibly outnumbered and poorly equipped army of farmers and ordinary citizens could have defeated the most powerful fighting force the world had ever known. Hearing firsthand the accounts of battles waged by these men, armed at times with nothing more than honor and courage, I understood for the first time in my life what it meant to be an American. It was at this moment that I realized that if the men who now defended Baltimore possessed this same passion for freedom, they surely would present the British a most formidable foe. A willingness to die for their right to be free cloaked these men in an armor that no Englishman could penetrate.

The cannons now reported a steady methodical pounding. Did the British guns still target Fort McHenry, or was the shelling now directed at the city of Baltimore? With a sudden intensity the fury of the attack roared out in a wild cry of carnage. The cannons screamed and the whole world seemed to shake. Not the slightest reprieve could be detected between the bombs which now called out in one long continuous chorus of war. My heart sank as I realized that no fort, no city, could withstand such an unrelenting assault. It was only the rage in Holyday's eyes that gave me even the slightest hope of an outcome not determined by doom.

Suddenly, as if being orchestrated by God himself, the sun broke the horizon precisely timed with the termination of the outrageous violence of England's mighty guns. We waited for the attack to resume but there was nothing. Plumes of smoke rose from the river as we looked intently in the direction of Baltimore. I had no doubt that the sickness that soured my stomach was shared by the others.

"I shall rally the militia," Smallwood stated. "If our towns are secure, we make ready to march on to Baltimore." He started moving toward the ladder to make his descent.

"Ho!" Holyday shouted. He was looking with a most pained expression through his spyglass.

The two heroes of battles long since decided stood side by side atop the platform and stared off in the direction of Baltimore. Those few seconds seemed an eternity.

"Ha," it could have been either man, or both, that offered a short laugh that instilled in me hope that something less horrific than expected was being observed.

"What is it?!" I could no longer contain myself.

I received no response. The two men stood motionless, two statues with spyglasses affixed to their faces.

"The British ships," Holyday exclaimed, "they move this way!"

It was mid-morning before the first frigate passed in front of us. She was at full sail and cut an impressive sight slicing through the calm seas. Smallwood informed us that she carried forty cannons on her deck. His spyglass aiding his inspection of the condition of the ship and her crew.

"Could blow my whole farm to bits from that position," Smallwood observed as the war ship sailed directly past our position not three hundred yards out into the river.

"It would surprise not a soul were the English to shell the mainland on their way back down the Chesapeake," Holyday said, still wearing a grimace of hatred even as he watched the fleet sail out of the mouth of the river and into the bay.

"I think the lead ship is spent," remarked Smallwood. "Every cannon sits beside an empty deck. Their guns could be loaded for all we know but there's not a cannonball in sight."

He continued to survey the ship. His spyglass, pressed forcefully up against his face, moved up and down the ship from helm to stern. I could imagine this man on the battlefields of the Revolution casting a similar pose.

"Her crew is spent too," he said while continuing his surveillance. "Those boys are ragged. Most likely been at sea for weeks. Hungry I'd think, and maybe out of drink, and tired."

Looking back up the river in the direction of Baltimore we could now see an endless line of ships sailing into view. I had not seen such a display ever in my life and was quite in awe of the size of the vessels.

When the first Man-of-War passed our treetop position, we stood mesmerized by her enormity. Smallwood counted more than sixty cannons on the four levels of the ship. But this ship, though thoroughly amazing in her magnitude, was akin to the other vessels in that her decks were absent cannon balls. The only thing to be seen anywhere near the cannons were men, exhausted and defeated, some struggling mightily with the immense sails while others appeared simply collapsed from fatigue.

The two warriors from years gone by continued to remember aloud their experiences. I sat listening to the men recount battles, both won and lost, that ultimately created America. It was an honor to be present and to hear them speak. I could not have felt more privileged were I in the company of kings and queens or indeed of George Washington himself. These men, heroes both, held honor more precious than life itself.

Thoughts of moving on to Baltimore tried to force their way into my mind. I beat them back. My people lie sick and dying in Somerton and I had not time to spare. But these hours, I was so acutely aware, were not being wasted. Never again could I expect to taste so precious and glorious a moment. It was but once in my lifetime that I would sit on the shore of this bay with the men who had wrestled this land from the English and built a new country with nothing more than defiance and blood. How often over the coming years would I think back on these priceless minutes spent watching the fleet of British warships retreat out into the bay? This was a scene so completely perfect and beautiful. It was as if I had stepped into a painting and become a part of history merely due to my good fortune of having been present. I would not rush this time away, knowing such an experience would never pass my way again. And so, I savored it, allowing not a single word to escape me. Every expression was captured, examined, and relished. I rolled it around in my mind to ensure these exquisite memories would burn themselves into my brain.

I alternated my attention between the awe-inspiring ships and the two veterans. One moment my mind would examine a passing ship, trying to envision its position in last night's battle. Then my focus would turn to whichever man was talking. I watched his expressions change and his body language. There was little imagination needed to see either, as a younger man, barking out orders to his command or charging a position in New York. In time, as more information was shared by these historians, I came to understand even more fully how monumentally important it had to have been for these men to witness for themselves the enemy in retreat. The American victory radiated from the old soldiers just as brightly as if they themselves had delivered the deciding blows.

We soon found ourselves begrudgingly and regretfully climbing down from the thick strand of oaks and poplars that had accommodated us so generously as we stood witness to history. To make the best use of the daylight we were forced to set out for Baltimore before the last of the British warships had yet sailed past.

CHAPTER 7
Baltimore

Captain Smallwood was going to summon the militia. He had been made aware of the pressing nature of my journey given the sickness currently torturing the people of Somerton. Having informed us that many of his men would be making the march to Baltimore on foot, Holyday and I bid him farewell. The embrace shared between the two Revolutionary War heroes was a moment lost to the ages. If history had been fortunate enough to witness the men's heartfelt and impassioned goodbye, there would surely be a statue commemorating it on display in one of the towns where the brave Americans accomplished feats so colossal.

"Godspeed," said Smallwood.

"Farewell, good friend," replied Holyday. He pulled on Thunder's reins and pointed him in the direction of Baltimore.

The horses were full of energy. Once we had them on the main roadway, we let them run. The highway was wide and smoothly paved. Thunder and Blue took full advantage of the firmness of the ground underfoot and it took us barely two hours to reach our destination.

My only other trip to Baltimore City was a year and a half ago in the spring of 1814. I had travelled with my Uncle Jedediah and had been wildly excited about the journey. With Jedediah leading the way, everything went exactly according to plan. We had used the main road without incident and arrived at Kent Island in only three days. We boarded the late ferry across the Chesapeake and entered Baltimore from the northeast under cover of darkness. No time was wasted securing the necessary supplies and the next morning we boarded the same ferry and crossed the bay back to the eastern shore. The adventure was thrilling for a boy who had never set foot outside the boundaries of the County Somerset. But the experience did nothing in the way of acquainting me with the city. Jedediah and I had arrived in darkness and climbed aboard the return ferry just as the sun was coming up.

On this occasion, however, Holyday and I approached the city from the south. It was a cloudless and glorious October afternoon. Nothing could have prepared me for the sight laid out in front of us. It would have been simply impossible for any print or painting to capture the awe-inspiring magnitude of the buildings that stretched out forever into the distance. It was not difficult to imagine that the remainder of the planet from this point forward was covered with similar structures. It stretched credibility there even existed this many bricks and stones in all the world. Yet here they were, amassed in one place and assembled side by side and one atop the other.

The incredible mass of people made the experience even more surreal. The excitement exhibited by the hoards sent a vibration through the air that pumped my blood faster, pulsating through my veins until I thought my heart might explode. Unlike my experience in Annapolis, which was only a fraction of this size, I was not at all overwhelmed but rather felt a sense of exhilaration previously unknown to me.

"It's really something hey lad?" Holyday had noticed my astonishment. It is likely any one of the thousands of people dancing through the streets, had they given me a second glance, would have seen the wide-eyed wonder etched across my face.

I followed Holyday through the streets of Baltimore. He was clearly familiar with the town and used the backstreet alleys to cross from one block to another. We moved at a respectable pace considering how crowded were the streets with citizens and soldiers alike, all still reveling in having turned the British away. There were a few occasions however, where the mass of humanity created such congestion that our horses were stopped in their tracks. The impasse would always be resolved rapidly as soon as the pedestrians took notice of Thunder, probably the largest animal any of them had ever seen. People pushed one another to get out of the way of the enormous creature. Only once did a man attempt to confront Holyday for riding his horse through such a congested part of town. But, upon looking up at Holyday's disfigured face, the grimace he wore constantly made even more sinister by his impatience with the heavy traffic, the man ended his reprimand in mid-sentence and disappeared into the crowd. I continued to marvel at the city and its many shops, pubs, and businesses and did not share Holyday's growing frustration with how the mob impeded our progress.

Holyday turned us down another alley, and we entered an expansive series of stables. We had evidently entered through the rear and Holyday maneuvered us through a maze of fences and stalls up towards the front of the establishment. Once there he addressed a man with whom he was quite clearly acquainted. The man took the horses and after commenting on their magnificence turned to take the animals back to an open stall.

"Bobby," Holyday called after him. "Stable them together in the best stalls available."

He reached into his pant pocket and pulled from it a thick packet of bills. Without counting it he stuffed the money into the man's shirt pocket.

"Thank you, sir."

"The very best feed and lots of it," Holyday instructed.

"Goes without saying sir."

"These animals have been supremely tested," he added. "Their performance has earned them every comfort available. Make sure they have plenty of water."

"These fine animals will be pampered so," the stable hand assured us, "they won't want to leave when you come for them."

"Very well," Holyday seemed satisfied.

The horses were taken away and Holyday started for the front of the building. His limp was more pronounced than it had been earlier. This was understandable as I too was stiff and sore from the hasty trip we had just made.

"Your horses are in the best possible hands," Holyday assured me.

It pleased me greatly that he understood how important the care of my animals was to me. I walked behind him down the crowded street. His limp now became so pronounced that I was tempted to ask him if he was okay. But he impressed as being the kind of man that would take offense at the question, so I refrained from such an inquiry.

Making our way through the town was much more arduous on foot than it had been sitting atop Thunder and Blue. The crowd swallowed us up and we were at its mercy as to which way it steered us. Fortunately, it pushed us in the direction Holyday wanted to go. We soon came upon one of the many back alleys that crisscrossed their way through the city.

Holyday walked only a few feet down the alley before stopping. He pulled a wrinkled paper satchel from a pocket on the inside of his shirt.

"Time for a smoke," he said, unrolling a crumpled bag and pulling out two well rolled cigars.

He did not ask me if I wanted one, rather just handed it to me.

"This is the good stuff," he said, lighting his then handing me the box of matches. "Smallwood Plantation Tobacco." He pulled long and hard and inhaled deeply. Our smoke break, I gathered, was as much to allow his leg a moment to loosen up as it was to enjoy the fine cigar, but there was no denying the quality of the smoke. It was superb.

We took our time smoking and leaned back against the brick wall. Holyday continued to move his bad leg around as if waiting for it to fall back into place. Not much was said as we enjoyed the cigars. We savored the flavor, fully appreciating the excellent tobacco. Lesser quality cigars were sometimes smoked about halfway down before being discarded and tossed on the ground. But this kind of superior product was smoked all the way down to the fingertips. Holyday took one last pull and flicked away the remains, which were so insignificant you could not have seen it on the ground even if you had known where to look. Noticing that I was scarcely a little more than halfway done with mine he instructed me to take my time. He settled back against the side of the building and repositioned his body to make himself, and his leg especially, as comfortable as possible.

"I know a good tavern," he finally said. "Right down the street." He nodded in the direction of the far end of the alley. "They will take very good care of us," he paused. "Get out of this noise and give us some time to think."

I nodded in agreement as I exhaled a thick stream of smoke. We then moved through the alley and in short order had arrived at our destination.

The doors to the tavern were thick and heavy and made of exceptionally fine wood. Once they closed behind us the deafening ruckus from the chaos outside was all but eliminated. The quiet murmur of the patrons and the silverware clinking against plates was calming and a welcome reprieve for our ears which had been under assault since first riding into the boisterous, jubilant city.

Holyday started toward the back of the room, walking right past the sign instructing diners to wait to be seated. He found a large round table in the corner. It was half encircled by a high-backed sofa seat. Despite passing several smaller tables set for two which were presently unoccupied Holyday opted to secure the larger set up. He sat down and slid awkwardly inward on the couch, motioning me to do the same on the other side. Holyday continued pushing himself around the table until he was almost to the halfway point. He then manually moved his leg, grabbing it with both hands and lifting it to his side where he set it on the soft cushioned bench. He elicited a loud sigh and allowed his head to fall back into the pillowed stuffing that adorned the top of the booth. Closing his eyes briefly, he seemed to be considering all the aches that coursed through his body. Strangely, though he wore a grimace, he appeared to relish the discomfort. It puzzled me to see a look of satisfaction framing his face, coexisting in complete harmony with the gnarled anguish of his pain. As the waitress approached our table, I was half tempted to implore her to let him sleep.

"Can I help you gentlemen?" she asked.

Holyday smiled at the woman. Whether by design or coincidence he was positioned sideways. Resting his leg on the cushioned bench required that he sit with his shoulder directed at the table. As a result, the gruesomely mangled portion of his disfigured face was nearer the wall of the restaurant, hidden from the other patrons and workers in the comfortable eatery. Looking at Holyday from this direction I could envision what he, as a younger man, probably looked like. His life had not been an easy one and evidence of this colored his face just as clearly as the scar that cut its way diagonally from eye to mouth. His was a face that had seen much ugliness as he worked his way down roads that lacked traditional privilege. But the story told by his wrinkles and scars was buffered by a flash of kindness and honesty buried behind eyes that sparkled sincere and genuine. This side of the man was seldom seen when his vicious wounds were on full display.

I had come to see the scars for the badges of honor they represented. Those who remained unaware of their origin either looked immediately away from the carnage or looked at it through a lens of ignorance. The bullet that had torn through Holyday's face some forty years ago insured that he would never again be a handsome man. Understanding that the disfigurement was one of sacrifice and bravery allowed me to ignore it so I could see a man that understood, like few others, how the world really worked. From this angle Holyday's horrific injury was completely invisible and his profile portrayed the kindness and wisdom that emanated from a soul who had known suffering and so was eager to help anyone and to do the right thing at all costs.

The place was now filling up to capacity. All the empty tables we passed on our way to the back table were now full. I found it peculiar that despite the dining room being so crowded, the place remained relatively quiet. The patrons engaged in low dignified conversation. There were no loud or boisterous folks defiling the pleasant atmosphere. I could easily overhear the two gentlemen at the table next to us discussing the attack on Fort McHenry. Even as they shared their opinions regarding the battle, they maintained a delicate soft-spoken demeanor. It was odd that these men, clearly excited regarding the event and its outcome continued speaking about it in almost a whisper. I am not sure why I picked up on it but the people that dined in this establishment appeared to be of a very refined nature. Everyone was dressed in a most proper attire. The only exceptions of course being Holyday and myself. Perhaps that is what brought it to my attention. There was a mild sense of being out of place although I would not go so far as to say that it made me uncomfortable.

As darkness now fully embraced the city, additional candles were lit throughout the tavern and lanterns were placed along the walls. The lighting bounced off the dark wooden paneling and gave the restaurant a certain ambiance. To describe the quaint diner as elegant would have been an overstatement but the soft lighting and seemingly upscale clientele served to provide a rather delightful atmosphere in which to enjoy a meal.

We ordered some ale, a couple steaks, and a bottle of whiskey. Holyday and I went at the meat like ravenous wolves, and it occurred to me that it was fortunate we were seated in a dark corner. We were not delicate with regards to how hastily we consumed our meal. Once we had finished our food we sat back and went to work on the ale and the bottle.

Holyday was a people watcher. His was an intense look as he glared at someone and sized them up. It is a skill I suppose that had been developed out of necessity over the course of his lifetime. Whatever it was that gave rise to his need to be a particularly good judge of character, he had refined the ability to the point where he enjoyed the exercise. People, I have noticed, tend to rejoice in doing things at which they excel. Everyone likes to be good at something and satisfaction is gleaned from engaging in the activity whether anyone is watching to marvel at the expertise or not. Holyday was a man that put a premium on self-satisfaction that far surpassed his concern with what others thought of him. I looked at him as he studied the man two tables removed from our position. It was fascinating to see him collect information and process it in a way that revealed his conclusion of the subject through the expression on his face. His current evaluation was of a man he found unimpressive. An expression of disgust tempered with pity graced his face. That I still could not see the more disfigured side of his face made reading him easier, what with his wound not providing a distraction.

"Do you believe in ghosts Steven Brixton?" The question seemed to come from nowhere.

"I suppose," I responded matter-of-factly.

"Sometimes," Holyday set his empty whiskey glass down on the table in front of him, "I know there are things I see and hear that aren't real. But it does not cause me great concern." He was looking for a reaction from me.

"It doesn't sound like too much of a problem," I responded in a way that was free from judgement while not being dismissive of his remark. It was unclear to me whether he was serious about the matter.

"On the other hand," he continued, "if there are no such things as ghosts, then I suspect that I am indeed quite a bit crazier than I would like to believe."

Ghosts played a significant role in life on the eastern shore. Everyone had a ghost story or two they could tell. To this end Holyday's confession did little in the way of startling me.

"Sometimes," he said as he licked the foam from the ale off the top of his lip, "I wonder whether the ghosts, or spirits, whatever you want to call them, are from heaven or hell." He took another long pull from his pint. "Or neither," he added.

"Or both?" I questioned, realizing now that this conversation was being promoted, at least in part, by the intoxication that was beginning to set in.

"What do you mean?" Holyday queried.

"Maybe some ghosts come from heaven, and some from hell," I offered.

"What if some people, after they die," it was now obvious that he wanted to pursue this present course, "come to find they ain't worthy of heaven, but God don't feel they deserve eternal damnation, that's possible I suppose."

"Yes," I said. "I suppose."

"Those people got to go somewhere," he reasoned. "Maybe they have to stay behind. Maybe they are stuck here with us. Until God figures out what to do with them."

"Or maybe," I returned to my previous comment for further explanation, "some people die and go to heaven, or hell, and come back from time to time to visit."

"You think God would let people out of hell to come visit?" he asked. "I must confess that I am not a believer. But if there were a God, I don't think He would do that. Or maybe He would. Maybe He would do it as punishment to make a person see how happy everyone is without him. Maybe he wants some people to see their wife with another man. Or maybe He wants them to see their children being hurt, knowing there ain't nothing they could do to help. That would be pretty painful I guess."

"I don't know," I replied after a short silence. "I'm not sure I think God wastes His time with you once He sends you to hell. I mean, you are in hell. You are engulfed in flames for all of eternity. I'm not sure there's anything anyone could see back here in the world that would hurt more than being on fire."

"I guess," he reasoned. "Maybe there would be time off for good behavior. Maybe you get to come back and visit if you behave yourself. Kind of like prison, or jail, or something."

"Then what about the people in heaven?" I pushed the discussion forward. "Why would they be sent back? If heaven is a perfect place with no misery, no pain, only glory and joy, why would God make someone come back here? Can there be punishments even in heaven?"

"Well, if there were a God, and to be clear," Holyday said, "I must emphasize that I do not believe He exists. I reckon' He could do whatever he wants with you."

Holyday refilled the empty whiskey glasses, and we had another drink.

"Ever notice how most ghosts just show up someplace?" I wondered aloud. "They just appear out of nowhere and then go away. They just show themselves to people, to scare them I guess, and they're gone."

"Your ghosts just show up and then disappear? Just like that?" Holyday asked.

"Well, I've never seen a ghost myself," I admitted. "But when you hear people talk about ghosts, I mean people that have seen them, they never talk about how the ghosts hurt them. Only scared them."

"You believe those stories? Or you think those people are crazy?" he wanted to know.

"I think some people have seen them," I answered. "You ever seen them?" I asked the question without really meaning to. He had already told me that he had seen ghosts. The liquor had loosened my tongue to the point where I was not hearing my words until they had already come out of my mouth.

"Yes, I've seen em'," Holyday answered without the slightest hesitation.

"Where?" It was a stupid question.

"I see my brothers every now and then," he lit two small cigars and passed one of them to me, "brothers from the war. Men I fought with and lived with. Men that died. Brothers that have passed on. I see their faces sometimes, hear their voices. But I suppose if I did not, that would make me even crazier. But some stuff, some stuff just cannot be explained. Or, I guess more accurately, the only explanation is that I visit the domain of the insane on occasion. But I always make it back and it does not much worry me anymore. I kind of embraced it. Accepted it and made it a part of my life."

"Well, a man would have to be crazy to begin with to go charging up a hill at 30,000 Redcoats," I said, trying to make light of our present conversation.

Holyday looked around the room and surveyed those sitting closest to us to see if they might be privy to our discussion.

"I don't talk about that to too many people," he said. His attempt was to make the remark under his breath, however intoxication rendered him incapable of doing so. Although it did not really matter as the couple sitting within earshot seemed to be engaged in animated debate and were paying us no mind.

"Serioushly?" I slurred. "I would make sure everyone knew who I was and what I did."

"Would you?" he asked. "Would you go around telling everyone that you left four hundred men dead and dying on a hill while you and a dozen others ran from death? Swam across a river to escape death?"

"What else could you do?" I asked in astonishment.

"Nothing," he said abruptly. "But not run around bragging about something I did that was only notable because of the sacrifices made by my brothers. The story is about them. The story is about Major Mordecai Gist and Colonel Sterling. It's about how the men of the 1st Regiment brought up the rear so that General Washington could save the Continental Army. And the country."

"I understand," I stated.

He emptied the last of the whiskey into our glasses and said, "That's a story for others to tell for I don't like to go there. Although sometimes they visit me."

"The ghosts?" I asked.

"To my brothers," he said, raising his glass and toasting his fallen brethren.

"To the Maryland Four Hundred," I raised my glass and made my toast quietly so that only Holyday could hear. He seemed to appreciate my discretion. We downed our whiskey and set the glasses next to the empty bottle on the table.

"How?" I asked.

"How what?" he responded. We both laughed at our drunkenness.

"How do they visit you?" I continued, the liquor now in complete control of my words.

"I see them walking down the street on some days," he began. "Sometimes they look at me and smile. Other times they do not smile. Sometimes they don't even look at me. I assume they know I'm there. I mean they're dad burned ghosts, right?" He began to laugh but its short duration implied sadness rather than joy. "I wonder sometimes if other people can see them? I expect not."

"Only natural, having gone through something like that," I reasoned. "Makes sense they want to come back on occasion and check in."

Holyday removed his leg from the bench and turned himself toward the table. The hole in the side of his face was something no one could ever get used too. I sensed he was aware that I stared at his deformity so to disguise the fact the whiskey asked, "How'd you get this?" I drew an imaginary line from above my left eye across my face to the bottom of my right chin. "That a sword?"

"No," he said, almost dismissively. "A bayonet. At the top of the hill, right next to the cannons, we fought hand to hand. Bastard gashed me across the face with the end of his rifle," he paused only for a second, "then I stuck mine clean through his gut. He spat blood even before I pulled it back out." This time his laughter was more genuine, although it was obviously being used to hide the memories of the most violent and horrible day of his life.

"I'll tell you a story," he snickered at his inebriation and inched himself closer to me. "I'm movin' through Virginia, a couple years ago. I'm makin' ready to cross the Potomac. Got three other fellas with me. We're looking for a place to cross that ain't too deep. Ain't got no horses. All the sudden we see Redcoats. Lots of 'em, and they seen us too. We got ourselves pinned back against the river. Water moving fast, no way to cross. So, we dug in behind some fallen trees and waited for them to come. We laid out the powder and the balls to reload quick as we could."

Holyday glanced around the room and in that moment I could see what his eyes must have looked like as he surveyed the forest in Virginia. The liquor revealed a southern drawl that had been absent to this point. This backwoods dialect, likely discarded very purposefully over the years, only served to enhance the story.

"We had six rifles and six pistols between us. We passed around our guns so that I had all six pistols and the other men each had two rifles. Easiest way for us to reload we thought. We got it all packed with powder and ball and ready to roll. Knowin' we are going to have to reload quicker 'an lightning, outnumbered as we were. Got so tense we were wishin' they would attack. Get it over with one way or the other."

"All at once the Reds come charging out of the thicket. All up and down the riverbed and they are blastin' away. The boys took aim and fired, dropped one rifle then picked up the other and fired again. Then squatted to reload. I was shooting one pistol at a time. I could not afford to miss and am much better shooting with my right hand than my left. So, I shoot one of em', he goes down. I pick up another pistol, aim, fire. By this time a few of em' are right on top of us so I picked up two pistols at the same time. Didn't even have time to aim. Just point, pull. Dropped those pistols and picked up the last two. Meanwhile the boys are spilling powder, dropping balls, and I'm thinkin' we're dead for sure. These guys is right on top of me. I dropped my hammers point blank on those sons of bitches and they 'bout come up off the ground. Dead as hell. I duck down and commenced to reload. Turns out I'm as shaky as the other fellas. It sure goes to figure that the one time in our lives when a fast reload was never more important and the whole bunch of us like we never handled a gun before. It feels like it takes forever before we are all reloaded. Me with six pistols, everyone else with two rifles loaded and cocked."

With the whiskey exhausted, Holyday interrupted his story to swallow down the last of his ale. I am on the edge of my seat and drunk as a monkey waiting for him to finish the story. And though it could only have been a few seconds I could no longer contain myself.

"What happened?" I pleaded.

Holyday smiled his broken smile as he resumed, "So we wait. I peer out from behind the trees. Nothin'. Where they at? We're peeking out from behind our positions scanning up and down the tree line. We can't see em'. We waited near an hour. Not a sound. We moved slowly. Out from behind our cover, guns all pointed at the tree line. Steppin' over the dead directly in my front. We canvas the whole area. They're all dead."

"Christ Almighty," I exclaimed, "you killed em' all!"

"No," he said, his voice having lost all its energy. "No, we didn't."

"What happened?" I asked, now somewhat anxious as I expected to hear how this man suffered the loss of one of his own, enduring the brutal heartache of war once again.

"We counted the dead," he proceeded. "There were sixteen dead British soldiers. At first, we were all so happy to be alive that we did not even take notice. But after a few minutes I got this strange feeling. Kind of feeling that something is off, and it paralyzes you. You can't move forward until you figure out what it is that is gnawing at your head."

"I know that feeling," I admitted.

"You shoot both your rifles Travis?" Holyday continued. "You shoot both yours Maxwell? Mark? They all answered in the affirmative. You shoot again after the reload, I asked em'? None of them did. Well, says I, six rifles, each fired once. Six pistols, each fired once. That there is twelve shots. And I looked at the boys as it slowly dawned on them that it didn't add up. Twelve shots. Sixteen dead."

"So, what was it?" I almost shouted.

"What was it?" he repeated. "Wish I knew! It didn't make sense then. It don't make sense now. It's not a riddle Brixton," he laughed. "It doesn't have a punch line. Ain't no answer. All I'm sayin' is that some things in this world can't be explained. Only thing I ever come up with is that we had some help that day. From shooters unseen. Who or what they were, I reckon' I'll never know."

CHAPTER 8
Merriweather Lewis

There was a bang on my door. I woke in a stupor. The world slowly began to come into focus. Holyday entered the room. He took one look at me and laughed out loud.

"Not much of a drinker are you Brixton?" he quipped.

I did not even remember leaving the tavern, such had been the state of my intoxication. Still groggy I struggled to my feet. My head ached in a most terrible way.

"I think you would be better served to take another hour of sleep," Holyday advised.

"I feel like shit," I muttered, again eliciting laughter from him.

"Ah, young Brixton, you held your own late into the evening," Holyday commented. "But if not for that bed you surely would have ended up face down in the street."

"I believe it," I confessed.

"I had heard that drunkenness was the standard down in Somerset," he stated, "and that the drinking started in the crib."

I snickered at his joke but felt too horrible to muster a response.

"I have a couple things I have to do," he explained. "Why don't you lay down for a bit? I'll rouse you when I return."

"No," I answered. "I've too much to do. I have to find a store called Wilson's and order the supplies." I pulled out my map and began to unfold it.

"I know the store," Holyday replied. "It's right down the street. Come on."

We walked out through the front lobby. Behind the counter there stood a tall, slender woman, probably thirty years of age and strikingly attractive. Beside her was a boy, younger than myself by a year I guessed. It could have been her son for the two shared some facial similarities.

Although, while the woman possessed a look of confidence with strong posture, the boy impressed as weak, and bent.

"We might be staying another night Marie," Holyday called out across the lobby as he reached to open the hotel's front door. "Can you change the sheets in room six? I think the boy here may have pissed the bed."

The woman did not even pretend to hold back her laughter. "We'll take care of it," she called after him as we stepped out into the street.

"What the hell was that for?" I protested, knowing full well I had not soiled the sheets.

"Nothing wrong with clean sheets young Brixton," Holyday smirked.

"Certainly not, but I didn't piss the bed!"

"Good for you," he said. "I did."

"What?"

"I'm in room six," he said with the look of a child who had played a practical joke on a friend. "You're in room nine."

I could not help but laugh. "Thanks a lot," I added.

"Don't matter," he assured me. "You'll probably never see that fine-looking woman again. She knows me well."

"Fair enough," I submitted.

"Okay," he said, stopping in the middle of the street. "There's your Wilson's. Salt, sugar, coffee, medicine too I guess, but I do not think they'll be selling you guns. Quaker folks. They steer clear of firearms."

"No," I answered him. "Jed told me to ask around for the McDonald's Raw Bar. Down by the water he said. Guy called Jack Quinn. Jed said he would direct me to the gun dealer."

"Why hell Brixton, I'm going right down there," he told me. "They serve real good food, and their ale is always fresh."

I cringed at the notion of ever drinking an alcoholic beverage again. Holyday interpreted my expression and replied that another drink was exactly what I needed.

"Let's get you your salt and sugar," Holyday recommended. "We can take it over to the stables and have one of the boys lock it up for you. Then we can walk over to the Raw Bar. I'm curious who might be sellin' guns down that way."

"Hey, I can't be gettin' none of Jed's contacts in trouble," I stated with concern.

"Not gettin' anyone in trouble boy," he assured me. "Always good to know another place to get a gun is all."

We did not discuss the plan further. Holyday and I walked into the small red brick and mortar street-front business. Upon entering there was not a soul in sight.

"Hello," I called out.

"Well, hello there!" We were greeted by an old woman who came walking up from the back of the store. Her name was Lucy and I had met her briefly on my trip with Uncle Jedediah some twenty months ago. It was obvious she did not recognize me. She was wrinkled and gray and despite walking with a distinct shuffle she appeared full of energy and blessed with a most pleasant disposition.

"How can I help you fellas this morning?"

Her smile was as genuine as her white hair. It was a smile her customers had likely been fortunate enough to witness for many decades. It was welcoming and somewhat infectious in nature. It was the smile of a woman that had long ago run out of time to worry about things that did not matter. She was happy to be alive and just as happy to have us standing in front of her, even though at this point she had no idea who we were. I could see behind the woman's eyes an authenticity that people wear when they understand they don't have any real problems. The woman's positivity was energizing, and I could imagine people thinking long and hard to come up with reasons to visit her store.

"Good morning," I said. "I am Steven Brixton of Somerton. Jedediah is my uncle."

"Yes! Yes!" she almost screamed. "I remember. My God, you've grown two feet since last time you was here."

Lucy continued talking as she turned away from us and shuffled across the floor. She disappeared around the corner. I followed her with Holyday behind me.

The back portion of the shop contained more product stacked high to the ceiling. There was a spot against the far wall that offered an oversized couch and several plush chairs. The woman positioned herself in front of the couch. Having turned around to face me, she allowed herself to fall backwards. It was comical to see the woman give way and collapse into the waiting arms of the sofa. The cushions collected her, and she adjusted herself not a single inch. She rested on the couch exactly as intended and beckoned us to join her.

"Come, come," she said. "Sit down, we must talk. Who is this gentleman?"

"I'm sorry," I apologized, "this is Cole Holyday."

"Hello Mr. Holyday," Lucy said. "Please, sit."

Holyday and I each pulled up a chair and took a seat across from her.

"How is Jedediah?" The woman's eyes sparkled.

"Uncle Jed is fine mam, he sends his best," I replied.

"What about Mildred? How is little Millie?"

"Aunt Millie is well. She sends her love too," I said. "There's a virus running through Somerton. Everyone is a little bit on edge. Aunt Millie is so afraid of it she's not left the farm in two weeks."

"Mildred always was a smart one," the woman told me. "This virus, went through here a while back, best to stay clear of it if you can."

"Well, Aunt Millie is sure enough steering clear," I said. "She is accepting no visitors until this thing passes."

"I don't blame her," Lucy agreed with enthusiasm. "This place was a ghost town just a month or so back. Folks would not even walk the streets for fear of catching it. Most unkind it was, I know it took some people away."

"You don't have to tell me mam," I said. "I was one of the first in Somerton to come down with it. I know I thought I was dying."

"I can only imagine, you poor thing," she sounded genuinely sympathetic, the way only old people can. "Me and Lew, we had to shut the store for a few days. People our age seemed to suffer mightily from it. In fact," she continued, "I think almost everyone that passed on from that horrible illness was elderly. Although, I did hear tell of a few little ones dying. Babies and old folks, that's who it takes away."

"When I was sick," I told her, "Jed and Millie set me up in the barn."

"Quarantine you did they, ha ha," she expressed a hardy laugh. "Best thing you can do if'n you have the space. City like this, with everybody livin' on top of each other, can't run from it. Nowhere to go. Only thing you can do is stay inside and hide from it. Try to stay away from folks until those nasty germs move on out."

"Jed and Millie," I laughed as I recalled, "when they would come check on me, they would cover up their faces with scarves."

"Don't blame em' one little bit," Lucy said. "Can't never be too careful when you got germs running about killin' folks, or making em' so God awful sick they was wishin' they was dead."

"Exactly how I felt," I said laughing. "I remember thinking I'd soon enough be dead then continue in the state I was in."

"That's how people was feelin' 'round here," she said. "Just misery. And can't do nothin' but ride it out. When it made its run through the city it spread like wildfire. They shut down the docks for a full week. Folks said it was to make sure we didn't import more of it from somewhere else, but I know just as likely it was 'cause half the captains was down sick with it and the rest of 'em couldn't find enough healthy souls to put together a crew."

"Well," I said, "it's running through Somerton right now and we're doing the same thing. Not letting strangers pass through. Making them use the road that runs outside of town."

"Smart," she replied. "People get contagious with it a few days before they even know they're sick. We had folks comin' to fetch the medicine for sick family. They see the sign on the store that says we was closed and dang if they didn't come a knockin' on our door anyway. Can't say as I blame em' though. Mighty hard thing to do, watchin' kin folk suffer. They would say, "We ain't sick!" But Lew and I knew if'n they had sick family they were probably already sick too, just didn't know it yet."

"Surprised they let you turn em' away, crazy as some people are," I said.

"Oh, we didn't turn 'em away," she said. "No, we couldn't do that. Cannot turn a blind eye to people's suff'rin less it comes back to you ten-fold. We would put the medicine in a basket and lower it down out the second story window, back all the way down past the other side of the courtyard. We own the second story of this building all the way down to the end of the block," she laughed as she pointed upstairs, "Always had to tell folks, take more than a drop of this and it'll kill you quicker than the virus. Told em' not to be givin' it to babies. Knew they wouldn't heed the warnin' but did our best to help em' understand they's dealin' with a pow'ful potion." She let go a hardy laugh, "Lew wouldn't pull the basket back up, figurin' it be contaminated. He would just throw the rope down after he lowered the medicine. A week or so into it there be thirty, forty baskets, hundreds of feet of rope settin' in the back alley down from our window. Once the sickness moved on Lew took the whole mess down the street and burned it all. Them germs only live for a few days, so they say, but weren't takin' no chances. Not for the cost of some baskets and rope."

At that moment Lew walked into the room. "What do we have here?"

Lew was a large man. He was not as tall as Uncle Jedediah or me but still stood well over six foot. The years had begun to bend him over, but his size was still imposing. His long gray hair had been turned white by his age and looked just a shade off from the blond hair my uncle and I wore. His arms were the size of most people's legs and despite his advanced years he still looked immensely powerful.

"Lew, this is Steven," the old woman answered. "You remember, Jedediah's nephew."

"Oh, sure," Lew bellowed. "Somerton folk. How the heck are things down there?"

"We're all fine," I answered. "This is Mr. Cole Holyday."

Holyday stood up and extended his hand. Lew shook it vigorously.

"Seems I've seen you somewhere before," Lew said. "Maybe down at the docks?"

"Quite possible," admitted Holyday.

"Not a face I'd forget" Lew commented nonchalantly.

"Lew Wilson!" Lucy scolded.

"It's okay mam," Holyday assured her.

"Damned fool says whatever thought pops into his mind," Lucy said.

"It's quite alright," Holyday repeated.

"Quit your worryin' woman," Lew said in a playful tone. "If Cole here were ashamed of that face, he'd wear a hood. I 'spect he won that face in the Revolt. Look to be about the right age. You fight in the war Mr. Cole?"

"Yes sir," replied Holyday.

"See Lucy? Without faces like Cole's here there would be no America," Lew said. "Freedom ain't free. Is it Mr. Cole? Freedom comes with price tags. Freedom comes with sacrifice. Lots of boys paid more than Cole did to win this country. But just the same, I thank you for your service. Quite obviously a warrior."

"Thank you, sir," Holyday answered.

"You should see the other guy, right Cole?" Lew laughed as he plopped down on the couch next to Lucy.

"I was just tellin' the boys 'bout how we lowered the opium in baskets while the sickness was runnin' through town," Lucy said. "They's dealin' with it now in Somerton."

"Oh, Christ almighty," Lew replied. "Never seen so many sick folks in all my life."

"Beg your pardon mam," Holyday interjected, a sense of astonishment in his voice, "you used opium to treat the virus?"

"Well," Lucy attempted to explain, "I don't know that the opium does anything to the virus directly. But it'll help you sleep through it. Avoid all the sufferin'. A drop or two a couple times a day. You wake up a week later hungry as a horse, but still breathing."

"Some of these illnesses," Lew chimed in, "it's the suffering that kills folks. The agony. Just too much for some people. Can't muster the strength to go on. Best to sleep through it."

"If you know how to use it," Lucy added. "In the hands of a fool the medicine is more dangerous than the virus itself. Treat the opium with respect and it'll do you right. Get careless with it and it'll make you pay. Kill you quick if you get stupid with it."

"We know too damned well don't we dear?" Lew asked. His words dripped with aching regret.

Lucy's answer was not verbal. Instead, her face became framed in a somber despondency, and she looked as if she might begin to cry.

"Meriweather Lewis," she whispered, closing her eyes.

Holyday looked my way and communicated his confusion by raising and lowering his eyebrows. The silence was quite excruciating until Lew finally attempted to clarify.

"I'm sure you've heard the stories," he said.

Everyone in the country knew of Lewis and Clark's journey to the Pacific. But at this moment Holyday and I lacked any information that could help us decipher his relevancy in the present context.

"We knew Meriweather very well," Lucy shared. "We were living in Albemarle County, only a couple miles from the Locust Hill Plantation."

"Virginia," Lew added, "where the boy was born."

Holyday looked my way once more. This time his blank expression conveyed no message.

"We were close to the family," Lucy said. "They were good people. Moved down to Georgia after Meriweather's father died."

"Meriwether moved back to Virginia some years later to live with Nicholas," Lew continued, "his uncle."

"Came back to get some education," Lucy said. The couple took turns telling the story. A habit typical of married folks who have been together for so long. "Had private tutors at first. Ended up going over to Lexington and graduating from Liberty Hall. Such a smart boy. We got to know him very well before he left for university."

"You heard about his death I'm sure," Lew spoke in a manner that implied they were not going to give us a complete history of Meriwether's youth.

"Lots of different stories made their way through Somerton regarding his demise," I stated. "Got so we figured most folks were just making stuff up."

"Yes, we heard all the different accounts as well," Lew said. "Murder or suicide?"

"Most people down our way seemed to prefer to believe he was murdered," I offered.

"I think that's probably true for most folks," Lucy said. "Speaks to the scale of the tragedy that the preferred version ends with his murder."

"He was a national hero," it was Lew's turn. "Folks don't want to believe that someone like that could take his own life. But we knew better. He continued to correspond with us over the years. And when he was getting ready to head out west, he would stop by and see us all the time."

"We were living up here in Baltimore by then," Lucy filled in the blanks for us. "He was living with Tommy Jefferson in the President's Mansion at the time, in Washington. Most folks don't know that."

"He was going up to Philadelphia all the time getting ready for that trip," Holyday and I had already shifted our attention to Lew before he even began to speak. "Stopped off to visit us every time he went through Baltimore. I guess we saw him quite near monthly the year before they set out."

"Meriwether was prone to depression," Lucy told us. "He confided in us on occasion, going into most specific detail. I, myself have severe spells of the melancholy. I think people like us, sometimes we take great relief in just being able to talk to someone who can understand. Most folks don't have any idea. Even the doctors don't really get it. If you have never been there, if you've never stood alone at the bottom of that black hole, there is just no way to describe the feeling to someone who's never seen it, never felt it."

"We heard the stories of his murder," Lew acknowledged. "Heard the stories that he might have killed himself. No one knows for sure. Like everything else in this world, people got to make up their own minds, come to their own conclusions. I find it hard to believe that anyone could have killed that man. He was so big, strong, and good with his weapons. Ain't no man alive could sneak up on him. He had the senses of an animal. I remember him telling us one time that he could hear you from a mile away and smell you from two. No, I don't believe anyone murdered Captain Merriweather Lewis."

"So?" I left the question hanging out there.

"Meriwether was a big man," Lucy said. "Everything he did was big, never any half measures with him. No moderation at all. It was always full speed ahead. I was not surprised one little bit when he told us he was going to the Pacific Ocean. It was exactly the kind of thing you would expect from him. He always had gigantic plans and the highest possible expectations of himself."

"Insatiable appetite," added Lew. "Seems he could never satisfy that appetite. Whether it was for work or play. He would always take it to the next level. That included his drinking."

"And his opium," Lucy said, her voice again growing quiet. "He suffered the chronic pain, as I do. Both mental and physical ailments plagued him. He had problems with his back and his feet. Of course, he also had to deal with the melancholy. The opium, if you use it right, take care of what ails you. But he took too much of it. I suspect the trip out west gave him cause to up his dosage considerably. Those men suffered the malaria and only God knows what other ailments they encountered along the way. I've no doubt that he and his men, the *Corp of Discovery* they called them, once stricken with the malaria, no other choice but to let the opium do its work. Without it, I'm sure they would have just curled up and died. But that stuff, magic in the right hands. Tamed the malaria and helped push those men over them mountains and all the way out to the Pacific Ocean. That's something you'll never read in the history books," Lucy chuckled. "If not for the opium, they never would have made it. Would be no such thing as the Pacific Northwest. Louisiana Purchase would just be a piece of paper."

"We knew something wasn't right from the letters," Lew said. "Once he got back to Missouri, he was Governor by that time, in the first letter he was on top of the world. Going to publish his journals. Had big plans for him and Tommy Jefferson. The next letter it was like someone else was writin' it. We knew he was dealin' with the bad place again. That was the last we ever heard from him."

"We talked to some folks who'd seen him in St. Louis," Lucy's eyes had started to tear up. "Heard a story about how he was on his way to Washington to see the President. They were in Tennessee when some of the horses ran off during the night. Considerin' the stories that followed, my first thought was that the horses had run off with his medicine, his opium. If he was still takin' those large doses, and by all accounts he was, you can't just stop. Might last a day or two before you completely lose your mind. That is what we think happened. Then to hear the awful details of the suicide. Shot himself twice, slit his wrists, cut his throat. People couldn't make sense of it. He must have been murdered they said. No. No, a person been takin' as much of that stuff as he was, for as long as he was, nothin' 'bout that suicide surprised me. As gruesome as it was, if that boy had been without the medicine for a few days, I can tell you he was in a dark, dark world. All that poor man wanted was for the pain to stop. All he wanted was to be dead."

"Its best folks think he was murdered," Lew figured. "He'd probably prefer that it not go down in history that he did himself in. But I'll tell you, when I heard that story, how he shot himself repeatedly and cut himself to pieces, I thought, of course he did. How else would such a man leave this world? Always to the next level, bigger than life, even in death."

"Mind you do not forget that story," Lucy stated emphatically. "I know sure, whatever else is on your list of provisions, Jedediah wouldn't send you all the way to Baltimore if he didn't think the folks in Somerton needed medicine. There is a lesson here. This medicine, people been using it for thousands of years. Countries gone to war over the opium. There is not a problem it can't fix. Broken bones, broken hearts, the melancholy, anxiety, you name it. Couple drops of the medicine, and everything is right with the world. These sicknesses that go 'round, the influenza and the fevers, sometimes they be so brutal all you can do is take a drop and sleep through it. It can turn a cripple into a healthy man and pull a person right up out of the doldrums. Surely it has saved a thousand souls for everyone its stolen. But treat it right. Don't go gettin' reckless with it. Before you know it, it will get you. And there aint' no comin' back."

"I have noticed that Uncle Jed is very careful with the medicine," I assured her. "We keep most of our stores in the main building. Salt, sugar, dried meats, preserves, all the jarred fruits and vegetables, all that stuff is there for the taking. The only things Jed keeps under lock and key are powder, balls, and medicine. That stuff is always locked up. Nobody gets to it without Jedediah's approval. Even then, that is the stuff we always run out of first. If someone is making a trip to Baltimore it is because we are low on gunpowder, shot, or medicine."

"You Somerton folk still don't have access to powder and balls through Princess Anne?" asked Lucy.

"We can get them in Princess Anne. Sometimes can get medicine there too, but they charge too much," I explained. "Uncle Jedediah says anything we buy in Princess Anne costs us ten times what we'd pay at Wilson's."

"Maybe we need to raise our prices," joked Lew.

Looking at the old couple laughing on the sofa I was struck by how they almost seemed to be the same person. Their conversations were practiced in a manner perfected over the course of decades. Each of them had a knack for finishing the other one's thoughts. It was as if they could read each other's minds. Even their expressions complimented one another. When one of them was speaking, it was the other's smile or look of surprise that added to the story, making the listener grateful to be in their audience. They were so deeply in love with each other, a sense of joy radiated from them. It felt good just to be in their presence.

CHAPTER 9
Francis Scott Key

The Wilson's appeared to be the kind of folks that took immense pleasure in the gift of gab. They both possessed an energetic eloquence when telling a story. Though lacking a polished command of the English language, their enthusiasm more than made up for mispronounced words or rudimentary grammar. And like all good conversationalists, they were adept at involving their audience in the activity. There was no desire to ramble on without eliciting input from others present.

"Will you return to Somerton by land or by sea?" Lucy asked.

I am sure her intention was as much to promote the dialogue as it was one of curiosity. I appreciated her steering us back to my most pressing need to secure the supplies, especially the medicine, and deliver them home as soon as possible.

"There is likely a ship sailing for the eastern shore this afternoon," Holyday surprised me with his remark.

His comment seemed to imply that he and I would be traveling together. Holyday did not comment further on the ship and the lapse in the discussion afforded me the opportunity to inquire about the supplies I needed to purchase.

"Jedediah told me there is a standard order with regard to Somerton's supplies," I redirected our conversation back to my business.

"Yes," Lucy answered. "Fifty pounds each of salt, pepper, sugar, and coffee, and two or three bottles of opium depending on the quality. The quantity of powder and balls seems to vary but Jed usually buys about twenty pounds of each."

"He asked that I double the order this time," this was not true, but I figured the windfall from Cornelius Armstrong should be put to good use. Not knowing with any certainty whether the British would vacate the Chesapeake after their defeat in Baltimore, it seemed wise to invest in additional staples. If England's warships lingered on the bay, it would likely be to the south, continuing to prevent merchant ships from venturing too close to the mouth of the Manokin River. If the ports at Devil's Island and Princess Anne were not going to be resupplied, purchasing additional weight would postpone the next trip to Baltimore. This would please Jedediah immensely.

"Okay," Lucy said. "We can get that together for you. The opium is especially good. How much of that will you be wantin'?"

"Jed gets three bottles when its good?" I asked.

"Yes," Lucy confirmed. "It's all liquid mind you."

She was referencing the opium in liquid form. Contained in glass bottles, transporting it was more difficult than when it is purchased as either powder or chunks. Still, it was my understanding that Jed preferred liquid medicine as it was easier to dose precisely.

"Better get six bottles," I said. "A lot of sick people in town."

"I guess a lot of folks waitin' on you," Lew interjected with a chuckle.

"Indeed," I replied. "Mister Wilson, I will confess that I experience a sense of dread previously unknown to me when I contemplate my neighbors, writhing in agony and counting every excruciating minute until my return."

"And powder and balls?" Lucy asked.

"Better stick to twenty pounds each on the powder and balls," I answered. With me in the saddle I was already a bit heavy.

"We'll get everything packaged up for you," Lew advised. "Shouldn't take an hour. You can wait right here if you'd like."

I informed the Wilsons that I needed to visit a gun dealer located down by the harbor and would be back in a couple hours. They assured me that upon my return the supplies would be packaged and ready for pick up. Our goodbyes were brief as we would see each other again shortly. Lew and Lucy remained seated on the large sofa. Holyday and I made our way to the front of the store and showed ourselves out.

We worked our way through the middle of the street, sliding around the waves of humanity still rejoicing in the defense of the city. If not for the fact that everyone squeezing their way past us was exceedingly jubilant the experience could have been terribly unpleasant. Pedestrians bumped into us, and we into them. At times it became necessary to grab those passing us by their shoulders and, as if dancing, turn them around so that our positions could be exchanged. There was a smile on every face and laughter filled the air to the point that Holyday and I struggled to communicate. I was eventually able to understand something to the effect that our destination was but a few blocks down the street and we had little choice but to forge ahead.

For a few more minutes we pressed on, at times literally leaning into the person in front of us to push the pile in the right direction. In time the crowd thinned, if only slightly. Still, it was enough to afford us the ability to walk side by side and to talk to one another without screaming.

"I have business on Pratt Street," Holyday said. "Maybe we can grab a table at the Raw Bar and order lunch. My meeting will be brief. I'll be back before you finish eating and we can go see about your guns."

"Okay," I agreed, looking up to see McDonald's Raw Bar right in front of us.

We passed through the front of the restaurant, a long galley with tables set along either wall. After making our way past a bar that afforded not a single empty stool, we stepped into a large back room that was separated from the rest of the place by a huge burgundy quilt embroidered with golden tapestry. The blanket hung from the rafters and served as somewhat of a curtain. Holyday pushed it aside and made his way to a small square table at the far side of the large room. There were two chairs tucked up tight. We pulled them out and took our seats.

A moment later a tall red-haired woman approached us with two menus in hand. Holyday, surprising me not in the least, knew the woman.

"Hello Kelly," he greeted her with that rough gravelly voice of his.

"Cole Holyday," she replied, a smile formed on her previously tired and disinterested face. It is fascinating how a person's expression can completely transform their appearance. This woman possessed no striking features. She wore a common face made even more mundane by the boredom etched across her brow. No doubt brought on by the endless hours of serving food and drink to the patrons of this pleasant but ordinary tavern. The smile that came to her face upon seeing Holyday gave her an altogether unique and intriguing look. She was, to be sure, a strikingly attractive woman. So taken was I by her beauty that I heard not a word Holyday said.

"This place makes the very best pizza pie," Holyday stated, snapping me out of my trance.

"Pizza pie," I repeated.

"Have you ever had pizza pie?" he asked.

"Ah, no," I admitted. "It's not something common to the woods of Somerset."

"You'll like it," he assured me. "Lots of good cheese. Do you like tomatoes?"

"Yes, sure," I answered.

"They bake it on a layer of thin white bread," he began.

"I know what it is," I informed him. "It's served in a restaurant in Princess Anne. But we seldom waste money eating in town. Uncle Jedediah believes in eating as sustenance and that food should not be taken up as a hobby."

"That's too bad," he said. "A good deal of joy can be derived from a tasty meal."

"I'm sure," I agreed. "It seems anything that could in any way be considered a luxury is avoided by our people. Cannot do anything that might slow you down. Never eat anything that sits heavy in the stomach."

"Always ready to spring into action," Holyday said, almost mockingly.

"Something like that," I agreed.

"Listen," he said rather abruptly, "I have to go see these people. Should be able to get us on a ship back to Cambridge tonight."

I was relieved to hear him revisit this topic. My return trip weighed heavy on my mind. Uncle Jedediah's instruction sheet spelled out an itinerary that included taking the Back River Ferry northeast of Baltimore City to Tolchester Beach on the eastern shore. From there it would be a two-day ride to Cambridge. Hearing that Holyday might be able to secure me passage back across the bay was welcomed information. It was one less thing I had to worry about and could have me arriving back in Somerton almost a week ahead of schedule. Jedediah would be impressed with such a timely return. More importantly, arriving several days earlier than expected could well mean the difference between life and death for some of my neighbors.

Holyday assured me his return would be imminent and he limped away towards the front of the eatery.

"Where did Cole get off too?" Kelly asked when she returned a minute later, setting the food and grog on the table.

"He's off to see about getting us on a ship," I answered. "He said he'd be back in a few minutes."

"I guess the bay is now safe for travel," she said. Her words rang tainted with a veiled skepticism concerning the whereabouts of the British warships. "Where are you sailing?"

"I need to get back to Somerton," I answered.

"Down past Annapolis?"

"Across the bay," I explained. "The southern peninsula. Almost to Virginia."

"Ships already sailing that far down the bay?" she sounded surprised.

"I believe he's attempting to get us to Cambridge," I said. "I'll do the rest by myself."

"Kind of a dangerous trip to be undertaken by your lonesome," she spoke as if she were familiar with the perils of travel in that part of Maryland.

"Well, if Holyday can get me on a ship," I stated, "I can get myself back home."

"He'll get you on a ship," she said in a most reassuring tone. "Cole is a man of his word if nothing else."

Her comment intrigued me. What could she have meant by wording her comment in such a way? It hit me with a sudden uneasiness how little I really knew about this man. He had proven himself to be honest and courageous. Otherwise, I cannot say I knew anything about Cole Holyday. He rode with the Maryland Four Hundred and for that he will forever be a hero. Still, his unwillingness to share that information with people was mysterious indeed. Most men, myself included, would have made sure everyone both far and wide had heard the tale of my heroics. I began to wonder how much this woman knew about Holyday.

"Can I ask you a question?" I started.

"Sure," and her smile was perfect.

"Do you know Cole Holyday well?"

"Not really," she admitted. "He comes in here once a week or so I guess."

"I heard someone refer to him as a pirate," I said. "Any truth in that?"

"No," she laughed. "Because of his face you mean?"

"Maybe that's what was meant by the comment," I decided to move past the subject as I had realized some time ago that Armstrong's initial introduction had been inaccurate. "Do you know about the Maryland 400?"

"Of course," she answered, "Cole doesn't like to talk about it. But a man like that, being a part of something so grand, every time he leaves a room someone whispers after him. He is a living legend. People can't keep secrets like that. I think deep down inside he knows that people know who he is. He knows people know what he did. The fact that he won't talk about it makes it even more impressive."

"Yes," I said. "I wouldn't be able to stop bragging about it had it been me."

"He told me once that General Washington assured the Four Hundred's place in history when he famously commented on their bravery," she said.

"Good God, what brave fellows I must this day lose," I repeated Washington's words.

"Yes," Kelly acknowledged, "Cole said that any further comments by the few survivors would only serve to detract from the legend of the battle. The Maryland Four Hundred will live forever because of what George Washington said about them. Cole only ever mentions it when he's good and drunk, and still only in the most discreet company. Do you mind if I sit?"

"Please," I encouraged her.

"He told me that out of respect for the men who died on the hill, the survivors swore an oath that the legend should live on under the perspective of General Washington," she resumed. "I remember him saying that the men that died on the hill deserve the eulogy that George Washington gave them. So, he leaves it at that."

"So aside from his heroics in New York," I pressed on, "what does he do? I mean who is he?"

"I've heard him referred to as a liaison," she said. "If he has an official title, and I do not believe he does, it might be that of an intermediary. I once heard one of our prominent officers call him that. Intermediary, I guess that would describe him as well as anything else. Truth be told, Cole is the kind of man that defies description. Maybe legend," she said laughing, the mesmerizing smile returning to her face.

She obviously was not being reluctant to share information about my travelling partner. It was possible, I contemplated, that my mysterious new acquaintance did not live the covert life which I had assumed. Perhaps it was only the unimaginable and bizarre circumstances that had thrown our lives together that had preoccupied me with such a suspicious curiosity.

"Intermediary," I said, putting the word out there to study it. "Yes, he would appear to have all the necessary skills to function in such a capacity." My understanding of the word, at least as it related to Holyday, was vague and afforded more questions than answers.

"I'm not even sure such a description does him justice," she replied. "Like I said, I don't know that he has a specific moniker assigned to him. There may not even be a word that accurately describes what he does."

"What is that?" I asked. "What does he do?"

"He helps people communicate," was her answer. "That's probably the best way to describe it. He communicates for people."

"For whom?" I asked in a tone that foamed of frustration.

"That's not it either," she added. "That makes him sound like a messenger and he is certainly much more than that."

"But who is it that he communicates with?" I tried as hard as possible to ask with a more benign inflection.

"People that don't want anyone knowing that they're talking to each other," she answered. "You know, politicians, military, families of the first order, the power brokers."

This description summarized exactly my thoughts regarding the work done by Jake McCabe. Maybe the two were of the same ilk.

"So, the nature of his associations is secretive?" I continued, almost involuntarily, to fire questions at her despite being aware that my line of inquiry was beginning to transcend curiosity and might at this point seem intrusive. Even so, she did not seem bothered by my inquisition.

"I think some of the things that happen in Baltimore are not meant for public consumption," she acknowledged. "Sometimes it's probably more accurate to say that the military and the politicians prefer their associations with the powerful to remain private. The government's relationship with the wealthy needs to be discreet."

"That makes sense," I said. "I would think maintaining the perception of being impartial would be beneficial come election time. But whose wealth are they so intent on distancing themselves?"

"The people that run Maryland," she answered in a way that inferred most people would have considered this obvious. "The rich and powerful," she continued, "the people that make the decisions, the families of the first order."

"Oh," for the first time some pieces of the puzzle seemed to fit together in a way that made sense. "Holyday provides a service for the rich to curry favor from the city's elected officials?"

"Well," she responded introspectively, "that makes it sound like it's the politicians that hold the power. That is not how it works. It is the leaders of the big families that decide what happens. It is the first order families that tell the government what to do. I mean, politicians come and go. The money and the power in some of these families goes back hundreds of years and will surely be around for hundreds more. These are the people who make all the decisions. The men and women of the elite families. They decide everything from land rights to tax rates to who wins the elections. People talk about Maryland's government being the most corrupt in America but it's really the big monied families that call the shots. It is the families of the first order that have turned Maryland into a political cesspool."

"And Holyday is the go between," I surmised.

"But see," she protested, "that doesn't do him right. Of course, I have never been to one of these meetings, but you can see these people around town. Senators and Councilmen, Captains in the Navy, the Governor himself, when they interact with Cole, they speak to him as at least an equal. On occasion you would swear that it was Cole who held the high card, so to speak."

At that moment, an impeccably dressed man, led across the room by another waitress, was seated at the table immediately adjacent to ours. He looked at Kelly and me as he took his seat and acknowledged us in a most proper and distinguished manner.

"Sir," he said looking at me and nodding accordingly. "Madame," he repeated the gesture toward Kelly.

He ordered some sweet tea and a bowl of seafood chowder. Then untying a small case for letters, he pulled several pieces of paper from within and placed them most specifically, as if they were in order, on the table in front of him. He then retrieved from the inside pocket of his very smart and expensive looking suit jacket a feathered pen and a small bottle of ink. Opening the bottle, he set it down and, dipping his quill to wet the tip, began writing on one of the pages. I found his behavior peculiar. He set himself up at the small table as if he were in an office somewhere. Being very well groomed and wearing a most impressive looking suit, what with him and his papers, ink well and feathered pen, you might expect that he was drafting a most important letter. I suppose it was that he appeared somewhat out of place that piqued my interest. Nonetheless, it was only with a concerted effort that I was able to conceal my frustration at having been interrupted by his arrival. Kelly had finally begun to share with me information about Holyday that, if not valuable in some way, was profoundly interesting.

I tried in vain to refocus her and return to our discussion regarding Holyday and the work he did as a confidant for the strategists of Maryland. Unfortunately, it seemed a lost cause as Kelly's attention now appeared solely directed at the handsome man sitting to our side. I was at first pleased to see that her overly unabashed flirtations went unrequited. The man seemed rather bothered by her blatant advances and dismissed them as nothing more than a nuisance. However, in short order that fascinating smile of hers worked its magic and the gentleman began to respond to her interruptions in an increasingly cordial manner.

It was not lost on me that the man, realizing that he had won the attention of the woman, gave me the once over to assess what kind of relationship I might have with her. His conclusion came quickly and was one that I had no choice but to find insulting. His assumption that this woman, articulate and beautiful, could not be involved in any serious way with the likes of me, I took as an afront. However, realizing that in my present state, unshaven, ragged, and unwashed, my sense of being disgruntled soon became more a feeling of self-consciousness. When Kelly took the additional step of sliding her chair slightly away from our table to position herself more in his direction this contest was over.

My thoughts then returned to Holyday. He had been gone much longer than expected. I knew not where he had gone and had no idea when, or even if, he would return. Kelly had furnished me with information about the man which I found particularly interesting. However, the issue that gnawed constantly on my mind was left unanswered. Why had he remained in my company for such a prolonged duration? The use of my horses assisted him in crossing the bay. Once that mission had been accomplished, I expected to be discarded. Being of no further use to him it would not have surprised me to have parted ways on the docks in Annapolis.

That I could supply him a horse might explain him allowing me to accompany him to the plantation of Captain Smallwood. Although surely a man with his reputation and resources could have easily secured alternative transport. Having been raised to always be suspicious of the motives of those outside my small Somerton community I struggled with the contention that Holyday was simply a good man and wanted nothing of me in return. To this point I had consistently given him the benefit of the doubt and it had worked in my favor on every occasion. The evidence now before me suggested only that he was a man, distinguished in both character and accomplishment, who had only taken interest in a young boy as a matter of convenience and a desire to see that my arrival in Baltimore went unimpeded. My suspicion that he had an ulterior motive for remaining in my company now appeared to be mute.

I began to plan my next move as it was imperative that I return to Somerton as quickly as possible. The thought of Somerton's struggle with the cruel and unforgiving illness disturbed me greatly. But any anxiety related to the tardiness of my return was constantly tempered by the knowledge that had fate not introduced me to the strange quartet of men in Cambridge I would likely still not have arrived in Baltimore. I remained ahead of schedule. It was a message I rolled over in my mind. If I could spend the night with Lew and Lucy, I could set out early to the north and depart from Back River. Holyday had said very definitively that the horses would be cared for at the stable for as long as necessary. It would make more sense to retrieve them in the morning. I would take them back to Lucy's, load up my provisions and begin the long journey home. It was probably best that I forego the purchase of the firearms. Attempts to coordinate how that might be accomplished confused me and I was growing agitated. It was Kelly's smile that interrupted my racing brain. She was laughing as she looked at me and I immediately rejoined the present conversation.

"How remarkable!" she exclaimed. "Are you hearing this?"

I had not been listening as my thoughts, riddled with anxiety, had consumed me. It was altogether deliberate on my part that I ignored the commentary of the dandy gentleman that had stolen the attention of the voluptuous woman.

"I'm sorry," I apologized. "My preoccupation is on my journey home. I have many days of difficult travel ahead of me. Just trying to sort things out in my head."

It did please me that Kelly had interrupted her shameless flirtation to include me, if only briefly, in their conversation.

"He was there!" she said. "He saw the whole thing!" She could not have been more excited had she found buried treasure. Whatever approach it was that this sophisticated man had chosen to use to seduce his new acquaintance had surely been successful. She was unabashedly taken by his charm.

I decided to give Holyday five more minutes but was convinced that the likelihood that I would see him again was remote. Until then I resigned myself to listen to the story that had Kelly so worked up. If nothing else, I reasoned, maybe a lesson in how to attract members of the fairer sex. It was with reluctance and a determination to remain unimpressed with anything he had to say that I lent my ear. However, my indifference to the man's anecdote lasted not a single minute.

The man had introduced himself as Francis. That was about the last thing I heard before tuning him out. He was apparently a person of some means, as evidenced by his attire, and a well-known and accomplished attorney. He regaled us with a tale that had him involved in a prisoner exchange. As it turned out he was aboard a British ship making such a deal when the attack on Fort McHenry commenced. Considering the circumstances, while the British did honor the exchange, they would not allow him to disembark their vessel for fear he would relay their plans. The consequences of this alleged transaction allowed this Francis to view the entirety of the battle aboard a British frigate positioned just behind the line of warships.

I consumed his tale with the utmost skepticism, but before long I was convinced by the detail of his narrative that his account was indeed factual. It coincided exactly with what I had witnessed. Although, to be sure, Francis was permitted to view the battle from a distance much closer in proximity to the action than was I.

Our small group, arranged atop the lookout posts, could hear the cannon fire. Visually, we were restricted by distance and saw only the glowing radiance of the bombs and rockets. While Holyday and

Smallwood proved more than capable narrators, Francis saw firsthand what we could only envision in our mind's eye.

Soon, despite my attempts to the contrary, I was engrossed by the man's narration. Some of his descriptions were so vivid that they complimented my own experience in such a way that it moved me from my position several miles downriver into the harbor and gave me a front row seat to a battle that would grace the pages of history books for centuries to come. So grateful was I for his rendition of the events of that night that my contempt for him fell swiftly away. Moments later when he happened to mention a wife and family in the Frederick Maryland area, I found that my appreciation of him had turned into outright adoration. He was a most impressive person and I realized it would be foolish of me to be critical of Kelly for having been infatuated with him.

He continued with his story until its conclusion and then shared with us that he was so overcome by the experience that he felt compelled to make notes of his emotions. These notes, it turned out, became the rough draft of a poem he was writing to commemorate the event. It seems he possessed some talent in this area and some of his previous work had been published.

As he went to work on his chowder, he passed the draft to me and allowed me to read it. I was genuinely appreciative of this gesture and silently reminded myself that I needed to proceed with caution when making assumptions about people based on first impressions. This fellow was obviously a gentleman and a scholar. My hasty assessment of him was born of both laziness and jealousy. Now I sat feeling somewhat embarrassed as I read his poem quietly to myself.

"Oh, can you not see? By the new morning's light
What we proudly were hailing at yesterday's twilight
Rockets' red glare
Bombs bursting mid-air
Proof at last! Our flag was still there
I pray that our flag still stands o'er the fort..."

There were several lines scratched out that were not legible.

"For this land of brave men who so fought to be free..."

It continued for several pages. Some of it written in verse and other notations made in between the lines. Francis had finished his chowder and seemed to be waiting for me to hand his manuscript back to him, so I obliged. I must confess to feeling quite flattered when he laid the paper out on the table and pointed to a particular phrase.

"Proof that our flag was still there," he said, "Pray that our flag still did stand o'er the fort. I wanted to get at the idea that as long as we could still see the flag, we knew that the battle was not yet lost."

"Say, that the stars and the stripes of our flag did yet wave," I suggested.

I do not know whether he was just being kind, but he at least pretended to be impressed with my thought. He went so far as to write it down in the margin of his draft. When finished making the note he looked at me and smiled.

Looking up I saw Cole Holyday walking toward our table. He wore an exasperated expression that indicated his meeting had not gone according to plan. I had already concluded that if he did in fact return, he would bring with him the frustration of an exercise that had not lived up to expectations. Nonetheless, I was overjoyed that he had rejoined my company.

Holyday grabbed one of the wooden chairs from an empty table and without lifting it from the floor dragged it across the room. Spinning it around so that it faced the table he positioned it between Kelly and myself. As this was somewhat of a tight fit, Kelly inched over a bit to make room for him. A wince accompanied his usual painful grimace upon taking his seat next to me. His fatigued posture complimented a face that surely was as equally uncomfortable to wear as it was to behold. He groaned as he sat. It seemed he was both acknowledging his pain and savoring it.

"Francis," he uttered cordially to the expensive suit. I was somewhat surprised that I did not laugh out loud for it was surely comical to witness his connections throughout every nook and cranny of the city.

"Mister Holyday," Francis answered, assuring me the two men were acquainted and held each other, at least outwardly, in high regard.

He turned his attention to me. For a man who had taken a beating from the world in which he lived, his calm peaceful eyes were outrageously out of place. His eyes suggested a subdued acceptance of all that had happened and all that may yet be headed his way. They glimmered with a smooth and relaxed satisfaction that was in no way consistent with the horrors they had witnessed.

"We can't get out tonight," the words, though raspy, were content, even cavalier. "No one is sure what the British Navy's intentions may be. Reliable sources have suggested this war may well be nearing its end. But that in no way offers insight into what the English may do as they depart the Chesapeake. If their course is charted to traverse the Atlantic it would not be out of character for them to violate every American enterprise unfortunate enough to cross their path."

"Francis was there," Kelly noted. "He watched the entire battle from the harbor."

"A prisoner exchange," said Francis in response to Holyday's inquisitive stare.

"Get stuck in the middle of it did you?" Holyday surmised.

"I'll say," Francis answered. "A most unnerving night. Had Fort McHenry fallen we would have gone straight from negotiation to incarceration. But the flag never came down. It was breathtaking, miraculous in every way. The British officers aboard the transfer ship could not believe the fort withstood such a pounding. I'm attempting to put it to verse for the sake of posterity."

"Ah," Holyday acknowledged. "Always the warrior poet. Good for you getting the thoughts down as they are still fresh. Never know what history will have to say about the battle. It could very well be that you witnessed a pivotal moment in the course of our great country."

"Time will tell," said Francis.

"I would be interested in taking a look at those firearms," Holyday stated, turning his attention back to me. "I did learn of an American naval convoy leaving the docks in the morning. We have space on a commercial frigate that will fall in behind them. But if that's the plan we've much to do."

"By all means," I agreed with great enthusiasm. Just as I had been about to abandon my plans, they all fell back into place.

"Then we'll have to bid you a good evening," Holyday said. Grimacing, he rose to his feet and extended his hand to Francis and shook it firmly. He bent over and kissed Kelly on the cheek while placing some money on the table in front of her.

"Godspeed," called out Francis.

We exited through the back door of the Raw Bar and stepped out onto a dank and desolate boardwalk. The air was putrid and took our breath away. Stinking dead fish and vomit combined to create a hellish aroma. The thought of retreating into the pub was interrupted by Holyday pointing to a large metal barrel that he surmised was the source of the stench. Together, breathing into our elbows, we moved quickly away from the reeking cannister.

CHAPTER 10
Original Sin

The narrow alley was lined with small shops and open-air markets, though the absence of pedestrians suggested minimal business. The address Jedediah had written down for me was, as Holyday had predicted, only a few doors down from the tavern. The shop itself was nondescript and had I not an address it would have been impossible to tell the windowless shack was the location of a gun shop. There was not so much as a name on the building. If the small numbers painted just above the door did not match those on the back of my crumbled map, I would have thought the place not a business unto itself but rather the storage unit to one of the taller structures on either side of it.

We entered the dimly lit establishment and were greeted by a skinny old man with long grey hair. His facial hair, a beard longer than his hair and absent a moustache, suggested he was a Quaker. This indicated to me that we were almost certainly in the right place. I've no doubt there was some line, however ancient and convoluted, that traced him back to County Somerset. Jedediah had informed me that the owner of the shop was a man named Henry and that I would be treated fairly if he were made aware that I was making my purchases on behalf of Jedediah Brixton and the people of Somerton. I initiated my greeting with this information.

"Hello sir," I began, "my name is Steven Brixton. I am the nephew of Jedediah Brixton. I am looking for a Mr. Henry."

The man spent a minute looking us over. He paused briefly to survey the mangled face of Holyday and, seemingly unimpressed, moved his attention to me. Until that point, he had remained as emotionless as a corpse. But once making eye contact with me his demeanor underwent a remarkable transformation. The yellow teeth revealed by his broad, open-mouthed grin looked exactly as I would have expected. His distant aloofness changed in the blink of an eye. He immediately became friendly and welcoming.

"I am Henry," he said. "Hank, to friends and family." He paused as he continued staring me down. His grin widened into a full-fledged smile which revealed more stained teeth. "My God you're the splitting image of your father."

"You knew my father?" I asked, though the answer was obvious.

"Aye," he answered. "Grew up on the shore. Never went back after the war. You be sure and tell Jed to come by and see me next time he's up this way," Hank requested. "Ain't seen him in a good five years."

"I will sir," I replied.

"Hank," he corrected me. "And Millie? Is Millie still around?"

"Yes," I said. "Aunt Millie is alive and well and keeping Uncle Jed on the straight and narrow."

Hank let out a howl. "I'll bet she is at that. I'll bet she is. You give her my best as well will you boy?"

"I will," I promised.

"Now, what are we lookin' for today?" He asked, his tone grew more serious as if to remind himself that we probably had other things on our schedule.

"Like to get some rifles," I said.

"And maybe a couple pistols," called Holyday from across the room.

"I'm sorry," I said, "this here's Cole Holyday."

"Good day sir," Hank replied.

"Good day," Holyday returned.

Hank's selection of firearms was impressive. He had hundreds of rifles and pistols displayed around his shop. It only took him a few minutes to match us up with exactly what we needed.

"We're going to need to pick the rifles up in the morning," Cole said. "We can pay you now if you'd prefer."

"No, no, pay me in the mornin," said Hank.

"What time you open up?" Cole asked.

"Well, usually open the doors about eight o'clock," Hank answered. "But I live right in the back there," he pointed to the back of the shop. "So, I'll be here whenever it is you need me to be here."

"We'll see you tomorrow morning at eight o'clock," Cole said as he motioned with the twist of his neck for me to follow him out of the shop.

"I'll see you tomorrow mornin'," Hank called after us. I turned to look at him and we exchanged smiles. The door creaked loudly as it closed behind me.

We walked for a moment in silence. I could tell Holyday's leg was bothering him. His limp was constant, but it varied in severity. Sometimes it seemed barely perceptible but now his gait was labored, and it was obvious he was in a good deal of pain. We were making our way through a back alley when he decided it was time to stop for a smoke.

Holyday leaned back against a wall and pulled out his satchel. Lighting two smokes at the same time he handed one to me. He spent a minute moving his leg around searching for a position that would relieve the pain. It was a fruitless endeavor and ended with an impatient sigh that suggested reluctant acceptance.

Holyday had a tendency of starting conversations by picking a topic out of thin air. I appreciated this habit. It demonstrated a diverse curiosity.

"When we first saw you walking your horses into Cambridge," he began, "we thought you were some derelict hailing from down Virginia way."

I laughed at the remark but did not comment.

"Of course," Holyday continued, "we were a couple hundred feet away and couldn't see your face. Your size alone suggested you were a grown man. Traveling alone through the Nanticoke it was Armstrong's guess that you were an Accomack trapper."

"Why would he have thought Accomack and not Somerset?" I asked.

"Don't see many Somerset folks traveling lonesome along the coast," Holyday answered. "I suspect the loners we see coming up from Virginia just don't know how dangerous it is."

"With regard to terrain or bandits?" I inquired.

"Either way," Holyday responded, "dead is dead."

"No arguing that," I agreed.

"When you walked into the tavern," he continued to explain, "and we saw you were just a boy we were more than just a little surprised. Couldn't make sense of who would send someone your age through such difficult land all by themselves. Especially with all those fine-looking furs."

"Well," I responded, "as I've explained, these are dire times in Somerton. It was an emergency. We did not have many options. We needed someone who had already been sick. Couldn't afford to risk someone falling ill on the trip. There was a good deal of reluctance sending me by myself, but there was no one else suitable to pair me with. Jedediah convinced the town that I was up to the task. But again, the decision was made of desperation."

"I'll admit, you caught us all off guard when we first sat at your table," Holyday stated.

"How so?"

"Folks comin' from south of Cambridge usually carry with them either the English accent of a Loyalist or the southern drawl of a Virginia farmer," Holyday continued. "You possessed neither and spoke with the confidence of an educated man. No schools down your way, are there? Not expecting you to be articulate. Threw us off a bit."

"There are a few schoolrooms in the county," I said. "The Quakers have one just this side of Pocomoke. There is another, a Protestant school, south of Princess Anne and a Catholic school to the north of town."

"Which one did you attend?"

"Somerton is not Quaker, Protestant, or Catholic," I answered. "We are not welcomed in any of them."

"So?" Holyday questioned, "where does the education come from? You don't learn to speak so well from birds or beavers."

"You'd be surprised what you can learn from the animals," I said with a grin. "Our town is blessed with a library," I continued. "Probably not more than a hundred books. The Classics, Uncle Jedediah says, are to be read over, and over again. They will teach you everything you need to know about how the world works."

"And you are able to present as a learned man simply be reading these books?"

"Well," I said, "they're the right books. And our reward is not a graduation ceremony or a diploma, rather the satisfaction that accompanies a hard day's work."

Holyday exhaled a thick stream of smoke. His inquisitive expression communicated to me that he wanted more information. I appreciated his interest.

"We find our classrooms on the Chesapeake and in the forests and the fields of the County Somerset. Our teachers are the tides, the sunshine, and the wind."

"Sounds like something an Indian would say," Holyday surmised.

"Our relationship with the Indians has always been a good one," I said. "They are good people, the Assateague. They have taught us much about the sacred nature of the land. It is their influence, people who have lived here for a thousand years, that models our character as much as anything else. Still, most days in Somerton have us on the water before the sun is up and then straight to the fields until it is again dark. To spend a few hours by candlelight in the company of timeless literature is a pleasure like no other."

"You are a most impressive young man Steven Brixton," Holyday replied, his tone genuine and sincere. "I would not have thought it possible you could present yourself as you do without a formal education. It speaks highly of the Somerton culture, and indeed of this uncle of yours, that such a fine boy can be grown in the woods of the lower shore."

"I think the County Somerset is a bit more sophisticated than most people would like to admit," I replied, "but I do appreciate your kind words."

"I am not a complete stranger to your county," Holyday said. "Before the current British infestation of the Chesapeake I visited Somerset aboard merchant ships selling tobacco. The people I met at the Devil's Island wharf, and those on the docks in Princess Anne, did a poor job convincing me there was a notable degree of civilization, much less sophistication, among the people."

"I would suggest that had you expanded your interactions beyond the men working the docks you likely would have found signs of intelligent life," I commented with laughter.

"Good for you," Holyday chuckled, "coming to the defense of your own."

Holyday and I flicked the remains of our smokes to the ground. Upon exiting the alley, the sign for the Wilson's store hung directly across the street from us. Entering the shop, we saw not a soul.

"Hello," I shouted.

"Back here," I heard Lucy yell.

Holyday and I walked through the front of the shop to the back of the building where we had been earlier. Still not seeing either Lucy or Lew I called out again. We then proceeded, following her voice, down a hallway that I had not even noticed before. The hallway curved slightly and without windows to let the light in, was almost completely dark. Once the long hallway straightened and illuminated our path, we saw a patio equipped with a cooking hearth and two wooden tables with benches on either side of them. Lew was working the grill. Lucy sat at one of the tables, a glass of ale set in front of her.

The enclosure where Lew had set up his patio was surrounded on all four sides by either brick or wooden walls. I had expected the rear of the shop to exit into a back alley. Perhaps that is what this area had been at one time. But now, with structures having been built to close off the throughway, a courtyard of rather impressive dimensions had been constructed. The area was accented with assorted shrubbery and flowers. Without a roof or any type of ceiling the open-air courtyard was at the mercy of the weather. On rainy days it would have been no use, but on days like this it was delightful. The way it had been set up and maintained gave the impression of a grand terrace or a garden. It was impeccably maintained and not a single weed or even a blade of grass could be seen squeezing its way through the stone floor that had been so precisely pieced together.

There were two doors and two sets of windows on the rear of the Wilson building. The three other buildings had not a single window or door on their walls facing the courtyard. The space provided Lew and Lucy complete privacy. The upper level of the building extended far beyond the confines of the courtyard. I could see the second story windows where the opium had been lowered down into the alley. It helped me realize how this space must have benefitted the two as they hid themselves away from the virus as it ran rampant through Baltimore. Being able to sit back here and enjoy the fresh air without going out into the streets where they would have been exposed to the contagion must have made the self-imposed quarantine much more bearable than it would have been otherwise.

I was fascinated at how they had created such a pleasant and private patio in the middle of the crowded streets of downtown Baltimore. They had managed to bring a splash of nature, albeit a slight one, into the midst of the jungle of brick and stone in which they lived their lives. Back in Somerton the sparse shrubbery and the few smartly placed flowers would have gone unnoticed. But here, amid the buildings and the paved streets, the scant plantings seemed glorious in their presentation. I was struck by the irony that those of us who lived in the country could not erect new buildings fast enough, while the city dwellers went to great lengths to bring into their world a slice of nature's beauty.

I am sure that it was my lack of such opportunities that made our dinner conversation so sublime. Lew and Lucy described life in the big city and would inevitably tie it to a story that included members of my family that went back generations. There were stories with which I was familiar, having heard them many times over the years. Other anecdotes provided me new information about my ancestors.

Lucy remembered her time spent in the Albemarle area and Lew recounted his days, long gone now, on the lower eastern shore. They shared stories about how our families came to Washington and Baltimore. I listened to the idle dinner conversation as if it were the stuff of legends. Indeed, at that moment, every word carried with it the significance of Greek mythology, Shakespeare, or the Bible itself. If I were to ever leave the woods for the city, it would not be for the food, or the conveniences, it would be for this, the conversation. I found myself wishing it would never end.

Having discussed life in Baltimore and reminiscing about their memories of County Somerset before the Revolution, the Wilson's eventually began to inquire as to the current state of the village of Somerton.

"Slavery still a problem for you down there?" Lew inquired.

"Only to the extent that it is practiced most enthusiastically by some of the wealthy families in the county," I replied. "It certainly would never be tolerated in our town."

"Of that I am sure," Lew acknowledged, "but I recall the differences of opinion causing a great divide throughout the county. To the point of hostilities as I recollect."

"I'm not sure I can speak to that," I admitted. "Somerton continues to be set apart from the county proper. Our interaction with the people in Princess Anne, and even Devil's Island, is rare. It is my understanding however, that slavery for the most part is tolerated only to the extent that it is confined to the great estates of the plantation owners."

"I know that when the Quakers held sway in Somerset there was no tolerance at all for the buying and selling of human souls," Lew stated. "But now that most of the Quakers have pushed north to Pennsylvania, I was curious what effect that had on the county's attitude with respect to slaves."

"Most of the residents of County Somerset, and everyone in Somerton, came to America as indentured servants, or is but a generation or two removed from being bound by contracts," I explained. "People in Somerset understand hardship. They have worked other peoples' land. But the freedom that comes from a cleared debt, a completed contract, that was the light at the end of the cave. People worked for years on end without so much as a single day off to reach the day when their obligation had been satisfied. To imagine someone working those fields without the promise of freedom waiting out there for them, it's just unfathomable. So, the County Somerset, and the town of Somerton in particular, remains abjectly opposed to slavery. The wounds of the work are too fresh and hit too close to home. But some folks, wealthy families, moved in more recently, their plantations still practice forced labor. But it's understood it is in their best interest to keep their business confined to their plantations."

"Out of sight out of mind," Lew's comment was made in jest, but his words were laced with disdain, making his thoughts on the matter clear.

"It is not too different from the county's attitude with regards to the Indians," I added.

"I had thought most of the Indians had moved north by now," Lew sounded surprised.

"Most of them, yes," I answered. "But the few small groups that continue to live in the county are tolerated. That is, they have not been run out. As long as they keep to themselves."

"You mean keep out of the way," Lew voiced a contempt for the white man's treatment of the Indians that was consistent with his thoughts regarding slavery.

"It's a shame, isn't it?" Lucy asked.

"What's that?" I responded.

"What we did to the Indians," she paused, "and to the negroes. We fled England in the name of tolerance and freedom. And the first thing we did was steal the land from the natives. Then we stole the black man's freedom and sent them to work in the fields."

"God only knows what waits for us on the other side," Lew stated in a tone so somber it gave me chills.

"At least Baltimore is more enlightened in their thinking with regards to slavery," I rationalized. "It is refreshing to see the black man walking the streets every bit as free as you and me."

"And yet just outside this city there are men and women that wear chains at night, unlocked only to labor in the heat of the day," Lew said, as if casting sentence. "And on the eastern shore, people who have lived on the same land since the Romans ruled England have been all pushed out of the way. Whole tribes driven north by the inhospitable nature of the entitled white man. And here we are," he stretched out his arms to include us all, "doing nothing."

"Well, this conversation surely took a turn for the worse," Lucy said. "How'd we go from reminiscing about our ancestors to the scourge of slavery and them poor Indians? My God, we have been at war for so long. Now it might be over, God willing. Can't we turn our attention to something more pleasant?"

"People have been turning their attention away from the suffering for so long," Lew said, "they have come to believe that it is the destiny of the natives and the Africans to be miserable. The Indians and the slaves are merely collateral damage. But something has got to be done. It is a problem of our own making. It is our responsibility to remedy the situation."

"One thing at a time," Lucy suggested. "Let's get out of this war with England before we start another one."

"It just seems wildly hypocritical," Lew added, "or at least ironic, that we fought for freedom and were willing to die on battlefields for the cause, but that freedom only concerned itself with certain people."

"Well," Lucy responded, "let us hope and pray that the war between England and America is finally over. Maybe then the American ideal of freedom will be made available to everyone and not just the white people that were so desperate to escape the oppression and tyranny of Britain."

"You believe," Lew answered back, "now that Americans have finally won their freedom from England, they'll turn their attention to the rights of the native people and to the negroes?"

"One can only hope," Lucy replied.

"It's going to take a whole lot more than hope," Holyday finally spoke.

"If we truly believe that all men are created equal," I interjected, "the war isn't over. I'd say it's probably just getting started."

"If there are enough people that feel strongly about it," Holyday stated, "it will change."

"And with that change, another war?" Lucy begged.

"There will always be war," Holyday coolly replied in a manner that suggested he knew this for a fact, "because there will always be injustice."

"One day," Lew said, "one day there will be enough white people that can no longer tolerate what is happening. One day people will stand together and cry out that none of us are really free until all of us are free."

"Somehow," Lucy said, "someone's got to figure out how to move that Mason Dixon Line from Maryland's northern border to her southern border."

"We need to move that line all the way down past Florida and out into the sea," responded Lew.

"One day," Holyday added, "the line will disappear altogether."

"I wonder sometimes how people can sleep at night," Lucy remarked, "knowing they have torn families apart and ripped children from the arms of their mothers."

"How do you see this thing playing out?" Lew directed his question to Holyday.

"Impossible to predict," Holyday said. "Greed seems to have become our national religion. Makes sense in a way I suppose."

"How so?" Lew continued his inquiry.

"If people can learn to pray at the altar of the almighty dollar, we may well become convinced that God is dead. There would surely be some comfort in denying the existence of heaven and hell."

"No sure I follow," Lew confessed.

"If there is an afterlife," Holyday attempted to explain, "well, I shudder at the thought."

"Our country's original sin," Lew spoke slowly, "our acceptance of slavery has tainted the land and stained the soul. But there are still many opposed to it."

"The sin is one that transcends forgiveness," Holyday preached. "The guilt is so pervasive that it spreads out across America. The vengeful arms of penance will reach into the massive tombs of the wealthy and deep into the graves of the Potters Fields."

"You believe we are all guilty?" Lew asked, continuing to press Holyday. "Even those of us who stand in opposition to slavery?"

"The slaveowners and the cowardly bystanders, paralyzed by indifference, will stand side by side in eternal hellfire. The flames that devour them will burn equally hot, and the screams of agony from each will sound identical." Holyday's words were stoic and foreboding.

"So, guilt by association?" Lew inquired.

"I am not a religious man myself," Holyday admitted.

"Could have fooled me," Lew remarked.

"A person cannot pretend to be outraged by evil but stand around and do nothing," Holyday responded. "If there were a hell, I am sure we would all be joining the slaveowners on a bed of hot coals. Whether it is the hypocrisy of fake outrage or the cowardice of inaction, I suspect our tolerance of Black America's suffering has sealed our fate. Better there is no God to sit in judgement of us."

CHAPTER 11
Ghosts of the Maryland 400

Holyday and I returned to the hotel well before midnight. The next day's arduous journey weighed heavy on my mind and a good night's sleep was the highest priority. The weariness born of my recent schedule and the almost obscene comfort of the bedding with which city folks afford themselves made my descent into sleep quite immediate.

So it was that I went unfazed when Holyday awoke me before the sun had risen. My rest had been sound and replenishing. Though the city itself was still asleep I was alert and full of energy. The coming day was a busy one. I welcomed it and could not wait to get started.

Holyday and I spoke sparsely and only in whispers as the other guests in the hotel were still drifting through the land of dreams. We walked softly down the hallway and out into the street making sure the heavy wooden door did not slam behind us. The town was dimly lit by glass-encased candles flickering atop tall wooden posts. The darkness coincided perfectly with the tomblike silence of the city streets. The black stillness that is at its deepest immediately before a new dawn was yet uncorrupted by sight or sound. I was not unfamiliar with this hour. The people of Somerton routinely begin their days without the blessing of sunlight. Living in the woods makes early risers of its residents. We are in our boats or standing in the fields, tools in hand, before the first glimmer of light.

Everything that can be done to prepare for the coming day's work is accomplished in the faint illumination of candles or the remnants of a campfire that survived the night. In the solitude of country life, by the time the land or sea is being kissed by the first rays of sunlight, the farmer and the waterman are hard at work. This is an expectation that eludes the city dweller and thus the darkness just before a new sun looks and feels much different on the streets of the city than it does in the fields and waterways of the countryside.

"Ready for this day?" Holyday finally broke the silence.

"Yes," I answered. "I am well rested and feel good."

"Good," he replied.

"And you?" I inquired as a simple courtesy.

"Ahh," he mumbled. "Don't sleep much anymore. Same dreams every night, they wake me constantly. Even when I sleep, I find no comfort in it. There is no rest to be found in slumber that is tormented by demons and the dead."

I was curious as to the content of his nightmares but did not know how to extract the specifics. One of the things I had come to understand about Holyday was that if he wanted to share information, he would find a way to do it. The details and the timing were always going to be on his terms.

Walking down the street, our footsteps echoed singularly in the waning moments of the night. The sun, though we could not yet see it, had poked its way up above the horizon somewhere. The dark had begun to transform the total blackness into a shade less intensely pure, signaling the approaching daybreak. By the time we reached the stables it was light enough for us to make out the rectangular shape of a sign that hung from barnlike doors.

Holyday disappeared into the weathered wooden structure. I waited in the street for him to retrieve the animals. My thoughts turned to the sounds of daybreak in the city. It was completely alien compared to a fresh morning in the country. I might as well have been on a different planet. The noises to which I was so accustomed were absent. There were no songs from the birds or rustling leaves. These sounds, so informative as to the weather of the coming day, or the presence of predators, were replaced by squeaking doors and shutters being opened. The feint voices of people beginning their day served as a sorry substitute for the chatter of forest animals. I stood thinking of how these people were so thoroughly unaware of what they were missing. To begin each morning deprived of nature's glorious welcome seemed a punishment. My pity for them was interrupted by Holyday's return.

The horses were happy to see me. I gave each a hardy rub across the face, and they whinnied with delight and bounced their heads up and down to welcome me. Because of Thunder's enormity I was unable to see that Holyday had a third animal in tow. I heard the new member of our party before I saw it. The mule was an animal of good size though mightily dwarfed by Thunder. Still, the sturdy, muscular specimen would suffice for the purpose of transporting the goods we were going to acquire.

"Every night I dream I am a slave," Holyday said. His propensity to resume conversations abandoned long ago no longer perplexed me. I followed the context of his statement as if he had never stopped talking about his restless night's sleep. "I'll not put too much energy into deciphering any meaning or message," he continued. "If these dreams are meant to be interpreted, I've no doubt one of my fallen brothers will get around to filling me in. I'm sure they will be joining me shortly."

I was not fully comfortable with Holyday's relationship with his ghosts. It was clear to me that he believed he was being visited by the dead. However, I was puzzled as to what extent he believed mental illness played in the existence of these apparitions.

"Have the visits become so regular," I asked, "that their arrival can be predicted?"

I made sure that I expressed myself in such a way that my remark could not have been mistaken for anything other than genuine interest. I was not making light of his situation and my tone asserted not a hint of ridicule. Rather, I asked for an update in a manner that assured him I fully believed him to be in concert with the dead soldiers.

Instead of answering me Holyday pulled the satchel from his pocket and passed me a smoke. After stopping to light our cigars we again began walking down the street. The early morning tobacco was delicious, and I enjoyed it immensely. I knew Holyday would pick up our conversation without ever acknowledging a lapse or even the slightest interruption in our dialogue. It seemed to be the way he worked. Adhering to a different set of rules, he did things at his own pace. His was a strange mixture of indifference and thoughtful intensity. It seemed he struggled occasionally to determine whether certain things were worth talking about. While he seemed to delight in disregarding matters deemed insignificant, he took great care to address anything that registered as important. He would not speak until he was ready and even then, it might be postponed. He surely would never talk if he had nothing to say and appeared to be magnificently inconvenienced if he were forced to suffer the rambling of a fool.

"My brothers have now included you in their message," his voice was so mundane he could well have been talking to himself.

"Me?" I questioned.

"They told me that you could help me get it done," he answered.

"Get what done?" I asked.

"I don't know," Holyday admitted. "They never talk to me in a way that makes sense. That is why I believe these spirits, or visions, are most likely a symptom of illness. If they were ghosts, if they were really my brothers, soldiers that died next to me on the field of battle, they would say what is on their mind and not speak in riddles. Right?"

I was at a loss. I was not sure whether he wanted me to reply or not. As he continued walking without saying anything I answered if for no other reason than to fill in the silence.

"I'm sure I don't know?" It was all I could think of to say and that I phrased it as a question made the response even more useless.

"The other day," he said, "I'm walking down the street and Thomas Ernst, a German fellow, taken out by cannon fire early in the fight, he passes me and says, 'Did we die in vain?' When I turn to answer he is gone. Vanished. Do not know what I would have said anyway. No, I guess. The Four Hundred saved the day. Saved the country. But a ghost would know that. Right?"

Again, I was stumped but this time Holyday mercifully came to my aid.

"Don't answer me," he instructed. "I'm just thinking out loud."

"Okay," I said, and he glared at me as if I were a child who had been deliberately disobedient.

"The other night I'm dreaming," he began again, "I'm a slave," he said. "I'm always a slave. I am digging in the dirt, on all fours, digging in the dirt for something. I look up and see Lieutenant Charles Greyswood. Charlie was a good man, hell of a soldier. He took one right in the gut during our second charge up the hill. The kind of shot where you cannot be sure if it is a mortal wound or not. If it hit an organ, you are a dead man, nothing you can do. If it went clean through, stop the bleeding and all you have is a bad memory and a scar. Well, two scars, in the front and out the back. I saw him on our retreat, ran right by him. He had bled out. Ball probably got his kidney, or liver, who knows. Anyway, he died right there on that field, bloody and alone. And he is in my dream. I am digging in the dirt, and he walks past me, looks down and says, 'Do something'. What does that mean?"

We exchanged glances. My expression indicated I would remain silent. His was a face that was merely making sure I understood to be quiet.

"If I think about it long enough it becomes clear that I'm not seeing fallen members of the 1st Regiment," he continued. "It makes much more sense that there's something wrong with my brain. What I am seeing, and hearing, are the shadows and the whispers of madness."

"I think you are asking of yourself the impossible," I said, not looking to him for permission to speak. "Who is there, anywhere in the world, that could explain with clarity the workings of the mind? What could anyone say with even the slightest hint of precision about hallucinations or dreams? As for ghosts, or spirits, their existence has been debated for centuries. I can tell you there are people in Somerton I have known all my life. People who I respect and admire, that will swear they have seen ghosts. Honestly, I have never questioned them, nor have I doubted them."

"You believe in ghosts?" Holyday asked. "You believe that the men that lost their lives on that hill have come back from the grave to haunt me?"

"I believe the people in my community," I replied. "I know they are of sound mind and are good, God-fearing people. To doubt them would be to call them liars, and liars they are not. To that extent I would have to say yes. Yes, I believe in ghosts. I will not pretend to understand them and do not expect to ever be blessed with such insight. Some things can't be understood, you have said as much yourself."

"Like God," he stated.

"Yes," I answered. "Like God."

"Then it is your opinion," he replied, "that it is ghosts that I see and not hallucinations."

"Yes," I answered even though he did not phrase it as a question. "Maybe not ghosts."

"Then what?"

"Ghosts, I think, means they intend to do harm. It is implied there is a reason to fear them. These friends of yours, the deceased soldiers, are they trying to hurt you? It does not seem so. It is more like they are visiting. I am not pretending to understand it. Maybe they are only spirits. The spirits of those that died in battle."

"I'm not sure what difference that makes," Holyday said. "And I don't know that I agree with your contention that they don't mean to do me harm. Maybe in the beginning. Maybe a few years ago when I would see them once in a great while, maybe then they were just visiting, just spirits. But now, now that I see them every day, now that they frequent my dreams and will not give me peace, now they are at least ghosts, if not demons."

Holyday seemed to be growing agitated as our conversation progressed, so it was with some sense of relief that I realized we had arrived at Wilson's store. Lucy stood out in front awaiting our arrival.

"Good morning!" she called out.

We exchanged pleasantries but Lucy and Lew both understood we were pressed for time. There was not a great deal of small talk. Because the back of the store opened into the fine courtyard, we could not pull the horses around to the rear. We had to carry the sacks full of dry goods and supplies through the interior of the store and out the front door. Lew and Lucy helped to the extent they could but most of the sacks were quite heavy, so Holyday and I did the bulk of the lifting. By the time everything had been brought out and secured to the animals Holyday and I had worked up a healthy sweat.

Lucy had prepared a large plate of baked ham and scrambled eggs. Holyday and I made short work of the breakfast and enjoyed several glasses of sweetened apple juice. When I pulled out my packet of money to pay for the purchase Holyday was already counting his bills.

"Put your money away," he told me. He then handed Lew a wad of bills. There was a couple firm handshakes and some strong hugs, and we were on our way down the street toward Henry's gun shop.

"You paid too much," called out Lew a moment later. "You gave me too much money."

"For the breakfast," Holyday hollered back as he turned to face them. "Real nice meeting you folks. Take care of yourselves."

Lew and Lucy both returned comment but we were now half a block away and the two spoke over each other. Neither of us could make out what was said. All the same we both turned back and gave them a friendly wave goodbye.

"Good people," Holyday said.

"Yes," I agreed.

"You should feel good about yourself," he remarked. "These families that moved up from Albemarle, the whole Somerton thing, born of good folks. Strong and honest, they understand what is important. People with integrity, folks can be trusted. They know how the world works, or how it should work. Americans. That is kind of what this whole thing is about. I enjoyed meeting them."

"Thank you," I replied. It was a nice thing for him to say, and I am sure he knew it meant a lot to me that he was impressed with my people.

"If there ever arises an occasion where I may be of service to them, please rest assured I will use any influence I may have to secure things work favorably for them," Holyday's words rang genuine and sincere.

"I appreciate that Cole," I said. It felt somewhat odd to call him by his first name. But his remark had been a kind one and it felt as though my response merited using his first name. I looked at him for his reaction, or maybe his approval, and he smiled at me.

The next couple blocks we walked without conversation. It felt good to do so. The streets were no longer empty. Merchants readied their shops for another day of business. One of those merchants was old Hank. He was busy sweeping off the area in front of his shop. He saw us approaching from down the street and gave us a quick wave. He hurriedly went back to sweeping so to finish before we arrived. He set his broom against the wall just as we stepped up to greet him.

We all threw hearty "good mornings," at one another.

"Who's the new fella?" Hank asked stepping up to the mule and running his hand down its side.

"Looks like Brixton will return to Somerton with quite a haul of treasure," Holyday said jokingly. "Got the mule to help carry the guns. Loaded down good. Our boy will be lucky if he can find himself a spot to ride. Probably have to sit on that sack of sugar."

The horses were packed well with sacks of sugar, salt, and coffee. Lew and Lucy had loaded me up with quantities that exceeded what we had discussed. I recalled Jedediah telling me that due to their loyalty to the Somerton people they would charge me much less than their regular prices and would always package more than what had been paid for. They had certainly met and exceeded those expectations.

Both horses carried burlap sacks filled with powder and balls. The supplies had been arranged cleverly and evenly distributed so I knew my horses would struggle not even slightly to carry the goods. There were sacks of spices and coffee and some premium bottles of whisky. Inserted into the bags of sugar were bottles of liquid opium and other medications. The packing method provided both a way to protect the glass bottles from being damaged and a covert method of transportation should anyone have reason to inspect the animals. I had been forewarned that even soldiers of the regular army or members of the militia might help themselves to a couple bottles of whiskey should they stop me. They tended not to be overly interested in spices or things of that nature. But the medicine, if it should be found, would be confiscated in its entirety because it was both expensive and exceedingly difficult to come by. Pirates, bandits, and Indians on the other hand, I was assured, would take every item I possessed, including my horses and possibly my life should I present the slightest resistance.

Currently, the mule was carrying only several reams of cloth which was evenly distributed on either side of him. Holyday had organized it in such a manner to provide the animal some cushioning against the rifles that would soon be added to its load. Hank seemed keenly aware of our tight schedule and wasted no time carrying the rifles outside where Holyday carefully placed them, one at a time, in between the layers of cloth that guarded the sides of the disinterested mule. Holyday arranged the weapons masterfully and to the naked eye no one would ever have cause to think that the material carried by the muscular animal concealed a dozen rifles.

Once the packing had been completed, we ventured inside. Hank offered us some fresh bread and cow's milk. We had just gobbled down ample portions of ham and eggs at Wilson's, but we took him up on the offer anyway. We were eating the warm buttered rolls when Holyday noticed some pistols on display that had not been there the previous day. It was clear these handguns intrigued him greatly.

"Fine looking pistols," he said. "May I?" he asked before picking one of them up.

"Sure," Hank said. "Everything you see," he continued, "is for sale. Hell," he laughed, "even the stuff you don't see is for sale."

Holyday inspected the guns carefully. They were spectacular pieces.

"Here," Hank said, handing one of them to me.

"Amazing," I said, taking the gold trimmed and finely polished wood grained pistol in my hand and pointing it at the wall. "How much for this one?"

"That pistol there is a Richmond." Hank said. "Looks like it's an antique but it's brand new. That is a beautiful weapon, outlive your grandkids," he said laughing. "I've been getting twenty dollars for guns like this."

"Oh," I said, and quickly put the gun down.

"I'll tell you what," Hank said, "you take this pistol, no charge. You give it to your Uncle Jed. Tell him I gave it to him and tell him I expect to see his big ass in my store thanking me for it come next spring."

"Thank you, Hank," I said, my eyes wide as saucers with appreciation. "Jedediah will be thrilled to own such a fine pistol."

"And here," Hank said, handing me one of the other fancy pistols from the counter. "This one's for you. No charge," he assured me. "Mind you come back and pay me a visit also. And sooner than later. Don't wait too long. Nothin' in it for me if you're just comin' to visit my grave. And I ain't gettin' any younger."

"Thank you," I said, holding one of the spectacular pistols in each hand. "I don't know what to say."

"Thank you, is what you say," Hank quipped. "And you already said it. Let's get you fellas on your way. I know the Somerton folk are counting the minutes until your return."

With the weaponry packed away I went for my money only to be informed that Holyday had already paid for everything.

"You tell everyone in Somerton old Hank said hello," Hank whispered in my ear as he pulled me close to him and hugged me tightly.

"I will," I promised.

These people, Hank, and Lew and Lucy too, they wanted the folks in Somerton to remember them. Maybe they were just afraid of being forgotten. Either way, I could not help but feel that all of them would have been happier in Somerton. They impressed as those that belonged in the woods. What is more, I got the sense they knew it as well.

CHAPTER 12
Kent Island

We approached the dockyard to see the first of the mighty American warships already moving up the Patapsco. Holyday explained to me that he had secured us passage on a merchant frigate that was to fall in behind the last of the military vessels. The line would consist of twelve heavily armed American battleships that would snake their way down the river and out into the Chesapeake Bay. Reports had come into Baltimore that the King's armada in its entirety had already sailed south of the port of Annapolis and were heading toward the mouth of the bay where the Chesapeake emptied into the Atlantic Ocean.

The American ships were well prepared to confront the British on the open water of the bay if that opportunity presented itself. However, there was no reliable information regarding the true intentions of the Royal Navy. It had been suggested that the English ships were moving down the Chesapeake to regroup at Tangier Island. It was impossible to know how many additional British warships, if any, awaited the defeated fleet at Tangier. The island had served as a British stronghold throughout the Revolution and now once more played a vital role for British ships throughout this Second War of Independence. The people of County Somerset understood the island was frequented by English ships, but that could be said for the mainland as well. At least as it pertained to any fast land to the south of the Wicomico River.

To describe Tangier Island as a base of operations for the British fleet once the Revolutionary War had ended had been regarded as a bit farfetched by the people of Somerset. The watermen of the lower shore spent a great deal of time sailing that part of the bay and fishing its waters. While there was never a shortage of stories detailing the coming and going of British ships from Tangier, no one had ever reported seeing large numbers of ships docked there at the same time. This led most to believe the island served as a friendly stopover, populated by people loyal to the crown, but nothing more than that. Nonetheless, without a definitive account regarding the exact status of Tangier and the British fleet, the American's plan was to survey the Chesapeake down as far as the Potomac River.

We were to follow the last of the warships down the Patapsco and out into the middle of the Chesapeake. The passenger frigate that would carry us was no match for the speed of the battleships. The fleet would quickly put great distance between itself and our vessel. When the American force turned in the direction of Tangier we were to cut and run, making our way across the open water to Kent Island. Knowing that somewhere out there on the vastness of the Chesapeake was an unknown number of Royal Navy warships was disconcerting. But Holyday and I knew that aside from sailing with exhausted and defeated crews most of the ships, at least the ones that had attacked Baltimore, were likely depleted entirely of all cannon balls and mortars. The concern we all shared was the possibility that additional ships that had not engaged in the attack of Fort McHenry may be lurking out beyond the horizon. More ships with fresh crews and full stores of ammunition could chase the Americans back up the bay and into the safety of Baltimore harbor.

Our ship, being a merchant vessel and without cannon, would be a sitting duck on the open sea without the cover of a military escort. After a stop at Kent Island, the frigate would proceed under full sail past Tilgman Island and up the Choptank River to Cambridge. It would be that last leg where we would be most vulnerable. Weighted down with cargo and passengers we would stand no chance of outrunning a battleship. We were expecting to have both the wind and the tide working in our favor but even at full speed we would have at least an hour on open water where we were completely defenseless. Once the final run into the mouth of the river was underway there would be nothing in the way of inlets or coves that might offer a place to hide from a hostile ship.

There were two gangplanks made available to board the merchant vessel which had been very lazily named, "The Merchant." The plank to the bow was narrow and served passengers only. I entered the secondary bridge as it was fitted more broadly and could accommodate cargo and animals. The harbor master was moving the navy ships out quickly and there was an excited rush to get everything on board in time to fall in line immediately behind the last navy vessel. The exercise had gone smoothly until I walked my animals across the boards.

Holyday had stopped to speak with a fellow on the dock. Judging by the man's attire I assumed he was affiliated with either the government or was a representative of one of the first order families. Either way, Holyday was having an impromptu meeting where he was undoubtably addressing some business arrangement or transaction that fell under his stewardship. He told me to go ahead and assured me he would be along in a minute. But as I attempted to board there was no sight of him.

The three men checking passengers and freight to this point had merely been asking people about the contents of their crates. The inquiries were brief, and the boarding process had gone without incident. The deckhands were less lenient with me for a reason that was unclear. They blocked the entrance to the ship by standing shoulder to shoulder and looked over my animals and packaging with great suspicion.

"What's your name?" One of them asked as he stepped closer to me.

"Brixton," I answered. "Steven Brixton."

Two of the men stepped up onto the plank and started to survey the sacks that Holyday had tied tightly to the sides of Thunder and Blue. The third man, a chubby Hispanic looking fellow, remained on the ship, and flipped through crumpled pages apparently looking for my name. I had no idea whether it would be on his list. Holyday had not confided in me any details regarding how he had reserved our places on the ship.

"Not on here," the chubby man with the list said.

"Where are you going boy?" One of the other men asked. He walked past Blue running his hand along the large sack of salt affixed to the horse's hindquarters and moved toward the mule.

"I'm going to Cambridge sir," I answered.

"Let's see," the man with the list started speaking again, "one passenger, three animals," he paused as he looked over the animals, "a shit ton of cargo, you're looking at about forty dollars."

Forty dollars was an obscene price. However, as I had pockets stuffed with money due to Holyday's unwillingness to allow me to pay for anything over the past few days I reached into my pocket and pulled out a wad of bills to pay the man.

"Well look at this!" Exclaimed the man when he saw my packet of money. "I think your fare just went up boy."

I was growing impatient with these men. They were being most difficult. More importantly, the gangplank, though seemingly sturdily constructed, was not intended to support the weight of two horses the size of Blue and Thunder, never mind the mule, my cargo, and three men.

"Can we step off these boards? A lot of weight here." I took Blue by his reins and started to step onto the ship.

"Hold on boy!" shouted the fat man. He continued to block my way.

"How much for passage?" I asked, holding up the thick wad of cash. I had come off sounding annoyed and while that was not my intent it was beyond my control. The men were being unreasonable, and I could feel myself losing my temper. I possessed the character flaw of a short temper, something born into folks on the lower shore it was said. Somerton people have no patience for disrespect.

"What do we have here?" I turned to see one of the men removing a rifle from where it had been hidden away in the cloth on the side of the mule.

I grabbed the rifle from the man's hands.

"Hey!" Holyday shouted.

We turned in unison to see Holyday limping up the gangplank.

"He's with me," he called out.

None of the men said a word. They all moved out of the way and stepped aside. Holyday and I led the animals onto the ship as the men scurried to remove themselves from our path.

"Sorry Mr. Holyday," said one of the men. "We didn't know he was with you. We thought..."

"Don't go thinkin'!" Holyday said. He glared at the man. "You three be no match for that Somerset boy. He's country strong. Throw you all in the harbor."

I'm not sure why Holyday had assessed the situation in such a way as to give the men no chance against me. It could have been the look in my eyes. Or maybe just his way of insulting the deckhands. I did not bother looking back at the men, but God knows I wanted to.

We took the animals below deck, following a much larger ramp that led us directly to the ship's makeshift stables. There was a crewman working the area, but we tied the animals up ourselves. Holyday carefully began unwrapping the horses and the mule. He removed all the boxes, sacks, and strappings, so the animals were completely free of any additional weight. Even the saddles and reigns were taken off. Each animal had its own stall separated from the one next to it by a single stretch of thick rope. Holyday laid out our cargo and the horses' gear in a fourth stall immediately next to the other three.

"These stalls are rented out individually," the ship's stable hand announced as he approached and saw that we had used one of the stalls to store our goods.

"Pay special attention to these animals," Holyday said. He was turned in such a way that I could not see how much money he handed the worker but could tell it was a respectful sum by the expression on the man's face. "Mind you keep an eye on the fourth stall as well," Holyday added, advising him to guard our property.

"Yes sir," he replied. "Yes sir. Thank you, sir."

We walked back up to the main deck and found ourselves comfortable seating that would allow us to take in our surroundings. It seemed no sooner had we seated ourselves than the ship floated away from the dock and drifted out into the harbor. We watched as the enormous sails were hoisted into the air. Pulled tightly, they filled with air and the ship straightened herself out and fell in behind the last navy ship. We were under way.

I looked back at the harbor as the line of ships sailed in single file down the long stretch of the Patapsco. Watching the great city of Baltimore grow smaller as we put distance behind us, I wondered whether I would ever again see this amazing place. I decided that it was with a high degree of certainty that I would return one day to Baltimore. Until then, I would cherish the memories of this adventure. As the ship rounded the first bend in the river and Baltimore disappeared from our sight there was a sadness that subdued me and rather took me by surprise.

It felt as though the city were leaving me rather than the other way around. The immensity of the sprawling neighborhoods and the massive stone and brick buildings were all still there, but I could not see them. I could not see the crowded streets and the people, black and white, pushing their way past one another. I could not walk across the street for a glass of ale or some prepared food. There was something sobering, almost chilling, with the realization that all the goods and supplies that I had traveled so far to secure were available to the residents of the city any time they wanted them. There were no rivers to cross or marshes to navigate. The possibility that Indians or bandits were lurking, waiting to make their move, did not exist on the city streets the way it did in the forests of the lower shore. I knew the nuance of city life would dissipate, and that the magical nature of the place would fade over time. But right now, leaving it all behind left me feeling hollow.

Holyday interrupted my thoughts with a nudge and extended to me a smoke. I gladly accepted it. I had grown fond of smoking his quality tobacco, but mostly, I was grateful that he had snapped me out of my grey mood. No good has ever come from ruminating on joyless thoughts. I believed wholeheartedly that entertaining unpleasant ideas was akin to welcoming darkness into one's life. That is a foolish undertaking. There will always be darkness and sadness and pain. These are the ingredients of a person's life no less than are happiness and love and peace of mind. But the unpleasant components of life always find their way into a person's soul. There is not a good reason to go looking for them or to think and obsess over them. It makes no sense to do so.

I sat back and enjoyed my smoke. Looking out over the majesty of the Chesapeake soothed the rough edges of my mind. It was impossible to behold such beauty and not be inspired. The glory of this sacred body of water helped me to understand that Baltimore was now behind me. The comforts and conveniences afforded those people belonged to them. I was a man of nature and born of the woods. My presence in Baltimore was fleeting and artificial. I belonged in the city no more than the politicians and their suits belonged in the forests of Somerton.

It took us surprisingly little time to reach the middle of the bay where we followed the staggered line of American warships eastward. The wind was warm and brisk. It filled the sails of the impressive flotilla as it powered its way further from us by the minute. Holyday and I watched the wondrous nature of the Chesapeake, its white capped seas lapping at the glorious sunshine. In the distance Kent Island came into view. The boom flew across the ship's deck and the vessel veered sharply away from the fleet and made straight for the channel that ran behind the island.

I did not know the captain of this ship. Just a few years ago merchant vessels such as this one frequented the port of Princess Anne and the wharf on Devil's Island so often that the captains, and even the crew, were familiar to Somerset locals. But with British ships patrolling the bay, especially in and around the waters off the coast of Somerset and the eastern shore of Virginia, merchant vessels no longer risked the danger of coming so far down the Chesapeake. When I looked at the captain of this ship there stood a man I had never seen before.

The captain swam the ship right up to the Kent Narrows dock, seemingly at full sail, and instantaneously dropped the sails and had us rocking gently back and forth floating in the water just feet from the wharf. Our stop at the island was a brief one. We took on no new passengers or freight and the few departing at Kent did so quickly. It seemed no sooner had the captain gracefully maneuvered the ship to a full stop than we were anchors away once again.

With the sails full of an easterly wind the ship cut through the back channel of the Narrows as if it were a canoe and not a twenty-ton frigate. The width of the waterway seemed barely that of the ship, but the captain wasted no time getting us back to full speed. In short order we left the wharf in our rear and sliced through the flat waters of Eastern Bay, heading to the western edge of Tilghman Island.

"See those pilings?" Holyday asked, pointing with his eyes.

I looked in that direction but saw only a few small fishing houses and a crab shack.

"In front of the shacks," Holyday directed, "close to the water's edge."

"Ah, yes," I answered seeing the ends of several thick poles extending from the water just feet from the shoreline.

"That's where the Virginia militia used to hang Marylanders when they made their raids," he said.

"Right there?" My response was one of keen interest, bordering on incredulous. "What did they swing them from?" It was a morbid but genuine question.

"The riggings are gone," Holyday stated. "There were once a couple trees standing only a few feet from the water. After the Virginians swung a few good men from their branches the Kent Islanders cut the trees down. The Virginians then erected scaffolding and stretched the necks from there. The remnants of the gallows survived until recently. The people of Kent preserved them as a reminder of the grave injustices suffered by their families. The Virginia raiders wanted to hang the men over the water so when they were cut loose, they'd fall into the outgoing tide."

I looked over the side of our ship and though we were being helped by a strong breeze it was easy to see the powerful tide racing out into the bay. The Chesapeake possessed notoriously swift and unmerciful tides. For those who knew how to use them they were a blessing, but for the novice they were a curse, being treacherous and often deadly. As the tide made its run east toward the Atlantic it carried even the largest ships at speeds that at times could be hard to believe. The water was channeled through the narrows and then shot back out into Eastern Bay. It travelled with such velocity that, if timed correctly, a ship would need no sail to move from the Kent Narrows out to Tilghman Island. The tide would do all the work by itself.

"Yes," Holyday continued, "once those ropes were cut, the islanders would hear the splash of the dead men hit the water and that was the last anyone would ever see of their beloved family member or friend."

"Ruthless." My thoughts were audible even though that had not been my intention. "It wasn't enough to kill them," I continued, "but the townsfolk couldn't even bury their dead."

"I know you've heard the story," Holyday replied, "all of Maryland knows the tale. But when I tell you that the battle that raged between Virginia and Maryland was as savage as any ever fought, I understate the point greatly."

"Yes," I acknowledged. "That fight has been the topic around a thousand different campfires over the years. I know most of us were hoping there was some exaggeration put to the narrative, but you are not the first to emphasize the brutality involved in the dispute."

"It was as cruel as anything I've ever witnessed," Holyday continued. "They would execute those with the largest families. The Virginians wanted to make sure the Islanders could hear the wailing of the wives and children as their men swung from the rickety gallows. Pure evil, nothing else, only way to describe it."

"And you were witness to these barbarous acts?" I asked.

"As a child," Holyday answered, "many years ago. I was in attendance one night during a Virginia raid. It was terrifying. But the murdering stopped when Lord Baltimore fortified the island's defenses. It continues to this day, down your way, does it not?"

It took me a minute to move my thoughts with him. Virginia's desperate attempt to win the province of Maryland as their own concluded when Lord Baltimore gave some of the same murderous villains from Virginia the power and prestige of being named government officials in

Maryland. It was a grotesquely unfair but effective way to bring the cutthroats to heel. Holyday bounced without so much as a hiccup to another topic entirely. However, now familiar with his penchant for doing so, I was able to connect the dots quickly.

"The oyster wars?" I asked, knowing that his implication was such.

"Killing still going on, is it not?" Holyday inquired.

"Huh," I answered with a muffled laugh. "Oh yes, they're still killing each other over who can fish where. And men continue to die because they're fishing or pulling oysters from the wrong side of an imaginary line."

"I swear to God," Holyday uttered through a clenched and crooked jaw, "I think some men just like to kill people. And the things they are willing to die for, well, I will never understand it, not if I live to be a hundred."

"It is a most heinous situation to be sure," I agreed.

"I have heard," he said, looking in my direction, "that for the most part Maryland is getting the best of them these days. Any truth in that?"

"Could be," I offered. "It's hard to say. Every now and then some of the men will return from a fishing trip with an extra boat. We know then that there will be a family in Virginia waiting for a crew that will never return. Other times, it is we that wait for men that we will never see again. But I will say that our fishermen return with an additional boat much more often than we experience the painful sorrow that comes from a group whose late arrival inevitably turns into the reality that our missing men are not delayed but rather gone forever."

"That must be hard," Holyday said, his somber voice relaying a deep sense of empathy.

"It cannot be put into words," I admitted. "The anxiety that accompanies a late fishing boat is difficult. But whence the certainty of their demise is finally realized, well, it is a hurt like no other." I paused momentarily before continuing. "As the Somerton community is one big family, the pain is searing. It helps little to know that the anguish is shared among all of us. The grieving is at times so intense that no one dare even speak of it. Words could not even be heard over the tormented cries and screams. The uncertainty of how the end came for the departed only serves to make the pain sharper."

"I'm sorry Brixton," Holyday offered, his condolence heartfelt and convincing. "It's a hard world we live in."

"It is indeed," I replied.

"You would think," he said, "that by now people would have learned to tame that wild instinct to slaughter and destroy their fellow man. I mean we are living in the nineteenth century for Christ's sake! But still, that savage rage that smolders in the souls of all living men cannot be wholly contained. Harnessed and controlled at times maybe, but it seems we are all but one insult, one slander or slight away from our base reaction to exact revenge, to avenge a wrong or to defend our honor. Oh, that we could learn to compete for justice in a more civilized manner. But alas, too many of us will always resort to the ways of ancient people and insist on immediate retribution. A primitive solution that I fear will always result in ripping out of a man's throat or caving in his skull with a hammer or sword. Deep down inside I think we are all too weak to walk away. Turning the other cheek, or forgiving and forgetting, I am afraid is not in our nature."

"To be sure," I engaged his debate, "it is difficult to imagine a world without evil, but if that world did exist, would it not also be a world without goodness?"

"Continue," Holyday requested.

"We are given free will so that we can decide for ourselves what kind of people we will be," I looked for his reaction. "We are tested so that we may prove ourselves. Happiness cannot manifest itself in a world without sadness." Holyday's curious expression compelled me to continue. "Why, there would be no need to summon courage or strength if not for the challenges inherent in our journey. If all men were rewarded equally, regardless of their choices, then surely happiness would be perpetually embraced by every living soul. How would that work? How could anyone rise to the occasion if failure were not an option? Who would be our heroes? How could there have ever been assembled the immortal Four Hundred?"

"Ah," Holyday mused, "the trappings of a young man's mind. You will learn, in time, the difference between courage and duty. And too, that sometimes cruelty is a necessary evil. Unlike the pure evil that lives in the hearts of some men."

"I understand this world," I replied. "It is a place that on occasion will give us only poor options from which to choose. Still, good men will always do the best they can."

"This is a conversation that would pretend to have answers no man will ever possess," Holyday stated. "I fear the puzzle will elude us well past our last breaths."

"I'm not sure I take your meaning," I said this in such a way as to implore him to say more. My yearning for the old man's wisdom was insatiable. In truth, I would have begged on bended knee to hear more of his thoughts and how his fascinating mind interpreted the bizarre and confusing world in which we lived.

"People will forever wonder why we were put here," he attempted to explain. "And how we should best spend the precious hours left to us."

"To fight the good fight," I answered definitively.

"Whose fight?" he countered. "And by whose rules?"

"The fight of righteousness, and freedom," I offered, though my words rang hollow, and weak. "By the rules set forth by God and country."

"Righteousness?" he sounded incredulous. "Freedom from what? And from whom?"

"Well," I had not a clue, but knew a response, any response, would invite him to continue. "Freedom from tyranny. Freedom to pursue happiness. Jefferson and the Founders explained it for us in the Declaration."

"The same document that declares all men are created equal?"

"Yes," I answered emphatically.

"All men?"

"Of course!"

"The poor as well as the rich?"

"Yes. All men are created equal."

"Even the Indian and the negro." Holyday did not phrase his response as a question rather as a statement.

I had no answer.

"No one can claim the Indian and the slave are treated as equals, as compared to white men," he continued. "If our contention is that we are all created equally, we must ask ourselves, what went wrong? At what point did some men lose the right to defend their land? When did some men become so much less equal than others that they must wear chains, and be sold like cattle? It cannot even be called into question. Cattle are treated with more respect than the slave. So where is the equality? Where is the freedom? For that matter, where is this God?"

"I cannot even pretend to understand how slavery continues to be tolerated in a country that was built on the premise that freedom is the foundation on which all people build their lives," I said. "However, I do believe that God is here. He is waiting for us to do the right thing. When that time comes it is God who will give us the strength to correct the injustices that have been leveled against the natives and the slaves."

"And you think there exists," Holyday further engaged the debate, "some strength, an energy that drives people to stand up for what is right, and to fight for justice?"

"I am sure that such a power exists," I stated emphatically. "You must believe it too," I insisted. "Surely you saw it in Brooklyn. How is it that you charged the British if not for the ability to call on your free will and summon that inner rage? Where does courage like that come from? What makes men race into the teeth of certain death if not for the need to defend goodness against the forces of evil?"

Holyday looked out across the Chesapeake with a furrowed brow. His eyes were set with an intensity that made deciphering his thoughts all but impossible.

"That day," he eventually began, "they say we were four hundred, but I would have guessed somewhat less, though not by much. But who am I to argue with the history books? Those of us that were there did what we had to do. Mind you," Holyday continued, "I mean no disrespect to the men that died on that hill, nor the lucky few that survived that bloody day. On the contrary, speaking truthfully about the matter pays homage to all that made the charge. But every one of us would have loved to hear we were going to make a run for the river with the rest of them boys."

I sat silently, absorbed in the narration.

"But that's not how it played out," he resumed his story. His eyes fixed up into the deep azure sky. I am quite sure had there been ten thousand geese blocking out the sun he would not have noticed them as his mind had carried him back to that day once more. "No, that day we were offered up. Sacrificed for the greater good, as they say." Holyday turned his eyes away from the cloudless sky and looked again out toward the sea.

"A sacrifice that gave birth to America," I offered.

"Well, you've heard this tale before," his tone conciliatory. "It doesn't change none. No less bloody. No less awful. The dead, they still died. The lucky, we still made it back across the river. The point is, free will had nothing to do with it. We did not volunteer to charge head on into that hail of bullets. We just followed orders. I will not," he went on, "pretend to speak for the others, but as for me, I would have much preferred to run in the other direction. But, like I said, we were just followin' orders. No heroes, not at that moment anyway. Maybe even cowards, chargin' up that hill with piss runnin' down our legs. Free will was not a factor. Not for one second. And I don't recollect God bein' on that hill. I sure didn't see Him. And I'll bet my very last dollar that none of them boys bleedin' out and dyin' with their guts all over the ground saw Him either. No Brixton, God was not there that day. Nor was free will. Just brave soldiers following orders."

Men stand humbled in the face of such speech and words are difficult to come by, but I found a few and spoke.

"With respect, I choose to believe that the only explanation as to how 400 men could go up against 30,000 and come away victorious is that God *was* on that hill."

A grateful smile slowly formed on his face, forlorn with the memories of the carnage.

"And there," he said, "therein lies my desperate search for a god, for a religion. You understand my frustration, my desperation?"

Given a moment I might have been able to put the pieces together, but his impatience prevented me from doing so. I must assume he saw I was perplexed and rather than wait for me to formulate a theory he described his struggle for me.

"Today," he began, "we look at the Battle of New York as a victory. We claim that the American forces were victorious not because Maryland's 1st regiment was slaughtered but because it allowed the remainder of Washington's army to escape across the East River. Because the Continental Army survived that battle, and only because the Continental Army survived that battle, America is a free country today. My heart aches, the pain sharp and unrelenting, when I think about my brothers writhing in agony and suffering, for they died not knowing they were heroes. Nothing did they comprehend of their victory. It would be impossible for them to understand that their sacrifice would pave the way for the birth of a new country. I cannot even briefly consider that lying there choking on their blood, shot full of holes, and breathing their last, there were any thoughts that even remotely resembled victory. I can only imagine their last thoughts were of death and defeat."

These words did leave me speechless. Holyday had a way of making the horror of the battle real and I could not add or detract a single word from it. As feeble thoughts stumbled aimlessly around my mind, I suddenly heard Jedediah speaking. His words were so clear and loud that for an instant I thought maybe it was Holyday who spoke. But it was Jedediah, and they were words I had heard many times over the course of my life. These were lessons ingrained in me so deeply they were as much a part of me as were my arms and my legs. They were messages related to strength and righteousness and faith. They rushed at me as if I were hearing them all at once. And so, I shared them.

"The purpose of religion, and then of God, is to guide people and to help them understand the value in being a good person," I said. "If it is a particular God or religion that you seek, I think the answer is one of faith. Believing in the unseen or summoning strength when you know you have none left, these are matters of faith. Believing in the impossible. For all the questions that cannot be understood, faith is the answer."

"Yes," he agreed, almost too quickly, as if to be dismissive. "That is a proper way to think of it. But for me it is not enough, for my dilemma transcends religion. My turmoil transcends even God Himself. My search is for heaven, and if not heaven, some evidence of an afterlife. I cast God out of my life many years ago and without Him I cannot find the peace that would come from believing in some form of eternal reward. I am burdened with being unable to be secure in the knowledge that those brave soldiers that died next to me, the men I ran past on my retreat, who continue to visit me to this very day, I cannot know that they rest in heaven. And oh, how it pains me to think that such brave men sacrificed themselves only to become food for worms. It is at times more than I can bear."

"You torture yourself," I did not hesitate. "You survived, you made it down the hill and across the river and your brothers did not. Is it guilt? I surely do not pretend to know. But I know this, I know that those fallen soldiers, your brothers, I know they reside in heaven. I know that those men were rewarded and now sit at the foot of God Almighty. And I know they are blessed with the full knowledge that the price they paid that day were the very seeds that grew into America."

"Do you really believe that to be true?" he asked. "In all honesty, do you really think there is life after death?"

"It has nothing to do with what I think," I said as firmly and as convincingly as anything I had ever said before, "It is what I know."

Holyday wore an inquisitive look that expressed a desire for me to continue. It was clear he wanted to understand how I was able to convince myself so thoroughly of my beliefs. That he had doubts did not matter. He could see that my conviction was real. My faith was unwavering and that excited him. If he could learn to blindly trust in something that made no sense to him, he might be able to find the peace for which he had searched so long.

Now the mask he wore changed yet again. The tantalizing intrigue that came with knowing the answer he longed for might be found among my experiences revealed the wide-eyed eagerness of a young schoolboy. That face had disappeared only to be replaced with a shroud of disappointment and frustration. Following this man's complex moods was daunting, even impossible. His propensity to steer sharply in and out of topics, jumping from one to the other without warning or reason, could leave a listener baffled and exhausted. But this time I understood the transformation almost immediately. I followed his gaze and saw the town of Cambridge straight ahead. The ship was bearing down on the docks. Despite the betrayal of a now unforgiving tide and winds that had the crew struggling mightily with the enormous sails we could be no more than ten minutes out.

Cole Holyday was a mysterious man in so many ways. His storied past had been revealed to me only in miniscule glimpses and his complicated way of looking at the world was at times foreign to me. Still, there were moments when I felt there were parts of him, small slices of the way he thought, that mirrored my own style of examining the world in which we lived. I knew he wanted nothing more than to continue our conversation. He wanted to interrogate me. He longed to question my religion and potentially even try it on for size. More likely than not, he would shoot holes in it and discard it as something that would not work for him.

There were many things about Holyday I did not know and some that I could not ever understand. However, there were other things that were as plain as the scar on his face. He was a practical man and selfless when in the company of those he deemed worthy of it. His sense of responsibility was overpowering and given to an almost obsessive need to plan and organize. These things I had come to realize about him. And because of this I could have predicted the next words out of his mouth. This despite him wanting nothing more than to investigate the structure of my spirituality.

"We must ready the animals," he said. "We'll be tying up shortly."

We descended to the lower deck where he methodically repacked the animals. It would have taken a team of men an hour to do what he did in a matter of minutes. His procedure was so precise, there were no wasted movements. His plan as to what articles went on which animal, and in what order, was done exactly as it had been on the streets of Baltimore. And the supplies, though set aside in a separate stall, were laid out in such a way that he put them back on the animals as if piecing together a puzzle. Even the ropes he used were left hanging over the sacks and boxes for which they were purposed. Holyday handed me the reins to the mule. He held Thunder and Blue each by their harness up near their jawline.

"Come," was all he said, and he led the way up the plank to the main deck.

The ship's crewmen had just thrown out the tie lines to the dock hands when we walked the animals up into the sunlight. Holyday walked us over to the gangplank that would be used for the animals and heavy freight. Due to the precision with which he had readied the animals we now stood in position to be the first to disembark.

"As we step off the ship," he instructed, "give the crewman to our right side ten dollars."

"Okay," I agreed. It would be the first time throughout our entire journey that he had allowed me to pay for anything.

Once we had stepped off the dock and had our footing solidly on fast land Holyday turned to me with an uncertain look in his eyes. It was as close to a blank stare as it was possible for the human face to form. He looked skyward, first straight up in the air, then to the east, and back to the west. Eventually he returned his eyes to mine.

"I understand your eagerness to be on your way," he said. "Your people in Somerton await your return with these supplies and much needed medicine. But you will not make it too far along the main road before having to scurry off into the woods to make camp. You understand the main road cannot be travelled at night for marauders and thieves. Were that I could accompany you, but I cannot."

"I could not ask that of you," I assured him.

"I am hard pressed to believe that a good night's sleep and an early start would not get you back to Somerton sooner than if you left straight away," he said. "Will you spend the night? It is the smart thing to do. I would sleep better knowing you and your supplies made it at least out of Cambridge."

"Shall I inquire about a hotel?" I did not hesitate. Although my intention had been to get on the road immediately, starting out fresh in the morning was the wiser play. Besides, I smelled rain in the air. The thought of sleeping in the wet forest did not appeal to me.

"Don't be foolish," Holyday quipped. "I am always welcome at the Armstrong manor, as will you be when he hears about the success of our journey. The young son of Somerset who helped turn back the British and win the war. Yes, you will likely have a private room permanently set aside for you," he said with a laugh. And with that we began walking the animals in the direction of the Armstrong estate.

CHAPTER 13
Cambridge

My initial ride to the Armstrong mansion, as a captive, had been long and winding. The elegant coach had followed a serpentine path that curved repeatedly away from and then back toward the banks of the Choptank River. However, as Holyday and I were on foot, it allowed us to take a more direct path. On several occasions we left the road and, cutting through pastures and fields, reduced our trip by more than a mile. The sun was shining brightly in the sky but had started its descent. With the calendar now approaching late October the sun no longer floated down to meet the horizon as it did during the long hazy days of summer. Rather, once it started to fall westward it seemed to accelerate before disappearing almost without warning. October on the eastern shore afforded spectacular sunsets, though they were known for their rapidness. A brilliant blue backdrop framed the fireball perfectly as it chased away another day. In the distance Armstrong's immense castle-like manor came into view.

"And there it is," I said. With a chuckle I added, "I believe you could fit every building in Princess Anne inside that man's house."

"It is most certainly massive," Holyday acknowledged. "And impressive," he continued, "in a grotesque and vulgar way. But speaking in purely architectural terms it is rather stunning. Each generation has added to the structure, as if it were not large enough already," he smirked. "Original house went up in 1661. Since then, I believe there have been six additions. The largest being the one completed just several years ago by the current owner."

I sensed an unmistakable contempt in Holyday's voice as he discussed the manor.

"This last renovation," he continued, "was said to have almost doubled the size of the building. It now stands at more than 20,000 square feet. It is just incomprehensible. I am still awestruck at times. It still amazes me. The elegance, the refinement, the style, and the arrogance of a man that would build something like that. More stone has been ordered from Scotland. He's going to make the thing even bigger."

"No!" I was stunned.

"People say he'll never stop," he added. "The house will never be big enough to insure he won't cross paths with his wife."

"Surely you jest," I laughed heartily.

"I have been in that house more than a hundred times," he said, his voice stoic, almost eerie. "I've never seen the woman."

"How many live there?" I inquired.

"He and his wife," he said, "that is all." He looked at me for a reaction.

"That's just wrong!" I exclaimed with a look of utter disgust. "What kind of man is this Armstrong that he should build such a thing?"

"Oh, make no mistake," Holyday confided, "Armstrong is a sick man. A monster really. Possessing all the worst possible traits a human being can have. He is a man of dark and sinister character. I swear to you he has not a single redeeming quality."

"How is it that work for such a man?" I asked sounding much more astonished than I would have preferred.

"Armstrong is extraordinarily wealthy," Holyday answered. "And I don't really work for him. He is a person with whom my job," he paused as he decided what he wanted to call himself, "as a liaison, brings me into contact. I arrange meetings with certain individuals. Usually, it is the heads of families of the first order, the patriarchs, and sometimes government officials. Anyway, I do not work for Armstrong. He is but an unfortunate by-product of my work. But his money is obscene. There is family of the first order money, and then there is Armstrong money. I am, admittedly, as broken as a man can be, emotionally. And feel no guilt abusing my relationship with him. If he wants to pay me a hundred dollars to deliver a message or set up a meeting, I do it. Or maybe I request two hundred. The man sickens me. I enjoy taking advantage of him. I find no dishonor in it. He earned none of his wealth. Inheritance, every penny. Inheritance and the sweat of slaves. He deserves none of it."

We walked around the side entrance of the estate and came upon the livery. Even the stables were made of stone and larger than any house in all of Somerton. Holyday squinted his eyes and looked from side to side.

Then, looking at me he released his grip from one of the horses and put his finger up to his lips signaling me to be quiet.

"We'll talk later," he whispered. "The man slithers around the property like a snake."

Once inside the stables we started to unpack the animals. Holyday moved so quickly that it was difficult for me to do much more than watch him. Occasionally he would hand me a sack of sugar or a roll of blankets and tell me to, "set these over there." Otherwise, I was but an observer. The animals had all been freed of weight and led to their respective stalls before the first stable hand appeared.

"Is that you Mistah Holyday?" asked the worker.

Holyday had been arranging the supplies in piles that made sense to him. "Leon," he called out. "Yes, it's me. Just organizing our materials."

"Yessa," replied the short barrel-chested black man. "Can I help you sa?"

"No," Holyday answered. "I've just about got it. Is Armstrong about?"

"I'm 'fraid you missed 'em sa," Leon responded. "He and Mista Morris left yes'day. Took the big coach. Goin' to Phil'delphia. Be back two, three days."

Holyday walked over to the black man and hugged him. The hug was returned.

"Good to see you sa," Leon said.

"And you my friend," Holyday grabbed Leon's shoulders and said, "You look well."

"Thank you sa," he replied.

Two other black men walked into the stable. Each carried a lantern and by the light that illuminated their broad white smiles I could see they too were happy to see Holyday.

"Hello Mista Hol'day," called the taller of the two men.

"Hello Willy," Holyday greeted him and then the other man, "Hello Josey."

"Any idea what Armstrong and Morris got goin' on in Philadelphia?" Holyday asked, having turned his attention back to Leon.

"You know he don't tell me nothin," Leon laughed. "Gone to Philadelphia. Get the big coach ready. Be back in two or three days. That about word for word what I got from the man."

"Hmm," Holyday pondered. "I'm sorry, this here's Master Steven Brixton."

"Good evenin' sa," the three black men said in unison.

"Good evening gentlemen," I replied.

"This stuff will be okay here?" Holyday asked, referring to the supplies.

"I'll make it safe sa, yes I will," Leon answered.

"Can I get you some dinner sa?" Willy inquired.

"That would be nice," Holyday accepted.

"Stayin' the night then, is you?" Josey then asked. "I can get some beds made up."

"Very good," Holyday said. "I'm going to bring this sack of sugar inside," he said to me as he picked up the sack that had the opium hidden inside of it.

"I'll get that," I offered.

"No, I'm fine," he replied as he tossed the sack over his shoulder and began walking toward the house.

"We'll see you inside then," he called to the three men.

They acknowledged that they would be in directly and we followed a fine stone path to a side door and entered the palatial estate. Holyday was familiar with the layout and made his way down a cavernous hallway and navigated us through a series of mazelike rooms and walkways.

"Afternoon Martha," Holyday said to an older black woman, passing her as she swept the floor of one of the dining halls.

"Well hello Masta Cole!" she exclaimed gleefully.

"Will you tell Josey that we'll be having our dinner in Armstrong's study?" he asked.

"I sure will Masta Cole," she replied. "Will ya'll be needin' rooms made up?"

"Already taken care of dear," he answered. "This is Steven Brixton of Somerset."

"A pleasure to meet you Mista Steven Brixton of Somerset," she said happily.

"Pleasure is all mine, mam," I answered her and continued following Holyday as he turned another corner. I recognized the colossal wooden doors of Armstrong's study.

We entered the well-appointed room with its fine leather furniture and impressive collection of books and maps. Holyday tossed the sack on

Armstrong's desk and limped over to the plush couch where he essentially fell over and allowed the plump pillows to catch him.

"Have a seat boy," he said. "Make yourself comfortable."

Holyday and I had just started to relax when Josey and Willy entered the room. If they had been a few minutes later in their arrival it is quite possible they would have found us sound asleep.

"Sa?" Willy asked.

"Yes Willy."

"What would you be havin' for dinner?" Willy was a large muscular black man and I surmised that his regular duties did not confine him to the kitchen. The muscles that rippled from his arms and shoulders suggested he spent his share of time in the fields.

"Whatever is handy," Holyday answered. "Don't go to any trouble."

Both black men broke out in laughter.

"Sa, Masta Armstrong is away," Willy reminded him. "When Masta is away, we servants do play," and there was more robust laughter from the two. "I don't reckon' there's a single thing you could ask for that ain't in that kitchin' cookin' up right now."

Holyday looked to me for suggestions. "Any requests?"

I shook my head no.

"We got some nice thick venison steaks on the grill," Willy started, "got some fish fryin' up, ducks in the oven, oyster stew, potatoes and beans, got some fresh pies, cornbread, grillin' some chickens..."

"Really doin' it up right," Holyday acknowledged with approval.

"Oh, I'ze just gettin' started," Willy assured him. "We got us some crabs steamin' and corn on the cob..."

"Just bring us a couple plates of food," Holyday said, interrupting his recital of the menu for a second time, "whatever's easiest."

"It's all easy sa," Willy assured, "we gonna be cookin' and eatin' all night long," followed by more infectious laughter.

"Some oyster stew then," Holyday finally consented. "A slab of venison. Cornbread. Potatoes and beans. A piece of fish," he looked to me. Again, I just shook my head, this time yes.

The men were back with the food in no time at all. We ate quickly. Everything was delicious. No sooner had we finished eating than the men returned and removed from our presence any sign that there had been so much as a morsel of dinner eaten in Armstrong's study.

"I made your regular room Mista Hol'day," Josey called, "and Mista Brixton is right across the hall."

"Very good Josey, thank you so much," Holyday said, "and thank you Willy, it was wonderful," he shouted to the muscular man who was now walking down the hallway with an arm full of dishes.

"Welcome sa," Willy shouted back to him.

"Shall I close the doors?" asked Josey.

"Please," Holyday answered. "And Josey..."

"Yes sa?"

"Any sign of Mrs. Armstrong?" Holyday asked.

"No sir," answered Josey. "Have not seen the Mrs. today."

Holyday gave me a knowing look and then turned back to Josey, "Very well then."

"Good night, sirs." Josey closed the doors, and we were left to the quiet stillness of Armstrong's regal and well-appointed study.

The silence was golden and the chair so comfortable that I feared I would dose off. I knew all too well that come morning I would arise early and be on my way. It was quite possible I would not ever see Cole Holyday again and I wanted more than anything else to have one more meaningful and thought-provoking conversation with him.

Holyday rose to his feet and, limping badly, walked over to Armstrong's massive mahogany desk. He pulled out two large cigars. He then turned and opened a cabinet removing a bottle of whiskey and a couple glasses. Setting them on the desk he opened the sack of sugar and removed one of the bottles of opium buried deep inside of it.

"Do you mind?" he turned to look at me.

"No please," I replied.

"My leg is ripe," he advised, the agony all too apparent in his voice.

He poured us each half a tumbler of whiskey and into his glass he let spill two drops of the liquid opium. After lighting his cigar, he walked over to me with his smoke in his mouth. In his one hand he held the other cigar and a pack of wooden matches. He handed them to me and then extended the two glasses which he had pinched together with his thumb and forefinger.

"Take the right one," he said with a wry smile.

He then returned to the sofa. This time instead of falling into it, he bent his old, stiff knees and slowly leaned back into the waiting cushions so as not to spill his whiskey. He winced and made a noise that I would expect to hear from someone who was being run through with a long blade.

The smoke was superb and the whiskey even better.

"Oh," he sighed. "That's the good stuff," he proclaimed as he looked at his glass. I was not sure if he referred to the whiskey or the opium.

We sat in silence as we enjoyed our smoke and our drink. He would eventually begin talking. As to what subject he would choose I could not even venture a guess, but I was looking forward to what could be our last conversation. Until then, the tobacco and the whiskey, and the silence, would suffice most splendidly.

I began to wonder if the long day had given way to exhaustion and might deprive me of the discussion I had so earnestly hoped to engage. But, as was always the case, Holyday did not disappoint.

"So," he broke the silence with such suddenness that his voice almost startled me, "you've had some time to contemplate the matter, after seeing the big city and all it has to offer. I'm curious, are you still enamored with life in the woods or did your brief taste of city life give you cause to consider that there might be a better way to do things?"

"It's quite possible that I'll go back and forth on this for some time, but as of this moment I feel rather certain that my life in Somerton affords me things I don't believe could be found anywhere else," I answered him.

"What kind of things is it that you consider so important?"

"Well," I spoke slowly to give myself time to think through my comments as I said them. "I like to know where I stand. In Somerton I will always know where that is. There will never be any doubt as to my place in the community. My expectations of myself and of my family, my friends, are very well established. There is no guesswork involved and with that comes a sense of security. A great deal of comfort is derived from understanding how all the different pieces fit together. I'm not sure that kind of stability, that sense of purpose and responsibility, would ever be available to me in a big city."

"And you are not worried that over time the comfort," he paused looking for a better word but not finding one just repeated mine, "that stability, will become too predictable? Is knowing your place so important that you would exclude all that a different life might offer?"

"I think so," my answer carried with it a sliver of doubt, as if the decision were not yet final. "I am sure that as life goes on and I come to understand more about how the world works there will be a change of heart with regards to how I feel and what I believe. But at this moment I feel I can say with great certainty that my home is in the woods. I know I will always be intrigued by city life. There will always be a fascination with the excitement that pulses through the streets. The conveniences are tantalizing. To have everything at your fingertips, or right across the street, is something I am sure I could get used to in a hurry. But as I sit here now, I feel quite convinced that the city is a place for people like me to visit. It is not where we live."

"I can't say I'm surprised," Holyday said. "You seem to have insights that few men ever acquire. Never have I met anyone of your modest age that can look at life from so many different directions."

"That is a kind thing to say," I said, "and I appreciate it. I have seen that you do not say things lightly. That is, you mean what you say. So, I will take your compliment as extremely high praise."

"It has been my experience," he said, "that the more hats a man can wear the better his position in life will be. Most men, and women, can interact with a certain type of person and their comfort is exclusive to such company. Taken out of that context most men flounder. It is a rare gift to have the ability to fit in, as if you belong, to whatever setting you find yourself. It is a skill that normally comes with experience, which usually requires many years to acquire. It's unusual to see someone of your age so adept at wearing the various hats of so many diverse walks of life."

"I don't have many years under my belt," I agreed, "but I do wholeheartedly believe that these experiences, or knack for wearing different hats as you say, can be acquired from reading. I think it serves a person well to read about people and how they behave and speak. I hope that is the case anyway, for most folks on the lower shore will never come any closer to certain places, or certain kinds of people, than reading about them in the pages of a book."

"Well," Holyday remarked, "it seems to have served you very well indeed. Most young people, once exposed to the excitement of the city, are taken in immediately. But if you think about the richest men in the world, men who could live anywhere they please, they choose to build estates in the country and live with nature. They almost seem to shun the big cities.

The heads of families of the first order for example, you will rarely see them in the city, and I have never known one to live there. Many of these leaders of first families are very smart men, very accomplished. They have built businesses and acquired wealth and power. These men can do whatever they want. They inevitably move out to the country. Even those who inherit their wealth and power seem to always remain in the estates of their ancestors. Convenience seems less important to them than peace and quiet, and beauty and solitude. Are these kings of industry merely avoiding the crowds and the chaos, or are they attracted to the pristine nature of the quiet countryside? It does not matter, I guess. For whatever reason, they choose the country life. And what is the one thing they all keep close to them?" He did not wait for me to venture an answer. "Family," he said.

"Very true," I agreed.

"I think your Uncle Jedediah knows what he's doing," Holyday stated introspectively. "I think he's trying to preserve something important. He understands that places like Somerton and the lifestyle it affords are quickly vanishing from our world and soon will have disappeared altogether. And I think he knows, as do you, that one day the responsibility will fall on you to keep it alive."

"Places like Somerton are good for the world," I answered him. "People grow up understanding the importance of loyalty and honor. They live their lives knowing that it is okay to ask for help. Everyone can expect their friends and their neighbors to be there for them."

"That's important," he replied. "Knowing that you can depend on people makes for a good night's sleep. Makes it easier to fall asleep and easier to climb out of bed each morning. This great country may finally be free from the oppression of the English. We shall soon know for sure. But even if the British are sailing back to England, there is a growing sense of skepticism among the people. I see it in Baltimore and in Annapolis. There is a reluctance to trust your fellow man. This is not just among politicians, where it can be expected, but among common people as well. Folks on the street, in the markets, in the taverns and the shops, they don't know who to trust anymore."

"That's what I mean," I said. "That kind of dark suspicion, it just doesn't exist in Somerton. Everyone in town is considered family. Blood relative or not, your friends and neighbors are your family. You know you can trust them. You know they will be there for you when you need them. There is never any doubt. The support is real. You pray for one another, and you genuinely want what is best for your fellow man. There is nothing I would not do for anyone in Somerton. And I know they feel the same way."

"The only other place I have experienced the kind of honor that you speak of is in battle," he said. "Soldiers, militia, in the heat and the fire of war you know the man next to you is your brother. You know you can count on him. He will die for you. At the same time there is not the slightest doubt in your mind that you would do the same for him."

"I can't imagine people feeling that way about one another in a big city, where no one really knows each other," I said. "I think it would be unreasonable to expect a stranger to lay down their life for you. Maybe it happens. But it would be foolish to expect it. It would be unwise to count on it."

"Again," Holyday smiled, "a young boy with an old soul. There is something different about you Steven Brixton. Something that didn't just come from reading books."

"I wouldn't know," I admitted. "All I know is that what I saw in the city was fascinating to me. It was an altogether different world, filled with excitement and oozing with opportunities. But it was unsettling just the same. It would never be possible to get to know everyone. And if you cannot know everyone, can you really know anyone?"

"I'm afraid the opium may have disabled the part of my mind that permits me to explore too deeply the universe of the philosophical," he confessed. "This I regret. At the same time, it has been so awfully long since I have been without pain. I feel almost naked without it. But it feels good. It feels exceptionally good."

"I'm glad," I replied.

"Me too," he said. "My pain has become so ingrained, so familiar, there are times I swear I seem to relish it. And as crippling as it feels sometimes, it would be a lie to say that there are not occasions when it gives me strength. I know that can't make any sense to you."

"I don't know," I countered. "I can see how constant pain can make you stronger. The world in which you live is more difficult. How could it not make you stronger? You are burdened with a weight that others are not forced to carry."

"It's not just that," he replied. "It's not just that it makes me stronger, I understand that part of it. But the pain has become part of who I am. It has been my loyal companion since the day we charged that hill. Sometimes, I am sure that it is the only thing I can truly count on. It has, in a way, defined me as a person. Some struggles are eternal, the pain etched permanently along the jagged edges of life's vast and brilliant canvas. Without the suffering, I would be incomplete."

"I will miss talking with you Cole Holyday," I said with a pang of deep regret.

"And I you, Steven Brixton," he replied.

Holyday closed his eyes and, leaning back into the oversized cushions, he appeared to be as relaxed as it was possible for any living person to be. If he were not already asleep it was clear that he would depart the conscious world at any moment. I wanted with all my heart to continue conversing with him. I relished being able to talk with someone whose thoughts and ideas about life were congruent with mine.

Holyday illuminated for me the void of intellectual stimulation available to me from the people I held so dear. For all the priceless beauty afforded the residents of Somerton, to banter philosophical was not a luxury afforded us. Of course, luxury, even basic comfort, was not what made Somerton such a magical place in which to live. There was no premium ascribed to literature, or philosophy, or science. Our emphasis was reserved for hard work, long days, and the gratitude that came from being a part of something much larger than yourself.

There were so many questions I wanted to ask of Coleman Holyday. Having only known him for a few days, he was in many ways still a stranger to me. And yet there was a curious, almost mystical feeling I had toward him that made me feel we had known each other all our lives. I watched as the liquor, the opium, and the exhaustion took him to a place where he would be unavailable to me.

"What was it that made you turn away from God?" I honestly felt that my opportunity had passed and doubted very much he even heard my question.

"It is not difficult," he answered without opening his eyes, "to turn away from something that has already turned away from you." His words came slowly, but at least they came. "Everyone, I am sure," he continued, "sees things as they pass through this world that make them wonder how

God could behave so cruelly. The longer a person lives the more likely it is they will have experiences," and he paused with great effect, "that will test their faith. Things that make a man question God's existence."

"My uncle once told me," I interjected, "that of all the things we ask of ourselves, maintaining a strong faith is the most difficult. But he also said it offers the greatest reward."

"Reward." Holyday repeated the word. "Yes, no denying that. The faithful are rewarded. Even if there is no God, the faithful are rewarded."

"But it has to be real," I added. "Faith must bring joy to your life. Spirituality without joy is not genuine."

"It seems almost a paradox," Holyday stated.

"How so?"

"Possessing one, either faith or joy, all but guarantees the other," he explained his contention. "But, lacking both, it would seem almost impossible to acquire either. But surely, their absence makes life more difficult."

"There is a decision to be made," I said. "Just as you made the decision to abandon your faith, so too can you decide to embrace it once more. To believe in something, anything, is a choice."

There was silence. It was my assumption that Holyday was mulling over in his mind the words I had just shared. I expected from him, whence he spoke again, a question that he knew had no answer, or a remark intended to dismiss my premise. I got neither.

"We were on our way from Philadelphia," he spoke with a pervasive sadness, "my wife and me, and our child. My son Joseph was but two years old. Born on Christmas day in the year 1799."

It took me by surprise that he was going to share the story with me. The thought registered immediately that Holyday's son and I would be about the same age. That might explain why he had taken such an unexpected interest in me and escorted me for the duration of my journey.

"We sailed down the river from Philadelphia and enjoyed good weather and calm seas through the Delaware Bay and out into the Atlantic," he was telling the story, I could tell, through a haze. "We enjoyed first class passage on a gorgeous new vessel. The *Triumphant Victory,* she was called, and making her maiden voyage. She would carry us from Philadelphia to Baltimore in less than three days. I refused to believe that a ship of such size could travel that distance so quickly. That was until I saw the size of her sails. They took up half the sky and blocked out the sun. When the wind stretched them full the gigantic forty-ton craft seemed to glide effortlessly across the ocean." He stopped talking and, keeping his eyes closed completely, he raised his empty glass. "Maybe another two fingers."

"Sure," I said, jumping to my feet. I took his glass from him and, setting it on the desk, began to pour.

"Three fingers then," he instructed. "And just a drop more of the opium."

I did as he requested, and he reached up and took the drink from me still without ever opening his eyes. I took my seat, and he enjoyed a healthy swallow from his glass.

"Ahhh," he licked his lips. "We left the Atlantic behind with the sun high in the sky and not a cloud in sight. I sat on the deck next to my wife, our son in her arms, and looked out across the Chesapeake. No one on this earth could have been happier than she and I at that moment. A new life awaited us in Baltimore. We would raise our son and probably many more, sons and daughters both. I had been appointed an Administrative Judge. A handsome salary accompanied the position as well as what had been described to me as a stunning two-story house on a hill. But it was not to be," he sighed in such a way that made it too clear the story was to take an unpleasant course.

"It was almost dinner time when we first noticed the sky begin to darken. I remember one of the attendants telling us that because we were expecting a little rain there would be no dining on the deck this evening. We thought nothing of it." He then inhaled the remainder of his drink and grit his teeth. "It seemed almost impossible how rapidly the storm took us. In an instant the clouds grew as black as night. Lightening flashed and thunder roared so ferociously that you would have thought that your fictitious Almighty Himself had fallen off His throne. Seas, as calm and serene as a sheet of glass just minutes earlier, jumped up over the rails and waves came crashing across the deck. We had just closed the door behind us upon reaching the safety of our cabin when the room itself turned upside down. I held my son tightly in my arms as the capsized ship tossed us about the room. Despite the terror and the chaos, we were able to grab the life jackets that had fallen off the wall and rested on the cabin's ceiling, next to our feet. I first tied Joseph into his jacket and then my lovely wife.

She held our son as I secured my own jacket. Before she could hand him back to me the ship disintegrated. It came apart completely and absolutely fell to pieces. In an instant we were engulfed by the waters of the Chesapeake, not afforded even time to say goodbye," his voice had grown angry. "So, I said goodbye to my God."

I looked at him in time to see him open his eyes. Their piercing intensity stood in such an awful contrast to a face left so relaxed by liquor and opium that I would have thought they were the eyes of a demon. Had I not known this man was my friend those eyes would have terrified me. As it was, all I could feel was abject sorrow for a loss so agonizing.

"I have never talked about it," he said, "to anyone. The day I lost my wife and my son. And my God."

Such a tale leaves one without words. The mind goes blank as there is nothing that can be said to make it any less tragic.

"My parents too were taken by the Chesapeake," the words came out on their own. I made no mindful decision to say them. To that end I was as surprised as Holyday to hear them.

"Explain," demanded Holyday, an expression of alertness returning to his face.

"I'm not sure I can," I began. "I mean, I don't remember it. I can only repeat the story I was told, and I know that as a courtesy to me, to protect me, the story was, ah, smoothed out. I am sure what happened was minimized, the horror of it. I have only been told the story twice in my entire life and not once since I was but five or six years old. We just don't talk about it."

"Talk about it now," he insisted.

"It has been so long," I began, "I'm not sure but I think they left out of Washington. I remember the story referring to the Potomac River. They traveled out of the Potomac and into the Chesapeake heading for the lower shore. It was early in the new century. Eighteen hundred and one, I believe. A lot of Quaker families were fleeing Virginia and Maryland back then, so I have been told. People looking for a more tolerant land in which to live."

"How many sailed with you?" Holyday asked.

"I don't know," I answered. "My mother and father as I recall were already living in Somerton. They had gone to Washington, or somewhere up the Potomac, to pick up another family."

"Related to you?" Holyday inquired.

"I don't know for sure," I answered.

"Do you know what kind of ship they sailed?"

"I don't," I replied and with a chuckle I added, "I feel as if I'm being interrogated."

"I apologize," Holyday said sincerely. "It's just that I have felt a kindred spirit between you and I and have struggled to understand it. And now to find out that we both lost our families to storms on the Chesapeake, just astonishingly coincidental, hard to believe."

"Oh, my parents were not lost in a storm," I said. "It was what Jedediah called a Chesapeake Wall, a rogue wave, that washed over the ship. Uncle Jedediah told me the wave was thirty feet high. Swept every single person off the deck of the ship. Jed saw the wave coming and grabbed me and my Aunt Mildred. He said some of the people never surfaced. My parents were among them."

"A rogue wave," Holyday, through the mask of his intoxication looked stunned. "And the ship?"

"I believe the ship was not too severely damaged," I answered. "I know that the survivors climbed back on board, and we were able to make port at Devil's Island."

"What else?" he inquired, seeming frantic for more information.

"That's it," I said. "That's really all I know. Like I said, we do not ever talk about it. I think it is a painful memory for Jedediah. Jed and his brother were close, and I am sure the loss of my father was much harder on Jed than it was on me. I don't think it's a memory he likes to revisit."

"And you?" Holyday beckoned. "You are satisfied with such miniscule details regarding the death of your parents?"

"I can't explain it," I said almost apologetically. "I never knew them. Jedediah and Millie are the only parents I have ever known. They have treated me like a son. I kind of think it may be unkind to make them dwell on it. My parents were lost at sea like so many others from the Somerset and Accomack lands. I do not know what else to say. We lost them, and a few other good people, and got on with it."

"Fascinating," Holyday ruminated, "that a thing of such beauty, the Chesapeake, that is the very life's blood of Maryland and all her people, can at the same time be so cruel. She is a giver and a taker of life. That the bay stole from both of us our families, it overwhelms me. I will try to let it go, but I cannot help but feel there is more to it. I am truly shaken by this and so deeply sorry for your loss."

"Thank you," I said. "But I dare say my loss pales in comparison to your experience. Again, I remember none of what happened."

"You know that a monstrous wave rose from the sea and took your parents away from you," he said. "And yet you still believe in God. That is amazing to me. The Chesapeake killed your parents. How does the mind reconcile that God allowed such a wave to erupt from the depths of the bay and steal your parents from you? How does such random cruelty fail to destroy, to shatter, any shred of faith that would yet linger in your soul?"

"We think differently," I said, "about some things, that is. On others, we clearly have minds that behave identically. But, with regards to the staggering misery you must have felt, still must feel, I do not see how you can carry such a burden without the help of God."

"Well," replied Holyday, "as I've said, pain is my constant companion. It is my friend, without whom I would be all alone, and lost."

"It seems to me," I countered, "that you, by choice, are making this life, already so hard and unfair, more difficult than it needs to be."

After a moment of silence during which he appeared to be contemplating my comment he responded.

"On this point young Brixton, I fear we are forever destined to disagree." He exhaled loudly and allowed sleep to take him. A moment later I joined him.

CHAPTER 14
Dorchester

The next morning began with the realization that I had overindulged in Armstrong's fine Scotch whiskey. *Aqua vitae*, or, the water of life, is more smartly enjoyed in moderation. However, given the circumstances I promptly forgave myself the transgression. To engage such an extraordinary and deceptively learned man in the blessing of intriguing conversation was an occasion that deserved to be celebrated. It was with a lack of regret that my sour stomach and pounding head were accepted as the price to be paid. Understanding that the liquor had enhanced our discussion by loosening our tongues and our minds it was clear to me that despite the sluggish start to this day it could not be considered anything other than a bargain.

Lying in the large leather chair I watched Holyday stepping across the room with nary a limp. He had walked the previous night in a most labored manner. It pleased me to see him moving more comfortably. He had his back turned toward me when he began to speak in that low, guttural growl that now so delighted me.

"A very long day awaits you my friend," I heard him say. "Your travel will be made easier with each minute left not wasted."

In an instant a sense of clarity embraced me and the dull, weary fog that can accompany the consumption of spirits was dismissed. Rising to my feet, I cast aside any lingering discomfort. I understood thoroughly that I simply did not have time to feel poorly.

We exited Armstrong's study and traversed the myriad of hallways that were now filled with the enticing aroma of a country breakfast. Holyday walked us through the main kitchen where we exchanged morning pleasantries with the servants working the kitchen. We enjoyed some delicious baked ham, some eggs, and a warm, freshly buttered roll. We devoured the meal so quickly that we did not bother to even sit down.

"Armstrong is not expected until tomorrow?" Holyday asked to no one in particular.

A large chubby-cheeked black woman responded, "Tomorrow or the next day," she said. "That's what he said anyway. But that man," she added cheerfully, "well, who knows?"

"Supposed to be some men from Easton arriving this afternoon with a shipment of fence posts and gates," announced an older feeble looking man who was busy working an enormous skillet full of eggs. He seemed to be enjoying his present assignment and I sensed he was not a slave that was frequently working inside the house. His weary face and tired posture, though full of energy at this moment, suggested his was a life of strenuous labor.

"Enjoy your day then," Holyday said to the kitchen workers. It occurred to me a rather odd comment to make to a room full of slaves. Nonetheless, the entire group, a dozen or so in total, responded in unison with wishes for a good day.

By the time we entered the stables several men were busy feeding the animals and cleaning out the stalls. The men were good natured and exchanged greetings with Holyday but did not slow, even modestly, doing their chores. Holyday went to work immediately affixing the supplies to the horses and the mule. No matter how many times I watched him do this I could not help but marvel at the proficiency with which he made the animals ready.

"Have our animals been fed?" Holyday asked.

"Fed and groomed," answered the man closest to us. "Got them taken care of first thing," he added. "Didn't know what time you might be settin' out. Knowin' you Mista Cole, we figured it be early."

"Thank you, Benjamin," Holyday replied. We left the stable through the doors opposite those we had used the day before.

We walked along a winding path that took us down to the river and away from the house. Black men and women could be seen scurrying all over the property. They each moved with great purpose, appearing to understand thoroughly their work assignments for the day. Brilliant white clouds graced the deep blue sky. Birds of every variety sang out as we made our way to the water's edge. The river rested idly in between the will of the tides.

"Are the slaves not supervised?" I asked. "I have not seen a white man since our arrival. What keeps the captives from fleeing?"

"They are trapped on the plantation," Holyday answered. "The wild lands of the Nanticoke present too formidable an obstacle to invite escape. The few who have tried are tracked easily and brought back to the whip."

We walked toward the dock where Armstrong's small fleet of ships sat motionless in the still water of the Choptank. I began to contemplate my imminent departure. The journey itself, though it would be a trying one, did not worry me. The challenges I would face over the next few days as I moved three animals packed heavy with supplies through the forests and marshes of Dorchester County intimidated me not at all. I knew that if I remained focused and travelled smartly, keeping clear of any that would interfere with my journey, I would remain safe. What did weigh heavy on my mind was the impending good-bye. I was preoccupied in parting ways with Cole Holyday to such an extent that no other thought entered my mind.

"You know," Holyday spoke softly, "if Armstrong is not expected to return for another day or two," he continued, an edge of strategy framing his words, "there is no reason I could not accompany you to Somerset. Together we could travel the main road. You would not have to walk the undergrowth hiding yourself away from thieves and ruffians. It would save you at least one full day, probably more."

"That is a magnificent plan!" I shouted. I could not even pretend to hide my enthusiasm. "You could meet Uncle Jedediah and Aunt Mildred. Oh, how they would enjoy making your acquaintance!" I laughed loudly. "This is so unexpected. Good fortune surely smiles on me this day. I cannot even begin to express my appreciation."

There was a smile on his face. I was sure he could see in my expression an unbridled jubilance. It was clear to me that he found joy in making me so incredibly happy. The journey would now be so much safer and less strenuous, not to mention the time it would save. But beyond that, and I knew it had occurred to him as well, another day or two of his company and magical discourse. I had become almost dependent on my dialogue with Holyday. The intellectual exchanges and impromptu debates alone were a gift so cherished that I found it difficult to contain myself. I was charged with excitement and a renewed energy pulsed through me making me feel positively exuberant.

The river was being graced by a gentle zephyr. The sun was warm against my face. Looking to the river I detected its stillness interrupted by a lazy movement inland heralding the incoming tide. Up ahead were several ancient willow trees. The breeze had picked up and the long wispy limbs of the willow danced playfully. Autumn on the lower eastern shore of Maryland cannot possibly have a rival in being the most spectacular place on earth. This glorious day possessed a beauty that I expected could otherwise only be found in heaven.

It was the suddenness with which Holyday came to a halt that caught my attention. I stopped and turned to see him looking up toward the river's bank. I followed his eyes, but his target escaped me. Far off in the distance were the slave's quarters, ineffectually hidden by a row of mighty oaks. But his gaze was not so far off. He appeared to be transfixed by something else, something much closer. My eyes scanned the bank in vain for the subject of his attention.

Seeing nothing I turned my focus back to Holyday and observed a man beset by terror. His eyes were opened wide, and he trembled slightly as he stood frozen, staring at something invisible to me. He surely looked as if he had seen a ghost.

"What is it?" I asked.

Holyday took a deep breath to regain his composure before addressing me. Once he had calmed himself, he turned to face me. He glanced back over his shoulder to check the bank once more before he began to speak.

"Did you know that black men fought in the Revolution?" The steady voice belied his unsettled appearance of a moment earlier.

"I did," I answered.

"Were you aware that there were many among the Four Hundred?" he asked.

"I'm not sure," I said, reaching as far back into my memory as I could. I could not remember having read anything about black members of the Maryland Four Hundred nor did I recall having ever heard it discussed. "No, I don't believe I knew that."

"There were black men in our regiment," he continued. "Can you imagine?" His voice grew more animated. "Risking your life for the cause of freedom only to return to see your brothers and sisters in chains?"

I knew in terms absolute that this was a question I was not to answer. I waited for him to continue.

"One of the black fellas was a freed slave named Abraham Rockhurst. I did not know him well. He was a quiet man and stayed to himself quite a bit. He had a reputation for being a good soldier, hardworking, always did more than his share. I remember his demeanor was one of sadness, as though he had suffered a great loss. Likely watched his family sold off to different plantation owners. That would have explained his fierceness on the battlefield, something I had witnessed on two separate occasions before Brooklyn." Holyday's speech was rapid and stretched with anxiety. "On that day when Mordecai Gist gave the initial order to charge the hill, Rockhurst was the first one up. It is entirely possible, even likely, that his was the first life lost that day. I ran past his lifeless body as I made my charge. There was not much left of him. Shot full of holes. Ripped apart by the lead balls and shrapnel from British muskets and scatter guns. I will never comprehend how some of us made it up that hill, and back, taking only a bullet or two, while others were shot a hundred times," he paused as he was becoming overwhelmed by the recollection.

"Providence will always work in her own mysterious ways," I offered.

"He stood on the riverbank just a moment ago," Holyday said, dismissing my remark. "Not a scratch on him. So, you must come back as you were just prior to your death. That is what I think. I'm guessing it has to be that way," he paused and again looked toward the bank, his hands still trembling slightly.

"He spoke to me," Holyday continued, his voice cracking. "War does not play out on the battlefield, but in the hearts and minds of people with the courage to stand and make a difference." Holyday swallowed hard. "What do you think he meant by that?"

"I'm not sure," I answered instinctively, not giving myself time to ponder whether to speak or hold my tongue.

"Why would Abraham appear to me?" he asked. "I hardly knew the man. Why must the dead speak in riddles? What could he mean?"

I looked around in different directions as if I might suddenly see something that would give me some insight.

"What is it I am supposed to do?" His voice was growing angry. "What is it I am supposed to understand? The courage to stand and make a difference," he repeated the words.

He looked skyward locating the sun and surveyed the sky from east to west. He was getting a reading on the time of day. Very suddenly, a strong gust of wind rushed past us. It was unusual in its strength and its duration. One of the sails on the ship closest to us flapped helplessly in the wind before falling limp once more at the cessation of the hurried autumn air. Holyday turned his attention to the river. It was now moving inland, or backwards, as the Indians would say. The tide was coming in. Holyday returned his eyes to the bank then again back to the river. Once more he looked up at the sun and followed its projected path westward.

"Of course!" he shouted with great excitement. Then, as he was so adept at doing, calmed himself completely before speaking again. "Son of Somerset, I need your help."

"Anything you want," I agreed without having yet figured out the puzzle.

"I can take us up to Potters Landing," Holyday was speaking loudly enough for me to hear him clearly, but he was not talking to me. He was making plans in his head and thinking out loud. "A couple miles south of the Denton Wharf," he continued talking, "bring us ashore at the bend in the river at Tuckahoe Neck. From there we are less than five miles from the Delaware line. Molly Cannon has men working that area looking for runaway slaves but if we stick to the edge of those fields, I know the area well, we can travel just inside the tree line." I could see the plan coming together in his eyes. "East into Delaware, then north to Pennsylvania," he snapped his head around to check on the river. "Tide is starting to run. We need to get moving."

He turned to me and spoke eagerly and with determination. "I can't get any of the bigger ships that far up the river," his speech now quick and anxious, "but, *The Glory Days*," he nodded in the direction of the schooner, "she'll get me through the shallows if we hit the tide just right." Again, he turned to check on the river.

"Brixton," he said, his voice enflamed with energy. "Run as fast as you can to the shacks." He pointed to the slave's quarters through the oak trees. "Tell them a ship leaves for freedom," he said. "It leaves now. Go!"

I raced across the field with long effortless strides, moving like a deer. I arrived at the first dilapidated structure in no time at all. The door, being unequipped with a doorknob or any kind of lock or latch, swung open widely as I pushed into it. The shack was vacant. The dirt floor had been swept clean and the sparse hand-made wooden furniture arranged neatly but there was not a soul in sight. I moved immediately on to the next shack. Pushing open the door I saw a young girl sitting in the dirt next to her mother. My entrance startled them, and they appeared frightened. I raised both of my hands, palms open and out, to signify I meant them no harm.

"Where is everyone?" I asked with a sense of urgency.

"They in the fields," the woman answered, her voice quivering with apprehension. "Workin'."

"There is a ship sailing for freedom," I said. "It leaves now. Get to the dock!"

I ran to the next ramshackle shed. It too was empty. In the next one I found a lone girl not ten years old. "Where is your mother?" I implored.

"Dead," she answered, her eyes wide with uncertainty.

"Your father?"

"In the fields, workin'."

"Go get him!" I shouted. "Get to the docks. There is a ship waiting for you. It sails for freedom. It leaves now!"

The girl tore out of the shack like a flash of lightening. I watched her race across the field. Her speed was amazing. I entered the next shack to find it empty, then the next with the same result. Finally, I pushed open a door where a dozen or so slaves crouched together in the corner of the small abode. The adults embraced the children. Everyone looked bewildered.

"There is a ship sailing from the dock," I spoke trying to sound calm but to also impress upon them the urgency with which they must act. "It sails for freedom, but it makes ready to sail at once. Come," I implored them. "Come, freedom awaits! Come now!"

I checked a few more shacks but they were all empty. I retreated to the dock to inform Holyday of my limited success. I ran toward the river. Some of the slaves followed me. Others ran off in the direction of the fields. I believed they went to retrieve loved ones.

"Most of the shacks were empty," I said to Holyday. I was panting and out of breath. "Some of them are coming," I huffed. "Others ran off in the direction of the fields. To collect family members is my guess."

I was bent at the waist with my hands on my knees and sucking in big gulps of air trying to catch my breath. I looked up at Holyday to see his reaction and to await further instructions. He smiled strangely as he looked over my head. Initially I had thought it possible that Abraham

Rockhurst, or perhaps another deceased member of the Four Hundred, had once more come to visit. But when I turned to look behind me, I saw dozens of slaves descending the bank. There were four of them out in front, followed closely by others that either pulled young children along by their hands or carried smaller children in their arms as they ran toward us. Behind them still others followed, and back even further I could see small groups of three and four racing across the field toward us.

"Help me!" Holyday demanded.

I climbed onto the ship and began assisting him with the rigging. In short order the passengers began to board the ship. Holyday would tell the women and children to remain on the main deck. He would send some to sit up front and others to the rear of the ship. As men began to board, having made their way in from the fields, Holyday would direct them below deck.

"Find a bench," he would tell them. "And grab an oar."

More enslaved people continued to climb aboard. I was surprised at the numbers.

"You there," Holyday shouted to three men as they prepared to board, "down below on a bench and grab an oar!"

He continued to tell the women and children to find a seat on the main deck directing them in such a way as to spread their weight around equally.

"Come with me," he said to me, and he jumped, bad leg and all, from the ship to the dock. "You see the marks," pointing to the various colored markings on the vessel's hull. He walked over to several ropes that were tied up to the dock. The ropes hung into the water and were anchored on the bottom of the river. "I need to sail this ship through channels six feet deep." He knelt to examine the markings on the dock and the boat. "We are mark twain," he said. "Twelve feet. I cannot take any more weight than the red marking. That is my six-foot marker. You tell me when that red mark hits the water."

Holyday climbed back onto the small ship. Four more passengers climbed aboard in rapid succession and the boat dipped down so that the red mark and the water line were perfectly aligned.

"There!" I shouted. "The mark and the water match."

"Stop!" Holyday shouted. "I can't take any more. We won't make it through the shallows."

There was no discussion. No disagreement of any kind. The slaves understood exactly what Holyday was telling them. But, as some of the families remained separated, those aboard the vessel with loved ones standing on the dock disembarked immediately. Not a word was said. They would not leave their family and they would not ask anyone to give up their spot on the ship.

"What's the marker look like Brixton?" Holyday barked.

"You've got an inch and a half," I replied.

Holyday turned and pointed to some women at the front of the ship and ordered them off the vessel. They disembarked without uttering a single word. Then Holyday turned his attention to the back of the boat and again ordered two women off the ship.

"Now?" Holyday asked urgently.

The ship was rocking, and the reading was fluctuating. Holyday knew that an inaccurate mark could spell disaster and waited patiently but anxiously for my report. The men bringing the fence posts from Easton or any white men visiting the plantation could arrive at any time. That would doom Holyday's plan to sail these people up the Choptank to lands where they could live as free Americans.

"Almost three inches," I shouted out when I felt the reading was secure.

Holyday yelled as he pointed, "you, and you there," he pointed to two men, "below deck and grab an oar."

"My family sir," one of the men protested.

"How many?"

The man pointed to a small woman with an infant in her arms.

"Come!" Holyday demanded. The three came on board. "Up front," he said to the woman and her child. The man went below deck. Holyday then directed the other man, small but muscular, to get on the boat.

"That's it!" I screamed. "She's dead on."

"Push us off Brixton!" Holyday ordered as he tossed the tie ropes onto the dock.

I grabbed the long pole and placed it against the side of the ship. I walked into it until I was at the dock's edge and pushed with all my might. The ship floated away and took right to the current of the incoming tide. Holyday stood on the bridge of the ship and stared at me. His eyes were discolored with a fiery passion when he spoke.

"Brixton," he called out.

"Sir," I responded.

"A favor," he said. "I implore you."

I did not hesitate. "Anything."

He pointed to the people standing on the dock. They were being left behind, but no one complained as they watched their friends sail off to freedom.

"Keep them off the main roads," he said. "Your animals will help you cut paths through the brush. Travel at night if you must. You know how to move through the thicket. Get them into Delaware. Arm them and send them north." He pointed to the passengers on the ship. "They'll be waiting for them in Philadelphia."

"They won't be waiting long," I said, forcing a smile.

"Brixton," Holyday called again.

"Yes."

"If they catch you, they'll hang you," he warned. "Be careful. Use all your skills," then the briefest pause. "It was not my intention to involve you in this Steven Brixton. I am terribly sorry."

"You have nothing to apologize for Cole Holyday," I shouted. "It is an honor. This opportunity is a gift from God!"

"Arm them," he yelled as his final instruction. "If it comes to getting caught, fight to the death. Do not surrender. They'll lead you straight to the gallows."

"Good luck!" I shouted.

"It is a great thing you do today brave son of Somerset!"

The oars hit the water and the ship straightened herself out and headed upriver. A moment later the sails unfurled. Holyday was able to catch the wind and in an instant the ship was under a full sail and on her way to freedom.

I turned to those standing on the dock. Most of them had tears in their eyes as they watched the ship flee up the river. I believed these were tears of joy, though certainly some had to be thinking it was the last time they would see their friends. Holyday had worked brilliantly to fit as many of the imprisoned Africans on the ship without making her too heavy to skirt the shallow channels they would encounter upstream. If the ship happened to run aground on a sandbar it would lead to Holyday's execution and, at a minimum, a return to the misery of slavery under shackles and chains for the others.

Holyday had been able to man the ten-oared schooner with strong hardy men without separating any immediate family members. Still, that did not mean that some on the ship did not move ever farther away from people with whom they had surely become intimately close over the years. It appeared almost orchestrated as those standing on the dock turned their attention in unison away from the ship and toward me. I had no time to consider the enormity of the task before me. I possessed not the luxury to be intimidated. The lives of these people were in my hands. I would either lead them to freedom or back to the fields and the whips.

"We go now to freedom," I began. "The journey will be a difficult one. Our chances for survival are diminished by each additional person that travels with us. But we cannot leave any behind that desire to join us. We begin on the main road but will quickly be moving into the brush to avoid the bands that will be hunting us. We leave from the end of the lane," I pointed to the ornate posts marking the entrance to Armstrong's long manicured pathway that curved its way up to the great stone house. "In ten minutes," I instructed them, "all that are assembled there will join our march. Any food or clean water will prove helpful, but we cannot wait for stragglers. We will need to travel lightly and quickly. Ten minutes."

I gathered my animals and moved toward the house. I took the mule by his reins and led him, knowing that Thunder and Blue would follow on their own as they were obedient and smart. The slaves seemed to be unsure of what to do so I instructed them in the most specific terms possible.

"Go," I said. "Gather your family and your friends. Be clear as to the hardship of the march. It will be a difficult journey. Food and water," I reiterated. "Ten minutes," then I turned toward the mansion. The group of slaves ran off together toward the quarters that had been their prison for so many years.

Upon reaching a side entrance to Armstrong's white stone castle I tied my animals to an iron gate that fronted one of a hundred gardens on the property. The garden was ripe with autumn's wildly colored flowers but also appeared to be used to grow herbs for the kitchen servants and cooks. I entered the door and found myself in a parlor of sorts. The room had no discernable purpose other than to make available three hallways, each leading in a different direction. I needed to get back to Armstrong's study and, as I had no better than a one in three chance of choosing the right hallway, I began walking down the middle one intent on asking the first person I saw for directions. However, as I moved down one hallway and then another, I saw not a soul. I was very nearly frustrated to the point of calling out when I saw those immense dark brown wooden doors that concealed behind them Armstrong's study. I did not bother to even close the door behind me but rather made my way at once to Armstrong's desk. I took a seat in his throne-sized leather-backed chair and, grabbing the edge of the desk, pulled myself up closely to its surface.

I had been in this room twice previously. Once, on the first night of this adventure when Holyday, Morris, Armstrong, McCabe, and myself gathered as Armstrong mapped out our route across the bay. The other was last night when Holyday and I ended up sleeping here. On both occasions I had taken notice of some of the artifacts in the elegant office. I had seen a fabulous looking polished sword hanging on the paneled wall. It probably had belonged to some high-ranking war commander and was displayed proudly in Armstrong's study to give the false impression that he knew how to use it. I had also reviewed his impressive collection of books and saw several that I would dearly love to possess if only long enough to read them. But there was no time for such endeavors. My business now concerned items I had observed earlier that sat on top of the desk next to what I imagined was a priceless, centuries old, hand painted wooden globe. There was a stack of fine paper imprinted with the Armstrong family insignia. Next to this stationary was set a delicate, hand painted, porcelain bottle of ink with an elongated feathered quill pen lying beside it. I wasted no time picking up the pen and wetting its tip in the ink. I slid the top piece of letterhead off the stack and positioned it in front of me and began writing.

"To Whom it May Concern," I wrote, "John Smith is hereby granted his freedom on this the...," I stopped as I was unaware of the exact date. I could recollect seeing a calendar in the room and busied myself looking around the room for it. I spied it hanging on the wall behind me. It was October 16th. I continued writing frantically knowing people who could foil our escape might arrive at any moment. If just one contractor or neighbor happened by, all would be lost. No sooner did I complete one letter than I slid it out of the way and began writing another.

"Jane Jones is hereby granted her freedom on this day, October 16, 1815." I was working at a frantic pace.

I had completed ten letters, all bearing the fictitious names of newly freed slaves. Having no way of knowing with any degree of certainty how many would be traveling with us, or the number of men versus women, I took even greater liberties with the last few letters.

"I, Cornelius Armstrong, do hereby grant the following slaves their freedom on this day, the 16th of October, in the year of our Lord, 1815." I then listed names as fast as I could make them up. Ultimately, I had close to twenty fabricated orders of emancipation. Roughly half of them were specific to one individual while the others contained lists of names. The only thing left to do was to sign them. I looked in vain for something with Armstrong's signature on it. Finding nothing I signed each letter in a preposterously elaborate and difficult to read signature. Once finished, I gathered my paperwork together and retraced the hallways back the way I came.

Exiting the building I found my animals patiently waiting for me. I grabbed the mule's reins and, making haste, headed for the end of the lane with my horses following behind me. As I passed the far wing of the mansion, I had an overpowering sense of being watched. Looking back, I observed, standing in a second story window, a woman looking at me. I could only imagine that this white woman, cloaked in a red robe, her long blonde hair spilling down around her shoulders, was the elusive wife of the plantation owner. I could not know what consequences, if any, her surveillance spelled for our mission. I was however quite sure that she smiled at me. Although at such a distance this could have been my imagination at work, or merely wishful thinking. Either way I turned away from the house and increased my pace to that of a slow methodical jog.

Looking toward the end of the lane I saw two dozen slaves awaiting my arrival. Glancing back at the house I saw the woman still standing in the window. This I considered fortunate as, if nothing else, it meant that she had not run off to report our endeavor.

Drawing ever closer to the slaves I counted them as I approached their position. My first headcount was twenty. I then realized one of the women held a child in her arms. Including myself there were twenty-two of us who would have to traverse thirty miles of the most difficult terrain, all the while remaining invisible and as quiet as snakes to avoid detection by the search parties that would inevitably be sent to capture us. The task was a daunting one and would have been immensely less difficult were we a smaller group. However, I forced myself to take into consideration that there could have just as easily been thirty or forty members in our group. This, I was sure, would have made our escape plainly impossible.

As I approached the excited evacuees I was greeted with anxious smiles. There was much I needed them to know regarding covert travel through the brush, but these lessons would have to be taught, and learned, on the run. Our very highest priority was to put as much distance between ourselves and Cambridge as possible. To this end I considered it prudent to put some of the children on the animals. I could not risk asking too much of Thunder and Blue, or the mule, as an exhausted animal would slow our movement to an intolerable degree. If a person became too fatigued to continue, they could be left to silently rest in the thick cover of the primeval forest. Once recovered they could attempt to catch up or I could go back for them. The same could not be asked of the animals for it is their nature to wander about and if seen would give the trackers insight as to our route.

To lighten the load on the animals I removed the weapons from their portage and handed out rifles, pistols, and ammunition to members of our party. In Holyday's rush to move the ship upriver he had forgotten, or more than likely, purposefully not taken any of the weapons with him. Except for the young children in whose hands a weapon would have been a liability, every member of our caravan carried with them either a rifle or a pistol. Being aware that we had a limited amount of time to keep to the main road I moved everyone along at an exceptionally good pace. Even so, to prevent fatigue, it was necessary to stop for a few minutes every hour or so to allow the weaker amongst us to catch their breath. I used these breaks to load the rifles and pistols. There is nothing quite as useless as an unloaded weapon. I made sure the group watched intently as I loaded the guns with powder and ball.

"You need to know how to do this," I said, "otherwise you don't have a weapon but carry only extra weight. Learning to do this as quickly as possible could be the difference between life and death."

I noticed that some, already weary from the hurried pace under a hot sun, were struggling to give me their full attention. I repeated the message more emphatically.

"Reloading a weapon quickly and properly can save your life," I said looking most specifically at those whose focus seemed to wander. "Being slow to reload will mean death," I paused, "for the children." I immediately had everyone's undivided attention. After small sips of water, we were back up and moving down the middle of the road.

It was now mid-afternoon and having put close to ten miles behind us I felt that to remain on the road any longer would be taking an unnecessary and foolish risk. So, I steered our party off the road and into the brush. Our progress immediately slowed to a crawl, but it was a prudent decision. There would be no outrunning a search party. Our only hope would be to hide from them. We pressed on through the thicket, being devoured by swarms of biting flies and mosquitoes. Whenever possible I detoured through marsh or standing water. Following us through the wetlands would prove a challenge to even the most skilled trackers.

On several occasions the underbrush became so thick that I had to mount Thunder and charge him through the hedgerow. His massive frame and immense power never failed to clear our path. Unfortunately, there was no remedy to cover the tracks of a charging stallion. Our route would be an easy one to follow should the slave hunters pick up our trail. We continued pressing our way through the Dorchester County wilderness until we found ourselves once more blocked by a shear wall of brambles and brush so thick that I questioned whether even my mighty horse could bust his way through it.

I made the decision to stop for the night. Tomorrow we would be swallowed up by the wild Dorchester landscape. The race to the Delaware line would mean running for our lives through land considered by most to be all but impassable. We had no choice but to find a way.

CHAPTER 15
The Nanticoke

"In the woods," I instructed everyone, "everything is food. Everything is trying to eat everything else. Things on the ground get eaten first." Normally this is good advice. Unfortunately, our biggest problem throughout the long night would be the mosquitoes and there was no escaping them. Getting up off the ground would keep some of the spiders and ticks away but we continued to be at the mercy of the winged pests. We tried to cover the women and children with blankets, but the exercise seemed futile. The cursed creatures gnawed at us incessantly making for a most unpleasant night, sleep all but hopeless.

I tried to keep everyone's attention off the constant attacks of the biting insects by educating them about the route we were taking. I helped them understand that while Delaware was a slave state the residents were, for the most part, sympathetic to our cause. While crossing into Delaware would not ensure our safety, it provided at least a modest sanctuary from the slave enthusiasts of Maryland. I continued to emphasize that no one would be free until they reached Pennsylvania. I reminded them that their friends, who had traveled with Mister Holyday, would be waiting for them in Philadelphia. This proved a satisfactory distraction, if only temporarily, from the misery of the long, hot, steamy night in the swamp.

Few of us got any sleep. Despite a state of near exhaustion, everyone rejoiced as the darkness began to give way to a distant sunrise. We were up and on the move prior to what could be considered first light, but no one complained. I could not even attempt to penetrate the compact wall of thicket in the dark and decided instead to find another way around it. This was a dangerous maneuver as terrain such as this could continue for miles. But I felt I had no alternative. Finding ourselves most fortunate and in natures good graces, we found a pathway, probably used by deer, through the insufferable thorns and vines.

At one point a long, thick black snake crossed our path. It surprised me how unphased the party was at the sight of such a large serpent. I was about to question the group's cavalier response when, as the snake had apparently taken too long to move out of our way, one of the women reached down and grabbed the snake behind its head and flung it into the woods.

"Not afraid of snakes I guess," I joked.

I got some muffled laughter from the group. One of the men explained to me that the quarters in which they lived were infested with snakes. Some, he explained, much bigger than that one.

"Besides," he added, "black snakes eat rats. Much prefer sleeping with snakes than rats," and everyone laughed.

I forced a smile, but it was not genuine. All I could think about was the cruel slaveowner. He lived in a castle with a polished wooden bed, hand carved marble sinks and fine silk linens. Armstrong slept comfortably night after night while these poor people, literally but feet from his house, shared their crumbling shacks with snakes and rats. The thought infuriated me, but my anguish was short lived. We promptly stepped out of the forest to see the Nanticoke River crossing directly in front of us. The Nanticoke was a formidable body of water. But we were a considerable distance from the mile-wide mouth of the river and stood looking at what could well pass for a large stream. It was no more than a hundred feet across. I felt greatly confident regarding our chances of finding a safe place to cross.

We broke up into separate scouting parties. I took three of the men with me and moved inland and sent the other group of four men toward the Chesapeake. We left the women and children, along with the animals, in a protected alcove that was heavily forested and could only be seen from the opposite shoreline. We told the women to rest and feed the children the last of our limited rations. If slave-trackers happened to stumble across the hiding spot, they were to fire off a warning shot, and we would come running. I was comfortable with their cover. It was as secluded a place that could be found anywhere along this winding course of the Nanticoke. Even a hunting party would have turned back thinking it impossible for our group to traverse the dense thicket and treacherous marches.

I explained to the three men traveling with me that there was a notorious woman who lived farther up the Nanticoke making her living by capturing runaway slaves and selling them back to their owners. This woman, Patty Cannon, who some said was a witch, employed teams of men that would patrol the Nanticoke and Choptank Rivers looking for runaways. The woman even engaged in the practice of kidnapping free blacks and shipping them down south to be sold into slavery.

One story had it that on Christmas Eve some years back, a barmaid and prostitute named Beatrice Homely could not quiet her child. Cannon became annoyed at the child's incessant cries and, grabbing the baby from its mother's arms, threw it onto a raging campfire. The mother of the child, it is said, was so traumatized by the event that she was never again able to speak. Others believed the woman could not speak because Cannon cut out her tongue so she could not report the incident to the authorities. The horror stories regarding Patty Cannon were thought to be myths by some, though others would swear to their authenticity. Either way, everyone steered well clear of the area of the Nanticoke where it was said she had built a house. I personally attributed the Patty Cannon stories to the variety of tales that usually included monsters or some manner of demons. That is, I believed them a bit too farfetched to be believed. However, given our present situation it would serve us well if the men did buy into it, so I conveyed it to them with the utmost credibility.

We spent two hours scouring the edges of the river for any sign of a crossable section of river before giving up and turning back. We met the other group at the alcove, and they too reported having no luck. We had tried to wade across the Nanticoke at the narrow bends in the river, but we would always step off a submerged ledge that sent us plunging into water well over our heads. At one point, attempting to determine the depth of the water, I swam down toward the bed of the river but was unable to reach the bottom. It had to have been at least twenty feet deep. If the depth remained consistent all the way to the banks on the opposite side, crossing here was not an option. There was no way for me to get my animals, supplies, and the people, across the river as none in the party could swim.

The river had halted our progress and it appeared there was no reprieve in either direction. It occurred to me the only option available to us was to head back the way we came. This was not at all what I wanted but seemed the only avenue available to us. The river was extremely lazy at this time of day. It flowed in neither direction, rather sat motionless much like a puddle in a field. I contemplated briefly making a raft but there were no materials readily available that would accommodate such a plan. I decided it would work in my favor to engage everyone in some pleasant conversation before breaking the news to them that we were going to have to turn around in search of a better route.

I began asking questions about their families in search of any topic I might explore that would serve to lighten the mood. However, as should have been expected, no one had any amusing anecdotes to share regarding life on the plantation. Stories were revealed detailing how Armstrong would torture some of the slaves for the amusement of his friends. These were stories that would have the opposite effect of what I had hoped to accomplish. I quickly changed the subject. Our unfortunate predicament being what it was, it occurred to me that postponing the inevitable would do more harm than good.

As I rose to my feet, I contemplated how best to share the news with them. Pondering my options, I stared into the murky waters of the Nanticoke and saw the water begin to move. The tide was beginning to roll out and the water slowly ebbed toward the Chesapeake. I thought nothing of this at first as it seemed to impact our current situation not at all. Suddenly something caught my eye. Several feet beneath the surface of the river I saw an enormous fish. A catfish, I thought. They were the only species in this part of the Nanticoke that could grow to such a length. I continued staring in disbelief. The size of the fish was like nothing I had ever seen. It was the size of a large shark. I remembered stories from my childhood about catfish so huge they could swallow a man whole. A chill went racing down my spine as I thought about how I had been diving to the bottom of this river just minutes ago. I watched in amazement as the outgoing tide seemed to reveal more and more of the monstrous fish. It was ten feet long if it was an inch. The tide continued moving out toward the bay, picking up its pace as it did so.

"You see this?" I asked.

"What is it?" asked the oldest member of our group, a man we called Mister John.

"A fish," I answered him. "I think." The fish did not seem to be moving. I found it odd that a fish would hold its position against an outgoing tide. Maybe it was a log or...

"Sand bar!" I screamed and immediately dove into the river. I swam only ten feet before feeling for the bottom. Once I secured my footing I rose to a standing position and was shocked to find myself in water that barely came up to my waist. I turned and walked toward the opposite shore and to my delight the sandbar took me right up to the other bank. Retracing my course, I approached the bank where our group was stranded and stepping off the sand bar, sunk down into water that was over my head. The depth of this narrow channel was inconsequential. It measured a very short distance from fast land to sand bar. It could be easily traversed. The smaller members of our group and the supplies could be thrown across the channel if need be. Our passage had been right in front of us the whole time, the motionless murky water concealing from us our escape route. I climbed up onto the bank and with great excitement went over to Thunder and climbed on top of him.

"Go Boy!" I yelled.

Thunder leaped across the deep channel with a single bound and landed squarely on the sand bar with a tremendous splash. A few more of his powerful thrusts and the horse rose effortlessly out of the water and was standing firmly on the other side of the river. I was certain we now stood in the northern reaches of Somerset County. The Delaware line could be no more than a few miles from our present position.

"Let's go!" I implored the group.

We moved the entire group and all the supplies from one side of the Nanticoke to the other in a good deal less than an hour.

I tied most of the supplies back onto the animals but some of the items were just as easily carried by members of our party. This provided more space for the women and children to sit astride the horses and the mule. The arrangement provided us the opportunity to travel at a much faster rate. The farther we moved away from the Nanticoke the more comfortable I became that a search party's attempt to track us down would be in vain. The incessant underbrush had given way to a pine forest and our journey became more akin to a stroll through the woods than the frantic escape from captivity we had endured to this point.

Everything was finally going according to plan. I was hopeful we would be crossing into Delaware before the day was over. However, as I reached into my pocket to retrieve my compass it was missing. I knew immediately that the cherished gold-plated compass, given to me by my

Uncle Jedediah, was now resting on the bottom of the Nanticoke River. It was likely already covered over by the silt carried by the outgoing tide. I was upset over losing my keepsake, but it was gone. I did not allow myself to fret over it.

I had not traveled this part of Somerset County prior to this day but, having studied maps of the area over the years, I knew our present location almost precisely. With the river behind us, I led our group through the woods in a line that had us moving directly toward the Delaware line. Aside from some of the children whining about being hungry, we found ourselves in a situation that was terrifically improved from our status of just an hour ago.

Luck continued to ride with us as quite by accident, while passing through the area of Mardela, we quite literally stumbled into a babbling brook whose water was crystal clear and delightfully refreshing. I could not trace the creek back to its source, but it flowed toward the river and not away from it. I surmised it was a tributary of the Mardela Spring. The natural spring and the creek from which we now drank was once the life source of the Wicomico Indians. The tribe had made its way north some years ago as the intrusion of the white man into the area had made life for them too difficult. I had studied the area well enough to know that the outpost of Salisbury was not more than a dozen miles to the south. But as our target was the Delaware line we moved east, and we moved quickly.

In time we came to a clearing that looked out over a large grassy field. Considering that we were on the run it was a blessing that we felt confident enough of our present situation to observe and admire the natural beauty of our surroundings. The sky had grown cloudy and while it did not feel or smell like rain the weather on the peninsula was entirely unpredictable. We had several hours of daylight left and it was my most sincere hope to cross into Delaware before nightfall so my new friends could begin their long journey north through Delaware and into Pennsylvania. I would then make my turn to the south and head toward Somerton.

It did not take long for me to understand that our present course was once again based on some guess work. Without a compass and with the sun blocked out by the clouds it was no longer possible to be convinced that our path to the Delaware line was a direct one. That we moved in generally the right direction would have to be enough for now. I was hopeful that we would soon see something that could be used to assist our navigation. In the meantime, I repeated the instructions pertaining to safe passage through Delaware. Some of the men and women understood how to travel by using the sun or the stars. Unfortunately, neither are available under the cover of clouds. I reiterated emphatically that the direction they would need to travel was north by northeast.

"You must maintain a course to the east. It is not possible to move too far in that direction," I said. "The worst that could happen would be to run into the Delaware Bay. From there it is an easy trip up the coast to where the bay meets the Delaware River. The river will escort you to the city of Philadelphia where your friends will be waiting for you."

The group delighted in being reminded that the others would be waiting for them in Pennsylvania. They relished the idea of being reunited with their people.

"Now, if you get to a point where you really feel as though you are picking a direction based on nothing but a hunch, you would be better served to just take cover in the woods and wait for a cloudless sky," I continued my instruction. "A clear sky, day or night, will guide you north," I said. "North, northeast," I emphasized yet again. "If you make the mistake of moving to the west you will find yourself back in Maryland. Back in chains," I said. "Your freedom short lived and vanished."

It was not a message they enjoyed hearing but was one on which their lives depended. Without a compass or a clear sky, the flatness of the lower eastern shore was impossible to travel unless you were familiar with the landmarks and these people were not.

"If you come across strangers, you will know immediately if they are good people," my lessons continued. "Those with evil intentions will be easy to spot. The people of Delaware are good folks. As I have said, it is still a slave state, but the practice is not a popular one. Folks you encounter who make Delaware their home will not interfere with your journey. They will likely ask if they can be of assistance. If you encounter bad men, their interest will be in money only. They would capture you and return you for reward money. I am going to be giving you a great sum of money. If need be, it is more than enough to buy your freedom from any that would try to take it. If things get ugly, you are a large group. There is strength in your numbers. Stay together. And as a last resort," I added, "you are armed with loaded rifles and pistols. You must use these as your last option as once you have killed men you face a whole new set of problems. But, if it is a choice between your lives and theirs, kill them. Kill them and be on your way. You can ask the Lord's forgiveness once you reach Pennsylvania."

Up ahead in the distance I saw a small graveyard. Its presence bewildered me. Family plots such as these were generally situated on private property. I could see no houses or structures of any kind for miles in any direction. We now crossed a vast grassland which afforded us a view almost to the horizon. There was a small section of woods off to our right and the fields were guarded by a forest running up its edge to our left. Generally, folks wanted as much notice as possible if strangers were approaching their property. Large, cleared fields gave the best protection against unwanted visitors. They provided a family with the time necessary to prepare themselves for whatever might be coming their way. The lone graveyard absent a residence seemed out of place and unnerved me slightly. I lowered my weapon from my shoulder and held it firmly in my hands as we moved forward.

The clouds that had been darkening and causing me concern looked to moving off to the north and that was a great relief. Bad weather was a formidable obstacle when traveling on Maryland's eastern shore. Everything was more difficult in the rain but of primary importance to our present circumstances was the limited visibility afforded by the squalls that frequently fired up over the Chesapeake and moved their way across the peninsula to the Atlantic. Visibility was often limited to a matter of a few feet during these torrential downpours and, as we were intent on determining our exact position in relation to the state line, a blinding rainstorm would effectively bring everything to a dead stop. However, on this day the storm clouds, struggling as they were to form, were being swept quickly away from us.

We walked together in a tightly assembled group, ever vigilant of any movement in the distance. Within minutes the sun was finally able to tear its way through the cloud cover. The gentle breeze that had been pushing at our backs for most of the day abruptly dissolved and the sunshine reclaimed the day. It was now a gorgeous fall afternoon on the lower shore. I was cognizant that Maryland's awe-inspiring beauty was a most fitting setting for these families to again taste the sweet flavor of freedom.

Moving closer to the small cemetery, it began to look as if it consisted of only a few graves. Each step brought the tombstones closer until we were able to clearly see that there were but three markers. My mind was busy putting together scenarios that would explain the presence of three lonely souls buried out in the middle of nowhere worthy of such impressive looking headstones. We could see there were no flowers left behind by recent visitors nor any kind of small gate or fence that was so common to family plots on the shore. It was not until the stones were immediately before us that we realized what they were. We stood before the final product erected to formalize the calculations of the surveyors Charles Mason and Jeremiah Dixon. The stones marked the Trans-peninsular Line and formed the boundary between Maryland and Delaware. The stones were positioned exactly halfway between the Chesapeake Bay and the Atlantic Ocean. The three markers were positioned so that the largest stood exactly at the intersection of the north-south Maryland-Delaware line and the east-west line. One of the smaller stones was fixed a few feet to the north of the big stone, and the other a few feet to the east of it. Together, the three very clearly marked the southwest corner of the state of Delaware.

I thought for a moment that I might explain the significance of these markers to my companions but seeing tears welling up in their eyes, it was exceedingly clear to me that my friends knew what these markers were and what they represented. Confined for years and forced to work the soil of Armstrong's fields, surely there had been mention of these magical stones that stood somewhere out there in the wilderness forming the boundary between the land where all people were created equal and the land that tolerated the abomination that is the practice of slavery.

While the free state of Pennsylvania was still a hundred miles away, setting foot in Delaware was a triumph, if only symbolically. To be sure, a sense of great relief accompanied leaving Maryland behind us.

Some of the travelers let their emotions be heard. Soft whimpering cries were intermingled with loud sobs. Others fell to the ground, kissing the stones and praising their Lord. It became obvious that my companions believed these markers to represent the famous boundary between slave states and freedom. There was no need to educate them regarding the difference between the Mason-Dixon Line and the Trans-peninsular Line. That the larger of the three stones was clearly and boldly inscribed with the names of the renowned surveyors only served to confuse the issue. What was important was that everyone understood that until Pennsylvania was under foot they remained in grave danger.

"So Mista Brick'son," asked a short and slender woman named Maggie, "I stand here and I a slave?" She took two steps forward and continued, "but I stand here and I a free woman?"

I explained to her that while she had the right idea, she and the others had another one hundred miles to go before they could step onto the soil of Pennsylvania. It would be at that moment that she stood on land that no longer wore the stench of slavery.

I straddled one of the markers and faced north. "There is a line that runs from this stone north to Pennsylvania," I pointed in that direction. "Any land to this side of the line," I pointed to my left, "is Maryland. And any land to this side of the line is Delaware," I said pointing to my right. "Land south of the marker is Maryland," I said stepping away from the stones to stand on Maryland soil. "North of the marker is Delaware," and I stepped over the invisible line into Delaware.

"But we need to be in Pennsylvania," Mister Johnny stated.

"And you will be," I assured him. "For now, it is good enough to know that Delaware is much safer than Maryland. Once you step past these stones you are done with Maryland. Maryland is not a safe place for your families. There are people in the state that possess cruel ways of thinking. But you are right Johnny, your destination is Pennsylvania. You cannot let your guard down until everyone stands firmly on the soil of that free state."

"Why don't God live in Maryland?" I heard an angelic voice speaking softly out from behind the safety of her mother's ragged and soiled, ankle-length burlap dress.

"Well," she had me stumped. "God does live in Maryland. God is everywhere. It's just that..." The child cut me off in mid-explanation.

"God wouldn't let nobody beat folks," the little girl whispered. "He wouldn't let nobody whip folks til' they jus' 'bout run outta blood. God wouldn't let no one get treated the way some 'us been treated. He wouldn'a let them beat Mista Petey to death like they done and He wouldn' make Masta Ar'strong put his thing in me all the time and hurt me like that. He would'n stand for it. I don't believe it."

The girl's mother began to cry, and tears poured from her eyes. She embraced her daughter and held her tightly. I knelt beside the girl and put my hand on her shoulder.

"None of those people are ever going to hurt you again," I told the child. "And those people that hurt you, God will tend to those people," I said, a muffled anguish seething from my voice. "God will sit in judgement of those people. They will be punished for what they did."

"Are you sure?" Her innocent brown eyes staring up at me for reassurance.

"I swear to you," I said, "and to your mother," my voice quivering slightly, "they will be held to account by the wrath of God."

"But Delaware still a slave state," Mister Johnny interrupted, feeling the need for additional clarification.

"But Delaware is a far more enlightened place to stand than is Maryland," I said. "Mind you keep yourselves over here," I said pointing to the east.

I unpacked my horses completely and passed out blankets and some material for making clothes.

"Why is you givin' us all your stuff?" asked one puzzled child. I smiled at her but looked to the adults when I answered.

"Everything you have can be sold," I said. "Some of these people, the bad ones, all they care about is money. Give them money or guns and they'll likely leave you be."

I reached into the saddle bag and pulled out the papers I had written and started to hand them out.

"These papers say that Mister Armstrong has granted you your freedom," I said.

There was a hearty laugh that echoed throughout the group as they acknowledged the absurdity of such a thought.

"How many of you can read?" I asked.

I was surprised to see all but two of the men and the younger children raise their hands.

"You need to memorize the names on these papers," I instructed. "You are now Ann Jackson," I said, handing the paper to one woman. "You are Jane Jones," handing out another. "John Smith." I gave the paper to Mister Johnny. I continued passing them out until everyone had paperwork. I then circled back around and handed out money to the adults. The money was substantial.

"Don't you need no money Mista Brick'son?" asked Johnny.

"No," I answered. "No, I don't need money." I continued passing out the supplies and reminded them of what I had been talking about all day long. "Don't wait until it's too dark to make camp. You need some light to set yourselves up for the night. If you decide to walk through the night be careful not to wander onto people's private property, or, be quiet about it. Do not ever travel at night unless you have a cloudless sky. Without the stars to guide you, you will end up walking in circles, or worse, back in Maryland. Do not travel on moonless nights. If it feels too dark to make any real distance you would be better served to stop. Settle down somewhere and start at first light."

"I want to thank you for what you done Mister Brick'son," Johnny said. "Ain't no way I can ever repay you, but you need to know I'll say a prayer for you ev'ry single night. Please know I will Mister Brick'son."

"Thank you, Mister Johnny," I replied. "That means a lot. And I'll take them prayers. But I am not giving you nothing that was not already yours. I can only apologize for the pain and the suffering you and your ancestors endured in British America and more recently in these United States. Rest assured it is my honor to undo the grievous injustice. Now, when you get to Pennsylvania, I hope you still have this money and these firearms. As I said previously, use them to buy your way out of a tough situation. But if you make it to Philadelphia with these guns and this money, you will have the means to buy yourself some land. You and your families can start whole new lives for yourselves. Be safe. Take care of each other. Love each other. Godspeed."

The group surrounded me and one by one hugged me and said goodbye. Tears flowed freely from my eyes. I had never felt more blessed in my entire life. I thanked God for giving me the opportunity to help these people. This was a memory that would surely follow me through the years. There would be a smile on my face and joy in my heart every time this occasion was recalled.

"Be on your way now," I said. "Make use of what sunlight you have left. Make the most of it. Go that way," I said pointing northeast. "And take this mule with you," I said. "He can spell some of the children from time to time. You'll not want to be stopping to rest more than you must.

Mind you do not forget to give the mule water. Don't let him get too thirsty or he won't be no good to you."

They began moving off to the northeast into Delaware. One of them would turn and wave every few seconds as I watched them. The waves became less frequent as the group moved farther away. Eventually I turned and headed south. I was now traveling much lighter and could afford to sit atop Blue, my faithful and beautiful midnight black horse. Thunder carried what supplies I had left, and he did so with ease as my load was so significantly reduced from when I had started out. Having given away the firearms, new blankets, and reams of cloth, I travelled now with only a couple sacks of sugar, one infused with bottles of opium, a few sacks of salt and coffee, and the one blanket, rifle, and pistol I had started out with. It was a far cry from the abundance of weapons and supplies I had hoped to bring home to Somerton. But I had the medicine and that was the most important thing. I knew Jedediah would be proud of me for giving the money and remaining supplies to Armstrong's slaves. We could easily make do without the additional stores and guns. On the other hand, the items could prove priceless to my friends.

Somerton was less than two days out. I thought that if I could put a few miles behind me and get to the other side of the Salisbury outpost I could sleep under the stars and with an early start might be home in time for dinner tomorrow evening. These thoughts made me realize how much I missed my family. I gave Blue a kick. The two horses and I began racing across the deep green field toward our home.

Having Mason and Dixon's markers pinpointing my exact location I knew exactly where I was and could plan accordingly. I did not want to move directly through the nearby Salisbury outpost as the people there would slow me down. Whether they wanted to buy some of my sugar or coffee or just engage a new face in conversation I wanted no part of it. The thought of a bowl of soup or a few bites of bread did briefly cross my mind. But, recalling that I had given away all my money I dismissed the possibility immediately. I did not know anyone up this way well enough to request credit. Besides, I did not want to delay the arrival of the medicine for a single minute longer than was necessary.

The land to the east of the Salisbury outpost was still very much wild and untamed and until recently it had been the sole domain of the Wicomico and the Delaware Indians. Those tribes had moved north but, much like the Nanticoke to the west, small groups of them had stayed behind to salvage a life for themselves in the vast and bountiful lands of northern Somerset.

I would move eastward until I was sure the outpost was well out of my way and then turn south toward Princess Anne and Somerton. If all went as I had drawn it up in my head, I would be able to climb up out of the bush and onto the main road between Princess Anne and Salisbury, or the road to Philadelphia as it was more commonly called, by mid-morning tomorrow. At that point, depending on my pace of travel, I could pass through Princess Anne early in the afternoon and make Somerton by dinner time.

I let the horses walk along at their leisure correcting their course from time to time. There was no need to rush things at this point in my journey. I knew that tomorrow would bring my homecoming and to press our advance at his late juncture would serve no purpose. It was a peaceful ride atop my loyal mount and gazing out at the County of Somerset in her natural splendor I could not help but to feel at peace. My voyage had been an adventurous one and I had not felt so relaxed since first setting out.

Suddenly, to my great surprise, before me not five hundred feet stood a most splendid looking church. The immaculate structure seemed stupendously out of place. It appeared it had been built in the middle of the woods. As I approached the idyllic building there was not a soul to be seen. I dismounted my horse and, knowing my animals would not abandon me, did not bother even tying them down. I tried the front door to find it locked securely. Walking around the side of the church I looked without success for another door. Making my way around to the back some movement caught my eye. I saw a man diligently working a shovel as he dug a grave in a small but lovely cemetery. He was completely unaware of my presence.

"Hello," I called to him.

He looked over at me. Being not alarmed by my appearance he set his shovel on a headstone and walked towards me.

"Hello," he said. "I have a feeling you are lost," said the old man, his face deeply aged with wrinkles.

"I am making my way to Somerton," I said. "Princess Anne, in the County Somerset." I added after my initial destination did not appear to register with him.

"Ah," he said, "sure, sure. You missed your turn off a few miles back. There is a road that runs right through the outpost and then," he paused to think it over, "ten miles or so I reckon'."

"I'm trying to avoid the outpost," I informed him. "Thought I'd move to the east of it. Circle back around and catch the road south of Salisbury."

"You an outlaw?" He looked me up and down a couple times.

"No, no," I laughed. "I've travelled to Baltimore to purchase supplies," I looked behind me to see my horses standing there.

"Princess Anne to Baltimore," the man sounded incredulous. "All by your lonesome."

"Yes sir," I decided to spare him the details, otherwise I might be detained for hours.

"Well," he said, "making the trip harder on yourself. No roads of any kind on this side of town. Nothing between here and Snow Hill but forests and creeks. Might pick up a deer trail if you're lucky but that's about it."

"By town you mean the Salisbury outpost?" I asked.

"Yes, the outpost," he replied. "They've built some houses on the river there," he added, "and a new store. Folks calling it a town these days. Though your description is a tad more accurate."

"Sir?" I asked, "With all due respect, what is this place?"

"Ha, well, yes," he laughed, a toothless smile coming to his face. "This is Spring Hill Church," he answered. "I'll grant you she serves more as a cemetery than a church these days."

"Kind of in the middle of nowhere," I said. "Again, I mean no offense."

"No, no offense," he said. "This church here," he said, "is one of a kind. Not claimed by any one faith. Non-denominational the fancy folks call it. For almost a hundred years this church catered to worshippers that found themselves unwelcome at most other places. There was a time when folks had to be mighty careful about what religion they confessed to belong. Then, Maryland got her statehood and the Catholics, well, they no longer had to run and hide. The Quakers, they mostly moved on, up north. The church, she has just about been abandoned. But not the graveyard," he gave a hearty laugh. "Can't abandon the graveyard, hard as they might try. No sir, membership here is permanent," again he laughed.

"Might there be any food about?" I asked, having not eaten since yesterday morning.

"Not unless you want to double back toward town," he said. "Although," he added, "seein' as you're goin' that way, there is a tremendous orchard two, maybe three miles," he pointed to the southeast.

"Indians used to settle there, the Wicomico mostly, grew the finest apples anywhere in the world it was said. Well, the Indians are gone now. But those apple trees, they are still there. Cannot miss it. Folks call it Shadow Hills 'cause it is the only land for fifty miles that ain't flatter than a pancake. You'll find a good-sized lake there with some small hills on either side of it where the Indians used to make their home. Apple trees all over the place. This time of year, ripe for the pickin'. Exceptionally fine land that, you'll see."

"No one's laid claim to it then?" I asked. "I mean after the Indians moved on. Fresh water, apples, sounds like property that folks might take interest in."

"No one put a claim in so far." Again he shared his odd sounding laughter. "Spooks."

"Spooks?" I questioned.

"Spirits, ghosts," he said. "There is an old Wicomico burial ground on the shore of the lake. The spirits of the dead Indians wander that land. I never seen 'em. But I know plenty of folks swear they seen the shadows of the dead walkin' round them hills."

"So, Shadow Hills," I said. "That's why they call it that?"

"Well shit for dinner!" the old man cackled. "I never put that together. Shadow Hills," and again he laughed and laughed. "Well young man let me get back to diggin'. I got a body on the way. Need a hole to put him in."

"Good day then sir," I said and climbed back on top of Blue and we trotted away. The old man continued his unusual laughter as he dug into the earth and threw shovels full of it to the side.

I found the lake with little effort. It seemed my horses could smell the water, or the apples. It was exactly as the old man had described it. Every tree was graced with big, ripe, juicy apples. Thunder and Blue were having a grand time. There was as much of the delicious fruit on the ground as there was on the branches of the trees. By the time we finished gorging ourselves on the fresh apples and drinking the crystal-clear water of the lake the sun was almost to the horizon. I reasoned that we would not find a more suitable place to get a good night's sleep than our present location. Foregoing the extra mile or so we might have been able to subtract from tomorrow's walk home, we bedded down under an apple tree. We slept by the lake on the old Indian village now known as Shadow Hills.

CHAPTER 16
Somerset

We woke to a glorious morning. A cool breeze helped the apples dance as they hung from the branches of the trees. More of the fruit was enjoyed for a quick breakfast before I loaded the supplies onto Thunder's back. With the last of the ropes being tied off I filled my canteen with fresh water from the lake and we were off.

Travelling without incident, it was well before noon when I decided to bring the animals up out of the bush and onto the road. Thunder and Blue seemed pleased to have solid footing under them and we moved at a brisk rate along the well-travelled road.

The horses realized before I that we were within a few miles of Princess Anne. Without any prompting from me, they gradually began to pick up their pace. It seemed they were acknowledging that our surroundings were now familiar. We were finally coming home and within minutes would see the outskirts of Princess Anne on the horizon. Looking to the sky I could see that it might be noon, but no more than a few minutes later. We had made exceptionally good time.

The horses now wanted to run, and I had to hold them back as we had a good ten miles to go past Princess Anne to our destination of Somerton. But, as Princess Anne came into full view, I found restraining the animals to be a lost cause and finally gave in and let them go. With a holler they took off. They ran with such speed I would have thought them to have been stabled and rested for days on end instead of having just endured the trials of such an arduous journey.

We raced into the town at full speed, the horses clearly holding nothing back. Down Main Street we flew, full of energy, full of life. It was at this point I first sensed something peculiar. The town was strangely empty. I saw no one anywhere. This at first did not overly alarm me as I seldom came into Princess Anne and for all I knew this was nothing unusual. But the longer we went without seeing a single person the more I began to worry that something was not right. I entertained for a fleeting moment the thought that the virus had raged rampant and blanketed the entire county in a rush of sickness and death.

I slowed the horses and we moved cautiously down the street. It would have been an outrageous understatement to say the emptiness of the town's streets bewildered me. Could everyone be at church? It was much too late in the day for that, I thought. All possible explanations for the lifelessness of the town eluded me. Not a soul could be seen anywhere. Then, from the eerie silence, there came a feint and distant sound, as if carried by the wind. Voices could be heard, muffled though they were. Turning the corner of Main Street and walking the horses out into the intersection of the crossroads, I saw a large assembly of people at the far end of the long avenue. They all faced the opposite direction and from my vantage point I could not detect what held the attention of the entire town so completely. My horses and I proceeded down the street toward the gathering at the end of the block.

The attraction, still unknown to me, had the undivided attention of the audience. No one even noticed my arrival. I tied Thunder and Blue to a side rail and began slowly pushing my way through the packed street. There was a great deal of commotion up ahead but even as I squeezed my way toward the front lines of the assembly, it was difficult to make out what exactly it was that had everyone so riled up. Finally maneuvering myself through the hostile and agitated crowd, I saw a man curled up on the ground. Several men stood over him. One of them cursed the man and kicked him repeatedly. With the mob loudly shouting their approval, it was impossible to make out the accusations of the aggressor. The subject of the abuse remained tightly wound in a fetal position with his hands clasping the top of his head and his arms covering his face. The defenseless victim was making every effort to elude the boot of his assailant.

With the next forceful blow to the back of the man's head, his hands, for an instant, were knocked away. Initially the profuse bleeding and swollen features continued to conceal the man's identity from me but with a sudden horror I was able to recognize the battered face of Cole Holyday.

"No!" I screamed and broke through the last remaining spectators that stood between myself and the assault. Finally standing detached from the crowd amidst the blood-spattered clearing I became aware that the metal-toed boots inflicting such brutal injuries to my friend belonged to none other than Cornelius Armstrong himself.

"What the hell are you doing?" I shouted as I rushed at him. I was within a few feet of my target when the butt of a musket impaled the side of my head knocking me to the ground. Bouncing off the street as if it were made of rubber I continued to go at Armstrong. He would have been in my grasp were it not for one of his guards stepping between us. The guard's rifle was leveled at my head, the barrel only inches from my face. Had the musket been affixed with bayonet it surely would have run me clean through, its tip likely visible sticking out the back of my skull.

"There he is!" cackled Armstrong. "The partner in crime. Arrest him!"

Two men came at me simultaneously, one from each side. I grabbed one of them and threw him forcefully into the other. There was a loud cracking thud as the two men collided, sending both to the ground. The man standing next to Armstrong had his rifle still leveled at me and pulled back on the hammer ready to fire.

"Don't shoot him God damn it!" Armstrong railed with the anguish of a lunatic. "I'll see him swing next to the other cursed criminal!"

I was being surrounded by Armstrong's men who appeared to number five, in addition to a couple of the Princess Anne authorities. Knowing that Armstrong wanted me subdued and captured rather than shot worked in my favor. I had no intention of surrendering peacefully. Looking at the men as they surrounded me it was clear none of them had the slightest interest in making the first move. I took a step toward Armstrong and in the blink of an eye had half a dozen rifles pointed directly at my head.

"You think you can steal from me?" Armstrong asked, his question dripping with disdain. "You pathetic inbred southern shore barbarian. It sickens me that filth such as you can breathe the same air as I. That your kind, pigs that you are, walk the same planet proves that even God himself makes mistakes."

I looked down at Holyday, his face a bloody mess, and through it all he smiled at me.

"And what?" I asked angrily, turning my attention again to Armstrong. "You're going to execute one of the Maryland Four..."

"Don't!" screamed Holyday. "Don't you take this from me!"

Armstrong for a moment seemed perplexed but he regained his arrogant composure in an instant.

"Oh, I'm going to kill this thieving, vile piece of filth. I absolutely am," Armstrong promised. "And I'll see your stinking worthless Somerset ass swinging right beside him!"

In his outrage Armstrong made the mistake of moving half a step closer to me and that was all I needed. He had a handsome pistol stuck inside his belt. Before he had any notion that I was making a move for it, the gold-plated weapon was pressed firmly up against his forehead. The hammer clicked loudly as I pulled it back into the fully cocked position.

"Stop! Don't be a fool Brixton!" Holyday begged. "I've already confessed. I stole the slaves. All of them. You knew nothing of my plans. Do not let him suck you into this. It is not your fight boy! Put the gun down!"

Holyday's words struck me like a kick in the teeth. My dire situation now becoming painfully obvious. I had yanked Armstrong's pistol from his belt almost instinctually. I had given it no thought whatsoever. It was purely an unconscious reaction, a reflex. But here I stood, with a gun pressed against the head of one of the most powerful men in all of Maryland. I found myself in a most precarious predicament. I took a step backward and removed the barrel of Armstrong's pistol from his forehead while keeping it trained on the imprint the gun's barrel had left on his large pale forehead.

"Someone dis-arm this pathetic parasite," Armstrong snarled. "The stupidity of these people never ceases to amaze me. Just when I thought it impossible to be any more hopelessly derelict, they prove me wrong," his face grew more deeply red with each word as spittle flew from his mouth along with the insults. "It is a wonder they ever figured out how to walk on two legs," he continued his rant. "I know the rats and other vermin feel cheated. How does this idiotic creature, this scum that lives in the woods on the underside of rocks, how does it manage to stumble stupidly around on two feet when clearly every living thing on Earth exceeds its intelligence a hundred-fold?" Armstrong bellowed incessantly. "I cannot stand to look at him another minute. The grotesque fool! The sense of a worm and here he stands pointing a weapon at the patriarch of a family of the first order. It surprises me that God himself has not struck down this blithering moron. Take the pistol from the imbecile!"

I was not in any way effected by Armstrong's words. I had learned long ago to dismiss insults. They always said much more about the person spewing them than they did about their intended target. No, it was the look on his face that impacted me. His pompous expression revealed to everyone in attendance that he did genuinely believe he was superior to all others. The common people were inferior to such a degree that the best he could do was to tolerate them. His utter contempt could not be concealed, nor should it be. It was his birthright, having been selected by God himself to be born into a family of influence. The world should forever bend a knee and cater to his every whim. And when not being of some useful service to him it was the obligation of the underprivileged to remain out of sight as their mere presence disgusted him.

It will be my contention until the end of time that I pulled Armstrong's pistol from his belt without giving it a thought. It was not the result of even the slightest contemplation, it just happened. But I cannot deny that when the entitled look on the cruel man's face became more than I could bare, I very consciously moved to aim the pistol away from his forehead where it would have caused his immediate death. He would have never known I pulled the trigger. I lowered the weapon to his chest. Thinking very clearly, I did not want the left side, not his heart, another instantaneous departure from this world. No, the wound must be to the right side of his chest. He must know that he is dying, and he must know that it was I who took his precious life from him. Me, a ragged peasant, had inflicted the mortal wound. Immense pain would fill his final moment as he choked on his blood and spit, trying to curse me. The last thing he would ever see would be the face of the lowly Somerset boy who freed his slaves and stole his life.

There were screams from the crowd when the hammer fell. The ball tore through Armstrong's torso. It entered the right side of his chest and came out his back. The exit wound was twice the size of the hole in his chest. The ball lodged deep into a tree directly to his rear. It was fortunate that someone had not been standing behind him. The shock of Armstrong being assassinated so publicly left the authorities at a temporary loss and they did not immediately apprehend me. Rather, it took them a minute to gather their wits about them before rushing to subdue me. It afforded more than enough time for me to see the life flee Armstrong's widely opened eyes, and to be sure the last thing he ever saw was my immensely satisfied and smiling face.

Holyday and I were rushed to the jailhouse amid the horror and screams of the crowd. We were simultaneously pushed and pulled through the chaos of the street. Some of the men that now handled me were being as rough as possible. Others escorted me more gently and tried to protect me from the angry mob.

The doors of the jailhouse slammed closed immediately behind us and with near completeness blocked out the deafening noise through which we had been paraded. The jailhouse itself was clean and smelled of disinfectant. One could not help but get the impression that the cells, numbering only two, were seldom used. Holyday was unceremoniously thrown into one of them. I was treated with a good deal more compassion and released from the grip of my captures and allowed to walk freely into the other cage. Our respective jail cell doors were swung shut with a heavy clank and the keys inserted into the locks and turned until a definitive metal bolt could be heard slamming itself into place.

The cells were simple, as would be expected. They were set side by side with only the familiar iron wrought bars separating the two. Wood-framed cots covered with flimsy cloth blankets and pillows encased with the same material were pressed into the corners of the sparse cells. Wooden boxes sat opposite the cots. The boards on top of them, when pushed aside, would surely reveal holes that served as toilets.

I sat stunned on my cot unable to fully comprehend what had just happened. Several minutes passed before I even raised my eyes to look at the men who stood rambling excitedly over one another. I could not have understood what they were saying even if I had been trying. My attention then turned to Holyday who sat bleeding on his cot staring at the blood as it dripped from his mouth and began to pool on the jail cell floor.

"Can we get the man a wet towel for Christ's sake?" I asked. The men looked somewhat stunned at how annoyed I sounded.

"You need not worry about the thief boy," the jailer admonished. I had seen this man before but did not know his name. Surely this town did not employ full time staff to tend to this rarely used jail. My recollection of this fellow had to be as it related to his real job, but I could not place it. None of the other men looked even remotely familiar to me and I assumed they had travelled with Armstrong as part of the impromptu hanging party he had assembled to exact his revenge for having been robbed of his property.

The men ignored my request and returned to their conversation. I slid my pillow out of its cover and threw the pillowcase between the iron bars to Holyday. It landed on his shoulder.

"Clean yourself up your honor," I said to him.

"Your honor?" One of the unknown guards questioned.

"Mind your business," I snapped. Looking at Holyday I observed that he beamed with the smile of a proud father.

"Quite the mouth for a lad that'll be swinging from the gallows before the sun goes down," he said.

"You work for Armstrong?" I asked. "Or worked, I should say," I corrected myself, "before I blew a hole through the bastard."

"Why you," he yelled, and he started towards me.

Rather than taking a step backward I moved toward the bars.

"Come on coward," I said, reaching my arm through the bars. "I dare you." That was enough to stop the soft, pudgy, middle-aged man in his tracks.

"We will need a trial, to make everything official" stated the man recognizable to me, though I still could not place him.

"A trial?" Another man asked incredulously. "The thief admitted he stole the slaves and the boy, hell the boy murdered Mister Armstrong in front of a hundred witnesses. I hardly think a trial is necessary."

"There's a matter of protocol," replied the local.

"To hell with your Somerset protocol," the heavyset man said. "We'll be leaving in the morning for Annapolis and these two criminals will most surely be dead by the time of our departure."

The group in its entirety exited the jailhouse to finish their conversation elsewhere. Holyday and I were now alone in the detention center, an ominous quiet our only companion. The silence was strangely both foreboding and comforting. The two of us savored it for a moment before I interrupted.

"So, what happened?" I finally asked, my tone more reminiscent of a casual conversation between two neighbors than that of a condemned man.

"We made it almost to Denton," Holyday answered. "I set us ashore, and we made quick work of the woods. Less than five miles to the Delaware line. I went to survey the situation once we had crossed into

Delaware. Damn if I didn't run smack into Armstrong and his slave hunters."

"How did they find you so quickly?" I inquired.

"He must have shown up at his plantation just as you were leaving," Holyday said. "I know he couldn't have missed you by more than a few minutes. But whoever gave him his information must have told him I had taken the slaves up the river. They could not have said anything about you. Otherwise, his men would have chased you down before you made it out of Cambridge. But whoever Armstrong talked to kept you out of it."

I thought about what a close call it had been. If I had taken just a little longer to write those letters or had not been fortunate to find Armstrong's study so quickly, I could well have been captured. All the folks that now made their way through Delaware would be back in Cambridge, most likely at the end of a whip.

"How was he able to track you down?" I asked him again.

"Nothing more than pure dumb luck," he answered. "I had seen them coming too, but it never occurred to me it might be Armstrong. They looked nothing at all like a posse. I mistook them for a group of workers headed to the fields. By the time I could clearly see them it was too late. Anyway, he was fumin' mad. He says to me that if I turn over the slaves, I will be free to go. Well, the slaves were hiding in the woods not fifty feet from where I stood. I told Armstrong I had left them on the ship while I came to check things out. 'Take me to the ship!' he screams and off we went in the other direction. The slaves, I am sure, waited until we were out of sight and ran off toward Pennsylvania." Holyday began laughing as he continued, "When Armstrong saw his ship floating there in the middle of the Choptank with not a soul on board he 'bout soiled himself. He knew he'd been had," Holyday mused. "His goons rounded me up and we headed straight for Princess Anne. I don't know how he figured out you were involved."

"I'm sure he figured you could not have squeezed fifty some slaves onto that little schooner," I said. "Not and made it through the shallows all the way to Denton. He probably jumped to that conclusion right quick," I surmised, "that I was an accomplice."

"Fifty slaves?" Holyday questioned. "How many went with you?"

"Twenty-one," I answered proudly.

"Twenty-one? You took twenty-one through the Dorchester marshes?" he asked in disbelief.

"I did," I replied.

"They all made it?" he asked, his voice stretched with great concern.

"Every last one of them," I answered and the two of us burst into a fit of laughter. The laughs were being used to defend against a horror that only the condemned can truly experience. After a moment, the forced jubilation gave way to an eerie quiet.

"First of all," Holyday broke the silence with a rebuke that I knew was inevitable. "That was a stupid thing to do. Damned stupid. And unless we are to be served up some divine intervention, I suspect you are going to pay the ultimate price for it." He continued, his voice growing more somber, "I will regret for what is left of my life that I involved you in this whole mess. Even then, if there is an afterlife, I will carry the regret with me right up to the golden gates of heaven or to the agony of eternal hellfire," and he paused as he was prone to do, with perfection, before proceeding. "But there's something you need to know," he said, "it might make what awaits us a little easier to stomach."

At this point he grabbed his leg and pulled it up onto the cot and, leaning back against the wall of his cell, fully stretched himself out so that he faced me directly.

"Armstrong has no offspring," he said. "No sons, no daughters, nary a niece or nephew. No one. The purpose of his trip to Philadelphia was to entertain offers for his Maryland properties. But he was unsuccessful. A messenger stopped him in Wilmington to tell him the meeting in Philadelphia had been canceled. He returned to Maryland without a buyer." He looked at me as if by that information alone I was to understand some great truth.

"Not sure I'm following you completely," I admitted.

"His lands," Holyday continued, "all of them, and he owns ten thousand acres in Maryland alone, all his properties will revert to the state. Apparently, he owes thousands of dollars in unpaid taxes. With a wife who has never wanted anything more than to return to England, from whence she hails, and without enough slaves to work the land, well, when you killed that evil man you not only freed his slaves, but you likely ended the practice of slavery on an exceptionally large tract of eastern shore land.

History won't record your name, but generations of children yet unborn will have you to thank for their freedom."

I would reflect on Holyday's statement in the hours ahead. In his words I would find immense consolation. But presently I had not the opportunity to respond as the front door opened slowly, squeaking of freshly installed hardware. This time the local man returned by himself. He turned and closed the door behind him just as unhurried and stoically as he had opened it. He walked in our direction taking short deliberate steps. He stopped in front of the jail cells standing equally distant between me and Holyday.

"You know me," he said, looking at me.

"I've been trying to place the face," I said. "Unfortunately, it continues to elude me."

"Elijah Travers," he stated. "I am the administrator of the wharf." Seeing that this information left my face blank he added, "I'm in charge of the town dock at the head of the Manokin River."

"Yes," it finally registered. I had seen this man registering merchants and logging inventory down on the river. "Yes, I've seen you on the docks. I have indeed."

"I'm afraid I have some bad news for you gentlemen," he said. "The men that were here earlier, they, ah," he stopped to clear his throat. "They have considerable clout in matters related to, well, matters such as these."

"You refer to matters related to giving people their freedom and executing a torturous maniac, do you?" Holyday inquired.

"Yes sir," answered Travers. "Although, those men have the power, or the authority, to classify it differently. They have determined the penalty and the course of its outcome."

"I'm going to take the liberty of reading between the lines here Mister, Travers, is it?" Holyday spoke.

"Yes sir," Travers was clearly uncomfortable.

"These men have taken it upon themselves to convict us of stealing property and murder. Am I correct?" Holyday asked.

"Yes sir, you are correct," Travers sheepishly responded.

"And these men have some kind of authority, or power as you called it, that permits them to stand in judgement of us," Holyday stated it as fact. "This power, I'm curious Mister Travers," Holyday rose to his feet as he spoke, "where does it come from?"

"Sir?" Travers was baffled.

"All power has a source," Holyday said. "Where does their power come from?"

"They are all members of families of the first order sir," Travers answered. "Very powerful and influential men indeed."

"Mister Travers," Holyday spoke as a man would to a little boy, "what exactly is a family of the first order?"

Travers' expression was a mixture of frustration and embarrassment when he answered, "I used to think it referenced royal blood lines, but that is clearly not the case. Now, the only definition that holds muster as far as I can tell is that of belonging to a family descended from the first settlers. The first families to cross the Atlantic and try to make a go of it on this wild and untamed continent are of the first order."

"Most of those families did not survive," Holyday protested. "I'll give you that, if it were in fact the case, if a family had crossed from England some, what, two hundred years ago and their descendants continued to this day thrive, that would merit first order status," Holyday continued. "But some of these families of the first order," his voice dripped with sarcasm and disgust, "they do not run three or even two generations deep. Some of these families, these members of this fictitious faction, they arrived only after the Revolution. Though they arrived more than a century too late to satisfy your qualifications they did arrive with enough wealth to purchase power and influence. Exactly the kind of thing our ancestors rebelled against."

"I suspect that is true," Travers said.

"I know for a fact that it is," Holyday insisted. "These self-proclaimed families of the first order that hold themselves to be royalty and present themselves as kings and queens, they're nothing more than rich immigrants. They arrived too late to make any meaningful contributions. They did not fight in the war and were not here to clear the land and plant the first crops. They are not the hearty souls whose ancestors braved the winters, endured starvation, and fought or befriended the Indians. The work was all done by the time they arrived with their trunks full of money. These imposters, hypocrites all, they appeared only in time to spread their wealth around and purchase the high standing of their families. Can honor and prestige be bought? I suspect not. So please Mister Travers, tell me, who are the revered members of these elite families?"

"I cannot answer your question," admitted Travers. "I know nothing of their family origins, only that the influence they yield is too imposing for any native of Somerset to oppose."

"Then tell me this Travers," Holyday demanded, "what have these all-powerful members of these mighty families decided should be our fate?"

Travers could not even look at us when he answered. "You are to be hanged at first light."

"And you people," Holyday's tongue was sharp and searing, "you Somerset people, so proud and strong, you'd let them hang a boy for defending his honor?"

Travers looked up with a questioning look about his face.

"I stole Armstrong's slaves," Holyday confirmed proudly. "I stole them and returned to them their freedom and if that is a crime, I am guilty as charged and am aware of the punishment for the offense. I shall hang and I will do so with a smile on my face. But this boy? This boy did nothing more than protect his honor. You yourself heard the insults. What man would stand to have such slurs thrown at him like so much vomit from swine? And you will stand by and watch this young son of Somerset face the gallows without so much as a trial because you fear these pompous arseholes?"

Travers looked embarrassed and ashamed as he stood in silence.

"I have sent word to Somerton," Travers finally mumbled. "Riders leave now to summon Jedediah."

Travers' words carried with them a glimmer of hope. If Jedediah were made aware of our current situation he would surely come to our rescue and run our persecutors out of town. But I found it hard to believe that Armstrong's henchmen would allow anyone to leave the confines of the city until after the execution.

"A cowardly lot that runs this town that you would have outsiders execute one of your own," Holyday fumed.

"I am not afraid to die!" I could hold my tongue no longer. "If that is my fate then so be it," I said. "There are worse things than death."

From outside came the sound of the first nail being hammered into the wood. They had begun the construction of the gallows. The brave words I had just uttered hung like a lump caught in my throat.

"I'm sorry," Travers said, his words ringing most sincere. "I'll get you a basin, some water and towels to clean yourself. And a last meal, anything you like."

"I won't need a basin," Holyday replied. "And we'll not be having anything to eat," he paused, "or drink."

Travers looked at Holyday with surprise and then turned to me to see if I agreed.

"There is one thing you can do for me," I said.

"Anything at all," came Travers' response.

"If my uncle doesn't make it here in time," I began, "tell him I died a proud man. Tell him I helped twenty-one slaves regain their freedom and that I executed an evil, hate-filled man. Tell him I ended the life of a man that tortured his slaves for sport and raped young girls in front of their mothers. Tell him that," I said. "Tell him I love him, and Aunt Millie too, and everyone in Somerton."

"I certainly will," Travers replied, his lip quivering.

"And please sir," I added, "please make sure Jedediah gets my horses and the medicine they carry. It is urgent. Tell him he needs to visit Hank, and that Lucy and Lew send their best."

"I should write this down," Travers suggested.

"Just tell him what you remember," I said. "It will come to you."

"Yes sir," Travers replied. "Anything else sir?"

"Say goodbye to my horses for me," I said. "They served me well and I will miss them. They are good animals, the best I have ever seen."

Travers just nodded at me. I could see his eyes beginning to water.

"One more thing," I added as Travers was about to turn and leave.

"Yes."

"Please see that we are not disturbed," I requested. "Call on us in the morning when it is time. Until then we would appreciate it very much if we were left alone with our thoughts," and I paused as I knew Holyday would have, "and our prayers."

I was quite sure that Travers was extremely near tears as he turned and walked out. The doors closed behind him and in the suddenness of the silence I looked over at Holyday.

"What shall we talk about?" he asked. A broad smile, surely meant to diffuse the terror of our present circumstances, was striped across his face.

CHAPTER 17
Manokin

We sat in the quiet stillness. Eventually the banging resumed as the construction of the gallows continued.

"What bothered me the most," Holyday finally spoke, "was that I didn't deserve it."

"Deserve?"

"I didn't deserve the glory and the honor of the Four Hundred," he explained. "We all felt that way. All that survived it. That is why we agreed to not speak of it. But people knew. People talked."

"Of course," I replied. "It was a great victory. Maybe the greatest of all time. Certainly, the most meaningful, when considering the ultimate outcome."

"It still felt wrong," Holyday continued. "I was afforded great opportunities in life because of the simple coincidence of having been there that day. And the dead, they got nothing. None of us chose to be selected. No one wanted to make that charge. It is hardly heroic merely to have obeyed orders. It bothered me a lot when people would say the survivors of the Battle of Brooklyn were heroes. The Maryland Four Hundred have become almost mythical. It always bothered me to be mentioned in the same breath with those that gave their lives."

I found it curious that Holyday, given only one more night to live, would choose to revisit the worst day of his life. But the battle haunted him. If he wished to reconcile unsettled thoughts that continued to torment him, I was pleased to oblige him.

"When I hear people speak of the Four Hundred," he went on, "I think of the men that died that day. It is difficult for me to explain, but having lived to tell the tale, there is a hollowness that makes the story not worth telling. I have spent my whole life believing that I did not deserve to be counted among their numbers. I was not one of the Four Hundred. I did not make the same sacrifice. I did not belong."

"You penalize yourself too harshly," I said. "Can your interpretation really be that because you made it out alive you didn't do your part?

"I don't know," he answered. "That has been my struggle."

"The word *retreat* does not just mean run," I said. "It means run as fast as you can, for all is lost. In any event, forward is no longer the way to go but rather back whence you came. Should you be condemned for surviving the Redcoats attempts to cut you down? It seems cruel and unfair to punish yourself for being successful in your retreat. You are guilty only of being fast, and possibly a bit lucky."

"Beautifully argued," the words edging their way through his crooked smile. "But it doesn't matter anymore. The glory is now deserved. I am finally worthy of whatever praise may one day come my way. I did the right thing. It was my choice. Not just following orders. By my own accord, the sacrifice was made. Whether at the suggestion of a ghost, or a delusion, I took it upon myself to see it through. Whatever kind words may be offered in remembrance of me will have been earned. I think that is all I ever wanted. Just to know I wasn't getting something that did not belong to me."

"Well," I said, "it belongs to you now."

"Yes," he said. "Yes, I guess it does. Still, my satisfaction is tarnished knowing that you too must pay the ultimate price. But most men are never fortunate enough to find themselves in a position to make such a difference in the world. I am convinced that the common man, given a chance to make a real difference in people's lives, always finds a way to convince himself that such a sacrifice is above and beyond the expectations this world should have of him."

"I would agree," I said. "Jedediah has advised me many times that a man need only always do the right thing to separate himself from cowards."

"It is a rare man that meets such occasions standing tall and square. There is no retreat in you boy. Your courage is the stuff of legends. The slaves are nearing freedom as we speak. Their joy and laughter, and that of their children's children, will echo out across the Pennsylvania hills. And people will remember that there was a boy, with his whole life ahead of him, who bravely stood firm in defiance of tyranny. It will be an honor for me to leave this life with a man such as you. Warriors such as yourself, you would have cursed yourself for the remainder of your days had you failed to act. I know this of you. You are of the same character as the men that charged the hill, every bit as heroic as any member of the Four Hundred."

We stopped talking for a moment. This allowed Holyday's terrifically high praise to settle into my mind. I was proud of myself. To be mentioned in the same breath as the revered war heroes was a compliment of the highest possible order.

I remained unafraid as I listened to the hammers beating down the nails and tried to imagine what part of the scaffold was being assembled. Was it the steps? Or, perhaps the platform itself, or the bar from over which the rope would be tossed? It did occur to me that these thoughts were too morbid to consume my last hours, but there are times when we have as much control over our thoughts as we do the weather.

Suddenly, there came a knocking at the jailhouse door. Four rapid thumps and then nothing. Holyday and I looked at one another with a stifled sense of hilarity.

"You want to get that?" he asked.

"Sure," I replied.

So it was that we were both laughing heartily when the door was slowly pushed open. Elijah Travers peeked his head around the door, which he had cracked only slightly.

"I'm sorry gentlemen," Travers began, "I know you desired to be left alone but there is a gentleman here who very much wishes to have a word with you."

Travers seemed to be waiting for a response.

"Enter," I stated.

The jailer, first knocking on the door and then seemingly asking permission of condemned men to enter the premises. The situation prompted more laughter. It must have struck both Travers and the visitor as quite odd to see the two of us, awaiting execution, to be in such high spirits. But the scenario was so absurdly ridiculous that neither Holyday or I could wipe the smiles from our faces even after Travers entered the room in the company of a middle-aged man and a young boy.

"I'll leave you to it then," Travers said before stepping outside and closing the enormous wooden door behind him.

"I'm sorry," the man said, "I understand you'd prefer to spend these last hours without interruption. But I cannot help but feel an obligation to share this information with you. I am sure I would have regretted the decision to refrain from seeing you."

I could not imagine what it was this man wanted. What information could he possibly have that would be of any interest to us at this late hour?

"My name is Owen Brown," the man stated. "I am a land speculator for the Pennsylvania Population Company."

Looking over at Holyday I could see he was as confused as I about why this man was standing before us.

"Land speculation affords me and the people I work with the perfect opportunity to travel into the southern states so we can coordinate efforts to help slaves escape and make their way north," Brown continued. "I just wanted you to know," he paused and looked down at the boy standing by his side, "I needed you to know, there are many of us in Pennsylvania and New York, Connecticut, all the way up into Canada that share your beliefs regarding the enslavement of human beings."

Brown had piercing blue eyes. It was impossible not to notice them.

"I just want you to know that this fight," Brown said, "this fight that you have so honorably and bravely engaged shall continue. And we shall not give up the cause until the practice of ripping apart families and selling human souls has been forever banished from our country. Please pass through the gates of heaven, where surely all the saints await your arrival, with the knowledge that one day this land will be a free land. We will follow you, and keep up the good fight, so that the Declaration of Independence can be the sacred document it was intended to be rather than meaningless words scribbled on so much toilet paper."

It was then I noticed the boy's eyes. Every bit as unsettling as Brown's. Piercing blue eyes that seemed to be perpetually startled. They were, in every sense of the word, outrageous.

Brown saw me looking at the boy.

"This is my son," he said. "Say hello, John."

"Hello," replied the boy. His voice was soft and subdued and not in any way consistent with his turbulent, wild eyes.

"Thank you," Holyday finally responded. "There is much work left to do if this country is to fulfill her promise. We appreciate you sharing with us the news that the battle will continue. It helps to know there are others who have grown tired of the pitiful promises and meaningless words. Condemnation is futile, absent the willingness to act. At some point words must be replaced with swords. Disgruntled people, weary of living with this country's shame, must one day stand up as soldiers. They must see themselves as warriors, intent on making a difference, willing to make sacrifices for the good of all descent Americans. It will make the walk to the gallows less terrifying, knowing that we are but casualties of war. Again, I thank you most sincerely."

I wish I had been able to participate in the brief conversation. Each man expressed himself eloquently and in a dignified manner. I would like to have contributed in some way to the men's powerful prose but could not entirely pull my attention away from the young John Brown. His eyes had me mesmerized, as did the expression on his face. The boy, roughly my age I guessed, wore the most genuine expression of jealousy. I found this disturbing. There was not a glimmer of sorrow or pity. Nor did he look at me with adulation, or remorse. His was a look that convinced me wholly that he would have given anything to have traded his place for mine.

The door suddenly opened, announcing itself with the squealing of the hardware under the weight of the heavy oak. There was no knocking this time, only Travers' face sticking into the room.

"The men return," Travers said. "You must vacate in haste."

With that, they turned and left the building. Nothing else was said. The conversation seemed to be left unfinished. Holyday and I, without saying a word, sat down on our respective cots. The silence was now deafening. Holyday sat motionless, lost in the words of Owen Brown. I was still awestruck by the boy's forceful yet dreadful eyes. A minute passed before I sensed Holyday looking my way. When I turned toward him a slight, contented smile graced his face.

"I think now would be a very good time for you to explain to me this religion of yours," Holyday requested.

"What is it that you do not understand?" I asked. "What do you want to know?"

"Your faith is strong," he answered. "I am envious. I would like to understand it better. Where does it come from?"

"And this is how you'd like to spend your last hours?" I asked. "Discussing something you do not believe in?"

"My belief has nothing to do with it," Holyday stated, almost as a reprimand. "I have no doubt that every soul who has ever been condemned to die, as they awaited execution, whether guilty or no, faithful and atheist alike, spent their last night contemplating spirituality. Life forced me to abandon my God. I never stopped being curious regarding His existence. I only knew that he was not there for me."

"Because He took your family?"

"Yes," Holyday replied. "But there is more to it. I have witnessed so much suffering and so much pain. It is incomprehensible to me that God, all powerful, would watch my brothers scream as they cupped their bowels in their hands. The agony and the horror, I can make no sense of it. And then slavery. God would have men chained and whipped? He would see their families and their freedom stolen away? I think not. Such cruel intentions. The work of a kind and loving God? There is no way to make sense of it."

"Some of it does not make sense."

"And yet you believe? I want to understand. I need to understand," he insisted.

"It just seems impossible to endure the injustice all alone," I answered. "There has to be a reason for it. There has to be a reward waiting out there somewhere."

"I would so dearly love to embrace that kind of thinking," Holyday's words were filled with regret. "But I have seen too closely the other side. There is no way for me to go back."

"What other side?"

"The cruel side," he answered, "the unforgiving side. I fought in the Revolution and was rewarded with the face of a monster. After the war I returned home and went to school. I endured the loneliness and the ridicule that comes with looking like this. But the bravery of the 1st Regiment carved out opportunities for me and I made the most of them. But it was a lonely existence. Hero or no, my appearance always kept people at a distance. I was always alone."

"If I may," I interjected, "once a person gets to know you, your scars all but disappear. For those blinded by first impressions, they are people not to be desired as friends."

"Kind words," he said, "and appreciated. But to be cursed with an ugliness that would guarantee I would never know the company of a woman was hard. And then I met her. It was like you said. She looked past my wounds. It was as if she did not even see the scars," there was joy in his voice when he mentioned her.

"Where did you meet?" I wanted to prolong the conversation. A happiness bubbled just below the surface of the stoic pain that permanently cloaked Holyday like a well-tailored suit.

"We studied Latin together at St. Francis," he said. "I often thought that it was the Latin, a language so elegant and generous, that concealed my face from her. We became wonderful friends, and in time, lovers. Hers was a beauty unmatched, both inside and out. And for her to be with me, it was, well, exquisite."

"Venereum," I replied.

"You speak Latin?" he almost screamed.

"Etiam," I answered in the affirmative.

"I suppose you will continue to surprise me up until my final minute," he exclaimed. "Venereum, yes, romantic. Heavenly so." And then He took her from me, along with my son. And the life we were to share was gone forever. All the laughter, and the love, and thousands of precious moments that would never come to pass."

"I'm sorry," I said.

"Yes," he replied, "me too. I tried to understand. But I could see only cruelty and hatred in this act. It became easier to blame the violent storm for killing my family than to put it on God. But that meant for me there could be no God. I have not seen Him since that day, and I have not looked for Him."

"That does not mean He does not look for you," I answered.

"Hence my curiosity," he said, "explain it please, this faith of yours that sees you through life's violent storms.

"Very well, although, I'm afraid it may fall short of your expectations."

"Most doubtful," he said, "as I have no expectations."

"I mean as it relates to heaven," I said. "We don't have thoughts regarding the afterlife per say. Nothing that will give you peace of mind regarding the Four Hundred. None that are in any way a significant part of our beliefs."

"Well Brixton," he quipped, "we'll have those answers soon enough."

"Yes," I said, "yes, I guess we will." We laughed, and it was not in any way forced or nervous laughter but rather heartfelt and real.

"So, if this religion of yours does not speak to the afterlife, what is it that you believe happens to you upon death?" he prompted.

I closed my eyes and thought deeply. It took me a minute, but Holyday was interested in my response, so he tolerated the silence. The quiet stillness of the jail allowed my thoughts to expand outward through the farthest reaches of my being so that when I finally spoke the answer came more from my heart than it did my mind.

"And then at once, everything, all that is known and all that will ever be known, is yours. A light so bright, so gloriously triumphant, that it is inconceivable that it will not burn for eternity. The comfort and bliss of spirituality realized. Heaven's warm and welcome embrace, and behold, the face of God."

"I'm going to miss you Steven Brixton," Holyday declared longingly. He stared at me with an expression that was at the same time regretful and triumphant.

"And I, you," I replied.

"But heaven's warm embrace?" Holyday questioned. "The afterlife. No?"

"Just my thoughts," I answered. "Nothing at all to do with the religion of the people in Somerton."

"Then tell me," Holyday requested. "Tell me of the faith of the, hmm, what is it that you even call yourselves?"

"We have been called the Pagan Quakers by some," I answered. "But that is a name leveled at us from detractors. A slander aimed at our acceptance of the local Indians. But ironically, it is the Indians, the Assateague, that gave our faith a name that seemed to stick with some. They called us the *Shiloh*. It is the Indian word for brother."

"In some native dialects it also refers to a *Place of Peace*," Holyday informed. "Either way, it would make sense in this regard."

"I don't know that it matters," I continued. "Whether called Pagan Quakers as an insult or the Shiloh by those not offended by our beliefs, these are names used by others. Not by us. We do not assign a name to our beliefs. We don't call ourselves anything," I said. "There were times, so recent by all accounts, in which many faiths, but Quakers and Catholics in particular, were so savagely persecuted. Over time people like Jedediah and his father, and his father before him, realized there was safety in the concept of unnamed worship."

"A nameless religion?" Holyday remarked with amusement. "Oh, how I adore it! Continue young Brixton, continue, please."

"Our service begins with a passage from the book of Sirach," I said. "Chapter two, verses one through eleven."

"This faith of yours begins with a passage from the Catholic bible?" he asked in astonishment. "Oh, this is good."

"You are familiar with the writings of Sirach?" I asked with my own expression of surprise.

"I am familiar with the bible," he said. "And yes, even the writings of Jesus, son of Sirach."

"Ha!" I laughed. "You do know it. And chapter two?"

"Verses one through eleven?" he said as if taunting me.

"Shall I recite it?" I asked.

Holyday had been leaning back against the wall of his cell with his eyes closed. He looked to be letting the conversation drip through his mind like a finely aged whiskey, savoring each word, every thought. At this point he opened his eyes and looked at me. His eyes glimmered, shining a knowing wisdom. I felt as though I could have been in the presence of Socrates or Aristotle.

He began speaking slowly at first as if he had to think deeply to recall the verses. The words then came more rapidly until his recital was delivered at such a pace that he seemed to be purposely ignoring any inflection. It was barely possible to understand the meaning of the words, much less the beauty and simplicity of the passage and how it so completely and profoundly captured the essence of faith and goodness.

"My son when you come to serve the Lord prepare yourself for trials. Be sincere of heart and steadfast, undisturbed in time of adversity. Cling to Him, forsake Him not, thus will your future be great. Accept whatever befalls you. In crushing misfortune be patient. For in fire gold is tested and worthy men in the crucible of humiliation. Trust God and He will help you. Make straight your ways and hope in Him. You who fear the Lord wait for His mercy. Turn not away lest you fall. You who fear the Lord, trust Him, and your reward will not be lost. You who fear the Lord, hope for good things, for lasting joy and mercy. Study the generations long past and understand, has anyone hoped in the Lord and been disappointed? Has anyone persevered in his fear and been forsaken? Has anyone called upon Him and been rebuffed? Compassionate and merciful is the Lord. He forgives sins. He saves in time of trouble."

Holyday looked at me with amusement, enjoying the perplexed expression on my face.

"How," I asked. "How is it that you know verses from the book of Sirach?"

"Why does it surprise you?" he asked. "Why would I not know these passages? Have you not read the bible?"

"Of course, but," I found myself at a loss for words.

"The bible is a book whose words are meant to be studied," he continued. "It presents itself for examination and contemplation. If the passages are thoroughly understood, recalling them can be done with ease."

"The readings of Sirach are ignored by many. Some consider them obscure, even obsolete," I replied.

"I don't know that I agree with you on that point," Holyday countered. "Maryland is a state born of protection for Catholics," he reminded me. "Completely understanding that everything is done differently on the eastern shore, there are plenty of Catholics on the other side of the bay, and a lot of people with an allegiance to the readings in that book. While my faith is now but a distant memory, there was a time when it was the most important thing in my life."

"Was it the Catholic faith?" I asked after reflecting on his comment briefly. "Was it the Catholic God from whom you turned away?"

"I was once a Catholic, yes," he answered. "But I think there are many people, regardless of their faith, that take a special interest in readings that are no longer popular. I would expect serious readers of the book to be curious as to why certain works have fallen out of favor. People will always be drawn to forbidden fruit. You might underestimate people's interest in the book of Sirach. And I know there are many people who do not believe in God that read the bible for the wisdom and the life lessons contained within its pages. They care nothing about what the church may say regarding which books, or which passages, should be studied and which should be overlooked."

"I should know better," I said, "than to underestimate you."

"I'm curious as to why the leaders of your faith chose to begin their worship with these passages," Holyday remarked. "You are not Catholics, but a decision was made to begin your service with verses from a book that is held in higher regard by the Catholics than by members of other faiths."

"I can't answer that," I said. "I don't know who made the decision, or why, it's just always been the way we start our prayers. There are stories related to how the verses were written by a common man," I offered. "That they are not divinely inspired makes them attractive to some. People seem to take comfort in knowing that a man, no different than their neighbor, could write such timeless instruction. I do know for certain that our faith was born of the three most oppressed people in this land at the time of its creation. We were Quaker, Catholic, and Native. This was long before the protectionism afforded Catholics by Lord Baltimore. It was decided to deliberately abandon the Quaker ways, Catholicism, and Paganism, and create something altogether new. A faith that would protect us from ongoing and brutal persecution. But in truth, we did not abandon all these beliefs. Rather, we combined certain elements from each. That is how it seems to me."

"You don't find it peculiar?" he asked. "With thousands of pages from which to choose your people decided to begin their celebration of faith with a reading from the book of Sirach."

"It is really not a celebration of faith, rather a celebration of life," I admitted. "Maybe it's not supposed to make sense. Maybe it is supposed to play into the whole mystery of faith. I really do not know. I can't explain it."

"Interesting," he said, "tell me more. What else do you include in your worship? What comes next?"

"After someone recites those verses there is silence," I explained. "We sit in silence and think."

"About?"

"Anything. Everything. Most of the time," I talked slowly, as if explaining it to myself as well as to him. "It has to do with nature. Sometimes people are moved to verbalize their thoughts. Others do not. The remarks are related to giving thanks for the warmth of the sun, or the beauty of the forests, or the abundance of the sea. Occasionally, some give thanks for the loyalty and the friendship of the community. Some will ask that God keep us healthy, or that He comforts the sick, or ask that the crops receive His blessing."

"Hmm," was Holyday's only comment.

"Other times no one says anything," I added. "On plenty of occasions we sit in silence. Nothing is said between the opening verses and the closing prayer. We sit quietly and enjoy the silence. Then someone will say the closing prayer and that's it."

"The simplicity and the silence," Holyday remarked, "I guess that's a Quaker thing."

"I guess," I replied.

"How long does this last?" he asked.

"Could be a few minutes," I said. "Could be an hour. If it is a nice day and the birds are singing, and the wind is playing music with the trees, we can sit for an hour in silence and just listen to nature. Depends a lot on how much work needs to be done."

"And who says this closing prayer?"

"Anyone who feels moved to do so," I said. "There are really no rules. The Sirach passage can be said by anyone. And the closing prayer can be said by anyone. In between, whether it is a minute or an hour, anybody can say whatever they want, whenever they want."

"Fascinating," Holyday said. "And what is it called? I mean do you call it a mass, or a service?"

"We simply refer to it as our daily prayers," I answered.

"I like it," Holyday acknowledged. "Just talking about it sounds peaceful."

"Yes," I said. "It is peaceful. At the conclusion of the final prayer everyone gets up and quietly walks away and goes about their day. There is a peacefulness to it. Absolutely."

"And the final prayer," Holyday continued his inquiry, "this can be said by anyone?"

"Yes," I answered. "Whoever feels compelled to say it."

"And they say whatever they want?" he asked. "Whatever comes to mind?"

"No," I told him. "The final prayer is the same every time."

"More from Sirach?" he grinned.

"No, the final prayer is not taken from the bible," I informed him. "It's a prayer that has been passed down for more than a century."

"Passed down from whom?" Holyday asked.

"There was a man, a preacher," I began, "this was back in the late 1600's when Somerton was in its infancy. There were different folks around at the time, different religions I mean. Some Quaker families had come directly from England and some Catholic families had moved up from down Albemarle way, in Virginia. Those early families, they are all pretty much still here, for the most part. But it seems they all got along. That is kind of when, best as I can tell anyway, the families started combining some aspects of their religions. And it was at that time there were relationships formed with the Indians, the Assateague, and the Wicomico. And their attitude with respect to the sacred nature of the land was folded into our daily prayers."

"The whole Pagan-Quaker thing," Holyday commented.

"Yes," I agreed. "Anyway, back then, like I said, both Quakers and Catholics were still being persecuted and that was something they had in common with the Indians. It is not easy to explain because I am not sure all the folks would necessarily consider it a religion. It has its origins way back when people were just trying to find their way. They found each other in this community, and it seemed to work for them. Best as I can figure, they fell in love with one another. In a spiritual way at first. In time, emotional and physical love followed. But these were hard times, very trying and difficult circumstances. It made people closer to one another. Formed bonds that ran deep. I can't explain it."

"I know exactly what you mean. They trusted one another" Holyday stated. "I have come to believe that in all meaningful relationships, trust and love mean the same thing. What about this prayer?"

"You want me to finish telling you where it came from? Or should I just say the prayer?" I asked enthusiastically. I was pleased that Holyday was showing such interest in my spirituality.

"No," Holyday objected emphatically. "I want to understand where it came from."

"This preacher," I continued, "his name was Lucas Boone. He was an artist. Some of his paintings still survive and hang on the walls of Somerton family homes. He was a nature lover and painted mostly pictures of the rivers and the woods and the Chesapeake. You know, animals and birds, sunsets, that kind of stuff."

"Alright," Holyday affirmed that he understood and coaxed my story along.

"One afternoon Lucas Boone takes his canvas and jars of paint, his easel and what have you, and heads down to the marshes in search of inspiration. He sets himself up in the tall reeds right off the beach where the Manokin River meets the Tangier Sound. After a while he sees this little girl walking down the beach. Girl's name was Diane. Diane Chantal, a French girl, orphan, came over from Europe with a German family. Diane, who everybody called Dee, is walking barefoot down the white sandy beach in her summer dress. She is letting the Tangier waves run up and play with her feet. Boone, hidden back in the reeds, is watching her, and thinking what a beautiful painting it would be if he could capture the angelic child strolling along the beach. Suddenly, the girl falls to her knees. Kneeling there on the powdery sand she makes the sign of the cross and begins to pray aloud. Lucas Boone is so taken by the moment that he dips his paintbrush into a jar of paint and hurries to write down the words spoken by little Diane."

"I can see it in my mind," Holyday said, his voice came as a pleasant-sounding whisper. I had no doubt that he was right there in the reeds with old Boone watching the little girl pray.

"That night Boone transcribed the prayer onto a piece of paper and took it over to the German couple's house. Their names were Armand and Hilda Baden. And though they adopted the little girl they let her keep her birth name. Different stories were told over the years as to why, but most folks believed it was because the girl's name had a lyrical, poetic quality to it. People simply enjoyed saying it. Dee Chantal, it is almost songlike. And Boone explains to the Badens how he saw Dee praying on the beach and asked them if this was a prayer with which they were familiar. They said they had never heard such a prayer. When Dee was asked about it, she explained she had made up the prayer on the beach that very day. Folks were so taken by little Dee's prayer that it soon became popular among the community and people have been saying it ever since. To this day, when we gather for daily prayers, we start with Sirach and end with the Dee Chantal. The little girl's prayer has been said aloud almost every day in Somerton for almost a hundred and fifty years."

"I prefer a story such as that to one of warships and battle any day of the week," Holyday said, as if he were dreaming of the young girl wandering down the beach all those years ago. "Let's hear it."

I too was momentarily lost in thought and did not take his meaning immediately. When it was not forthcoming Holyday prompted me.

"The prayer," he said.

"Oh, of course," I said. "I'll say it the way Dee said it that first day. When it is said today, whoever is praying will speak for the group and recite it in a plural form."

"No, no," Holyday emphasized. "I want the girl's version."

"Dear God, thank you for another beautiful day in paradise, and thank you for all the wonderful things you have given me. I am truly grateful. Please help me to live my life by your will and help me in my quest for spiritual understanding. Heavenly Father, please give me the courage to achieve my potential, and the power to attain the goals you have set for me. I trust in you Lord, and through your kindness I stand unshaken. God bless my friends and family. Please keep them safe and healthy. Through your grace I pray. Amen."

CHAPTER 18
Home

Neither of us spoke. The hammering outside had stopped, and the jail's thick stone walls and heavy wooden doors kept any noise that might have disturbed us outside where it belonged. Inside we shared the interior with only the unbroken quiet. I knew that Holyday had traveled back in time with me. We were looking out over the immaculate beach and watching the little girl say her prayer.

It might have been only a few minutes, although it seemed much longer, before Holyday spoke and shattered the serenity. Alas, it must have occurred to him, as it did to me, that while we were connoisseurs of quiet repose, we all too soon would have the rapture of silence at our eternal disposal. Let us fill these last hours with speech.

"How old was the girl?" Holyday wanted to know. "When she first said the prayer, how old was she?"

"She was twelve," I said.

"Yes, there is a childlike simplicity to it," Holyday acknowledged. "But it goes right to the heart of the human struggle, regardless of age. I can see why your people embraced it so. The prayer speaks straight to the essential needs of man as if shot like an arrow from the bow of an angel. She gave thanks, asked for help to be faithful and for the strength to be a good person. She must have been quite a girl."

"Yes," I said, "by all accounts she was." There was another pause, but I was determined not to let this one lapse into extended meditation. "Tell me," I said, "once you turned away from the church, or religion, how was it you found the strength to carry on? Did you really find a way to deal with all of life's struggles by yourself? Is it even possible to do battle with reality all by your lonesome?"

"I don't know," he answered in a way that told me he was pondering my question and whence he formed an answer he would share it. I knew it would not take long.

"I don't know for sure that I ever completely abandoned my faith," he started. "I turned away from God," he said, "but that was basically to punish myself, I guess. For what I do not really know. But I never lost my spirituality, not entirely any way. And it is funny," he went on, "but there are times when God, religion, spirituality, faith, they all mean the same thing. Other times, one has nothing to do with the other. I continued to think about things like that. I guess I always had a sense of spirituality even if I couldn't understand it."

"I don't know if anyone fully understands it," I offered.

"I would suggest they do not," Holyday said. "If you live long enough, and it does not appear you will," this comment drew anxious laughter from both of us, "you would have learned that with age you are destined to acquire a predisposition toward wisdom. It is through wisdom that people come to understand that happiness is not possible without peace. Happiness is peace. And peace is happiness. We are all destined to be happy for it is inevitable that we shall all be at peace."

"Yes," I said. "Yes, I see that."

"I thought you should know this," Holyday shared, "as you might not get a chance to figure some of these things out for yourself. You should know that life has a way of bringing us all to the same place eventually. I do not know how big a role God plays. I am finding with every passing minute that I do so want to believe in life after death. Now, not only for my fallen brothers but for myself as well. But I cannot fool myself. I've neither the time nor the patience to play games. Pretending that there is something else, it seems insincere to me, hypocritical, goes against what I have believed for so long. It reeks of desperation and cowardice. Not to say that I did not take solace in the spiritual. But life after death? Heaven and hell? Seems just as absurd at this moment as it has throughout the course of my life. But spirituality is an entity unto itself, far removed from any god or religion, at least for me."

"So, it was spirituality that saw you through the tough times?" I asked him.

"Sometimes you must rely on the way you think about the world to help you navigate it. A person's belief system is their guide through life, their map. What you think is who you are," he answered.

"What do you think?" I wanted to know.

"We are gifted life, whether worthy or not," he said. "Henceforth, there are but two charges. The first is to live well. Color everything you do, everything you say, with honor. If you do this, you cannot help but to make a difference in the world. The second charge," he said, "is to die well. Acknowledge to yourself that you have done the best you could. Then, a time will come for you to die. Meet death head on. Stare death in the eyes, and smile. Death cannot smile back as his is a dark and joyless world. Hence, your last battle in life will be a victorious one."

"Yes," I said. "I like it."

"To live with honor is to change the world," Holyday went on. "To die with honor is to never die."

"I see it," I agreed with him. "I will die with honor. I just wish I could have had a little more time. Otherwise, I have no regrets."

"Brixton," he said, "you were worthy of so much more time. To be sure there is nothing fair about this life. Not even the young are spared regrets. But given fifty more years, a hundred more, could you have done anything more magnificent? Possibly, for there is surely greatness in you. But people will remember your courage. Your memory will exist among the legends of our time. One thing is sure, you made a difference. You had an impact on this world like few men ever do. It is now of vital importance that you die well."

"I will die well," I said.

"I know you will," he said. "I'll make sure of it."

"What do you mean?" I asked.

"Did you not wonder why I told Mister Travers that we did not desire food or drink?" he asked me.

"I was curious," I admitted.

"Surely growing up in the woods you have seen a man die," Holyday inquired.

"Of course," I said.

"What's the first thing they do?" he continued his line of query. Seeing the puzzled look on my face he pressed on. "What's the first thing they do upon dying?" he asked again. Receiving no reply, he answered for me. "They piss and shit themselves," he said with a wonderfully wry laugh.

"Yes, I've seen it," I said. "Most foul."

"You'll have friends and family collecting your body," he reminded me. "You'll not want that to be the last impression you make."

"No, certainly not," I said, and we both began to laugh at our situation.

"We'll leave them with one last surprise," he said in a terrifically mischievous tone.

"What is it?" My inquiry wore the excitement of a child opening a gift-wrapped present.

"You watched Armstrong die. What did you notice about his face as he passed?"

"What did I notice?" I asked.

"You saw him looking at you," Holyday spoke, a film of venom coating his words. "You saw the horror and the disbelief that you, a harmless boy, could take his life from him. You saw the anguish as his mouth filled with blood. The murderous rage consumed him as the realization set in, he was dying and there was nothing he could do."

"Yes, I saw it."

"Then what?" Holyday implored. "Then what did you see? As Armstrong exhaled his last breath what happened to his face?"

"What happened to his face?" I did not know what he was after. "I don't know. Nothing. He just died."

"Nothing," Holyday reiterated. "Nothing happened to his face. Because when you die, you are done. Did he close his eyes when he died?"

I thought for a minute, "No," I said. "His eyes remained open."

"If the execution is conducted properly," Holyday continued, "and I expect it will be, our necks will snap and the expressions we wear on our faces at that very instant shall be frozen in time. That expression, that look on our faces will be the same minutes later as they take our bodies down from the gallows. When that floor gives way tomorrow morning, we will have smiles on our faces. We will be smiling as widely as it is possible for us to smile." He then made a tremendously exaggerated smile.

"Like this," I mimicked him.

"Just like that," he said. "The audience will see the condemned men smiling. Laughing at them. And Brixton, years from now, a century from now, when they speak of how these cowards executed an old man and a young boy for returning to freedom the enslaved victims of the madman Armstrong, they will talk of how we laughed at death. Long will live the legend of the men, executed without a trial, who laughed at them from beyond the grave." And he again displayed the crazy forced smile.

They came for us while it was still dark. It would be in the best interest of the henchmen to hang us before the light of the new day. But, due in part to a Somerset County ordinance dating to 1768, an execution cannot be carried out until the sun has risen to the height of the Manokin Church's steeple. Holyday and I climbed the steps to the gallows in the dimly lit morning. There were no people anywhere. For a moment it seemed our plan to smile at the crowd and laugh at death would not come to pass as the covert nature of this hanging would happen before anyone was even out of bed.

When the hoods were offered to us, we declined. Holyday remarked that there was no need to cover our faces for there would be no one in attendance to view the spectacle. That is when Travers told us of the so-called *steeple statute*. The church stood off to our left and turning our heads just slightly we could easily see the steeple which the sun had to touch for this to be considered a legal execution.

"When the sun is high enough on that church," Travers said, "this yard is going to be packed full of people. You're sure you won't be wanting the hoods?"

"Positive," I answered.

Holyday was pleased at my assertive remark. When I responded to his expression of approval with a contented grin, he briefly flashed the enormous smile he planned to show the crowd. At this we both laughed, and the hangman looked at us as if we had lost our minds.

People were slowly gathering in the hanging yard as the sun cleared the horizon. It was obvious that as the people gathered, they were more than a little surprised to see us already standing on the gallows with ropes around our necks. I could see a few folks running off to inform the town residents that the execution was near its commencement.

The sun continued to rise, and people continued filling the yard. Holyday and I realized we would have many eyewitnesses to pass along to future generations the story of the laughing dead men. The more often the story was told the more it would change. A hundred years from now it will have been distorted so that even Holyday and I might not recognize the tale. But the one thing that could never change, as it would be a matter of public record, was that we were executed for helping enslaved people escape to freedom.

"Without the smiles," Holyday had said, "it's just another hanging. Folks will talk about the dead men laughing as they swung back and forth from the gallows. The rope will snap our necks and those expressions will lock in place. That is a story that every witness will tell their grandchildren. The haunting smiles on our faces will ensure the story will be repeated forever. As the story gets passed from one generation to the next and moves from one century to another, people will be tormented by the smiles of the dead. Slavery is part of our story Brixton. The tale cannot be told without revealing man's most horrific sin. People not yet born will speak about the day when two white men lost their lives, and died happily, and laughing, for releasing from bondage those cursed to suffer the heinous and evil practice of slavery. One day someone will read the Declaration of Independence and realize that if all men are created equal, the rich men cannot force the poor men to work in their fields. They'll talk about us Brixton," Holyday had continued throughout the long night, "and one day they'll do something about it."

The yard was now packed and the sun just inches from the steeple. I looked for Jedediah and Millie, but they were not in attendance. No one from Somerton stood in the yard and it was clear that Armstrong's men had denied anyone permission to leave town. I think deep down inside both Holyday and I knew this would be the case. We never discussed it, nor was it mentioned even once. We needed to prepare ourselves for this moment and holding onto the false hope of some remote, last-minute reprieve would not allow us to do so. If, somehow, word made its way to Jedediah, and he arrived in time to save us, we would rejoice. But we were not expecting to be rescued. The moment Travers had mentioned there was going to be an attempt to reach Somerton it had occurred to me, and I am sure Holyday thought similarly, that the road out of town would be closely watched. No one would be allowed to depart Princess Anne until after the hanging. The people of Somerton were completely unaware of the execution. This realization impacted me not in any way. I was proud of myself, if I am being honest, for how little fear I experienced on that brisk October morning. My strength was summoned from the knowledge that I had made a difference in this world. People's lives were better because I had walked this earth. My name would likely not be remembered but that did not matter. I knew what I had done and somehow that made dying a whole lot easier.

When the hangman pushed the lever forward the floor fell out from beneath us. My only thought was to keep smiling. Smile as widely as I possibly could, and the rope would do the rest. But something had gone wrong. The scaffolding came tumbling down on top of us. Covered with wooden planks and boards it was difficult to tell which way was up. Finally, after pushing the crumbled pieces of the gallows off me I scrambled to my feet. There was a sudden hard pull on my shoulder. I turned to see Holyday standing next to me.

"Let's go!" He screamed at me, and we took off running. The people yelled with what seemed to be delight. Holyday continued pushing me through the crowd. The people would step out of the way until we passed and then close in behind us so that the authorities, now all in earnest pursuit, found it difficult to make their way through the mass of people.

"Lead the way boy!" Holyday implored me, and we ran.

Down the street and across the field I ran as fast as I could. My arms and legs were yet shackled but this did not impede my progress. The energy that coursed through my body as I ran for my life gave me the strength of ten men. I grabbed the chain that connected the shackles on my wrists and pulled it close together, holding it up by my chest and out in front of me.

The leg irons around my ankles were joined by a thicker chain of considerable length. Though it did not allow me to take the long strides I would have preferred I was still able to move much more quickly than I would have expected, given that my feet were bound together.

Holyday and I had probably run close to half a mile before the initial jolt of adrenaline began to fade away. The chains became more cumbersome with each step and the irons around my ankles were cutting deep into my leg and causing considerable pain. Looking downward I could see the metal had carved into my ankle deeply and a large flap of skin had been folded back and could be seen protruding from underneath the shackles. Blood coursed freely from the wound and sent excruciating pain shooting up my leg.

I knew that slowing my escape was not an option. The fatigue and the pain had to be ignored. There came from within me an animalistic growl. My life was at stake and so too the survival of Coleman Holyday. The strength to carry on was within me. I needed to dig deep and find it.

I raced through the woods and descended the sloping terrain down into a stream. Splashing my way across the creek I refused to let myself slow the pace even slightly. Reaching the other side, I began my ascent upward. Understanding that no consideration could be afforded my exhaustion, or the burning in my lungs, I pressed on. The searing pain no longer seemed confined to my wounded leg but was now shooting up throughout my entire body.

"Run Brixton run!" Holyday was screaming in my ear. "Faster boy faster! Go!"

I ran as I had never run before. Now sweating profusely, my clothes were soaked and heavy with perspiration. The leg irons continued to dig deep into my flesh.

"Go Brixton go!" The orders from Holyday continued.

My current path seemed so much higher and steeper than ever before. This was an embankment I had scaled so many times in my youth. As a boy I would fly up out of this creek bed in half a dozen steps, but now I ran working as hard as I could and running for my life and the climb seemed to go on forever. Then, just when I thought I might collapse, there came renewed strength. I began thinking about how Cole Holyday walked through every day of his life with similar pain. This thought, its origins unknown, helped me continue onward. My aching wound and tired limbs were used as motivation to push me up the hill. There was inspiration in this agony. The chains became less heavy until I would have thought them made of paper.

"Run!" Holyday shouted and he began laughing loudly.

The laughter, now echoing throughout the forest, was bewildering. Was Holyday taunting our pursuers? Or, had his descent into madness been completed? The laugh did possess a most hysterical quality.

I turned to make sure he was keeping pace to see him right there with me. Catching a glimpse of his face I saw him wearing the exact same desperately exaggerated expression he had practiced last night. He ran after me, staying with me step for step, and laughing all the way. His bizarre smile stretched from ear to ear. I raced on, a newfound energy lifting me up and washing away all ill feelings.

Sensing the summit is near I turn again to see that crazy smile. Looking over Holyday's shoulder, in an instant I understand completely, and everything makes perfect sense. Screaming out in a wild cry of victory they follow us up the hill. Leading a glorious and triumphant charge come the Four Hundred.

ABOUT THE AUTHOR

Craig Stofko retired as the Director of the Department of Health for Maryland's Somerset County. He was a Johns Hopkins University Associate and member of the Maryland Association of County Health Officials. Stofko served on the Legislative Committee and the Administrative Committee. He was the Chairman of the Health Policy Committee.

While working for the state of Maryland, Stofko developed and implemented the first public tele-psychiatry program in the country. His tenure as a government official inspired his research into Maryland's forgotten history.

Stofko's passion for literature predates his distinguished professional career. His short stories have been published in magazines, newspapers, and on-line.

NOTE FROM THE AUTHOR

Word-of-mouth is crucial for any author to succeed. If you enjoyed *Of Sacrifice and Surrender*, please leave a review online—anywhere you are able. Even if it's just a sentence or two. It would make all the difference and would be very much appreciated.

Thanks!
Craig Stofko

We hope you enjoyed reading this title from:

BLACK ROSE
writing™

www.blackrosewriting.com

Subscribe to our mailing list – *The Rosevine* – and receive **FREE** books, daily deals, and stay current with news about upcoming releases and our hottest authors.
Scan the QR code below to sign up.

Already a subscriber? Please accept a sincere thank you for being a fan of Black Rose Writing authors.

View other Black Rose Writing titles at
www.blackrosewriting.com/books and use promo code
PRINT to receive a **20% discount** when purchasing.

www.ingramcontent.com/pod-product-compliance
Lightning Source LLC
Chambersburg PA
CBHW010734100726
47899CB00009B/3049